Still Water Saints

Alex Espinoza was born in Tijuana, Mexico, the youngest of eleven children. At the age of two, he migrated to southern California with his family and grew up in the city of La Puente, a suburb of Los Angeles. Earning a BA from the University of California at Riverside with honours, Espinoza went on to receive an MFA from UC Irvine, where he was the editor of the university's literary magazine. He now teaches creative writing at UC Riverside. *Still Water Saints* is his first novel.

Still Water Saints

A Novel

Alex Espinoza

PICADOR

First published 2007 by Random House, an imprint of
The Random House Publishing Group, a division of
Random House, Inc., New York

First published in Great Britain 2007 by Picador

This edition published 2013 by Picador
an imprint of Pan Macmillan, a division of Macmillan Publishers Limited
Pan Macmillan, 20 New Wharf Road, London N1 9RR
Basingstoke and Oxford
Associated companies throughout the world
www.panmacmillan.com

ISBN 978-1-4472-4830-9

A CIP catalogue record for this book is available from
the British Library.

Printed and bound by CPI Group (UK) Ltd, Croydon, CR0 4YY

Visit **www.picador.com** to read more about all our books
and to buy them. You will also find features, author interviews and
news of any author events, and you can sign up for e-newsletters
so that you're always first to hear about our new releases.

Para mi padre, Federico Espinoza (1923–1989).
Your hands and heart shaped me.
I have not forgotten.

Feast of the Epiphany of Our Lord & Día de los Reyes

Magi and Kings of Africa, Arabia, and the East

Patrons of travelers.

She could walk on water.

She roamed the banks of the Santa Ana, among the long green stalks, chanting to the moon, to the gods of Night and Shadow. She rose and stepped onto the river, her footsteps gently rippling the surface.

She summoned the spirits of the dead. They whispered their secrets to her, and she scribbled their messages on scraps of paper and in the margins of her phone book:

Tell Ramón the locket fell on the floor between the bed and the nightstand.

I'm all right. It's like Disneyland up here, only without rides.

I don't miss my ears because they were too big.

She fought the Devil. Every night he came to her, his head crowned with horns, his skin covered in scales. He cursed and called her names. She beat him back with her bare hands and sent him running, his cloven feet tapping against the tile of her kitchen floor.

She was a Bruja. A Santa. A Divina. A Medium, Prophet, and Healer. Able to pass through walls and read minds, to pull tumors from ailing bodies, to uncross hexes and spells, to raise the dead, and to stop time. When doctors failed, when priests and praying were not enough, the people of Agua Mansa came to the Botánica Oshún, to Perla. The shop sold amulets and stones, rosaries and candles. They bought charms to change their luck, teas to ease unsettled nerves, and estampas of saints, the worn plastic cards they carried in their purses or wallets for protection.

As thanks the customers brought her booklets of coupons and long strips of lottery tickets. They gave her fresh bouquets of roses and carnations. They showed her pictures of aunts and uncles she had helped see through heart surgeries and hip replacements. They brought in the children she had saved from drug addictions and prison sentences. They told her of the abusive husbands and gambling wives she had chased away for good. Men often grew uneasy in her presence. The women always opened up.

"I think I have bilis," Gilda Mejía said, walking up to the register where Perla stood. "Look." She stuck out her tongue. "It's all yellow. Plus my stomach's upset."

"What happened?"

"Where do I start?" Gilda rested her hands on the glass countertop. She rented an apartment over at the Agua Mansa Palms. Her brother and his new wife had moved in a few weeks ago, after he lost his job. The couple was making it hard for Gilda to relax when she came home from work because they were always in the living room watching television with the volume turned all the way up.

"You think they'd turn it down, but no. They're not deaf. And his wife. I can't stand her. The way she talks to my brother. And she's cheating on him. I see the way she looks at that guy from 312. There's something going on there." It was too crowded for three people in a one-bedroom apartment, she explained. Her brother and his wife fought well into the night, making it hard for her to sleep. She was irritable all the time, and her nerves felt ready to snap at any moment.

Simonillo was perfect to cure strong cases of bilis, to relieve tension and stress. Perla stepped away from the register and walked over to the packets of herbs that hung from pegs on the left wall of the botánica.

"I want you to make a tea with this," she said, handing the bag to Gilda. "Drink it on an empty stomach. It's bitter, so suck on a sugar cube or put some honey in it."

"Okay," Gilda said, handing over money for the herbs. "I just want to be better."

Perla took a blue seven-day candle from the shelves behind the register. She pointed to the picture of Our Lady of Regla on the glass candleholder. The Virgin, holding the infant Jesus, floated on a bed of clouds high above a cathedral. "Light this veladora before going to bed. Keep it lit all night while you sleep."

After Gilda left, Miriam Orozco's van pulled up. She got out, but her husband stayed in the car.

"Hi, Miriam. How can I help you?" Perla said.

"It's not me this time." She pointed to the van. "It's him. He's embarrassed to talk to you."

"Embarrassed? Why embarrassed?"

Miriam shrugged her shoulders. "Men. You know how they're like. Big babies."

Perla walked out into the parking lot. The car door was locked. "Talk to me, Jorge," she shouted and knocked on the window.

He rolled it down. "Hi," he said, resting his elbow on the door.

"What are you embarrassed about? Miriam says you don't want to come in."

Miriam stood behind Perla, jiggling the car's keys. "Tell her. Don't act dumb." She crossed her arms and sighed.

But Jorge stayed quiet.

Miriam said, "Here's what happened: Jorge went to a doctor who said he has depression. The pills the doctor gave him made his mouth dry. Jorge, tell her! You've missed work." Miriam walked over and leaned against the van's hood, watching Jorge through the windshield spotted with mud. "He doesn't touch me anymore."

"The doctor," Jorge said, raking his hair with his fingers. "He says I'm going through a midlife crisis. Menopause for men. Is that for real? I cry a lot. I'm no fun to be around. I can't look at my wife in that way. When we're in bed. Together. You know?"

"Come with me," Perla told Miriam. Back inside the botánica, Perla asked her, "Has he been eating anything strange?"

"No," she said.

The oils, bath salts, and scents were kept on the shelves next to the herbs and teas. Perla picked up a bottle of "Love Musk" cologne. "Has he been drinking?" She took a prayer card of Saint Job from the plastic rack on the counter.

"No," Miriam said. "He's been sober now for fifteen years."

"I'm only making sure. Have you been putting a lot of pressure on him? To do things? Around the house? Are you fighting over money?"

"No. Everything's good. Except for this."

They walked back out to the van together, and Miriam got in. Perla handed the bag to Jorge and said, "This is a cologne I want you to wear. It'll help you with your love problem. There's an estampa. Job." She showed him the picture on the card. "He's the patron of depressed people. Pray one rosary to him. And I want you to keep taking those pills the doctor gave you. Even if they make your mouth dry."

"He's bad at following directions," Miriam said. "I'll make sure he does, though."

"Good," Perla said. "If he's not better, have him go see the doctor again. If still nothing, bring him back here."

Miriam started the car, took the rosary wrapped around the rearview mirror, and handed it to Jorge. "Hold this," she said as they pulled away.

Perla helped a man whose daughter was fighting hard to kick a drug habit. Someone else needed luck in starting up a new restaurant. An old woman Perla recognized but whose name escaped her memory brought in her grandson because the boy was wetting his bed.

"He's thirteen," the old woman said. "Too old to be peeing in bed. I think he needs a limpia."

"I don't wanna do this," the boy protested. He crossed his arms and glared at Perla. "It's stupid."

The old woman tugged at his shirt. "Stop it, Tony."

Perla took the sign that read BACK IN A FEW MINUTES and taped it to the door. She led the boy and his grandmother behind the counter and through the curtain that separated the front of the store from the back.

The small kitchenette, with the mini-refrigerator and microwave Darío had given Perla when he left her the store, occupied much of the cramped stockroom. The rest of the space housed three bookshelves about six feet tall on which Perla kept her back stock. The narrow hallway separating the kitchenette and shelves from the bathroom and utility closet was where she held private consultations.

Perla worked slowly to gather the items, trying to remember what Darío had taught her. "Limpias are delicate because you're cleansing a body and chasing away evil spirits," he had said. "So it's important to concentrate." He had used a cigar, feathers, and an egg. He had chanted and whispered, rocking back and forth on his heels.

She covered the floor with a sheet and stood the boy in the middle. She coughed when she took a puff from the cigar, then blew the smoke around his body, letting it drift and settle around his head. After beating the air around him with a gray plume she pulled from her feather duster, Perla told Tony to close his eyes. She took an egg from the refrigerator and rubbed it over his body and face.

"This is lame, Grandma," the boy said, then opened his eyes. "Can we go?"

Perla turned to the boy's grandmother. "There."

The old woman pointed to the egg. "Aren't you supposed to break it and look inside?"

"Oh," Perla said. "Yes." She cracked the egg and poured it into a Styrofoam cup.

"Tony," said the boy's grandmother, pointing. "See that red swirl? Inside the yolk? That's what was doing it. That there."

The boy looked. "Yeah, right."

His grandmother pinched Tony's arm, leaving two red marks on his skin. "We'll see what you say when it starts working."

Perla covered the cup with plastic wrap she kept on the shelf above the kitchenette's sink. "Throw this out before you get home."

"Why?" Tony said.

"Because if we don't," the old woman said, "the spirits will stay with you. So we have to get rid of it to lose them. Right?" She looked at Perla.

"Yes."

"So we're just gonna, like, throw that egg out the window of a moving car?" Tony asked. "What if it hits somebody?"

"Would you rather we not? Would you rather the spirits follow us? Keep making you pee in bed? All your friends will find out and make fun of you, Tony. And that girl you like. You want her to know?"

The boy blushed. "No."

"All right then," the old woman said. She took some money from her purse and handed it to Perla.

Perla walked them outside and found a group of customers waiting for her in the parking lot. She sold a "Quit Gossiping" candle to a high school girl and a jar of "Adam and Eve" love oil to a man who rode up on a ten-speed bike. Then Rosa Cabrera came in with her four-year-old daughter,

Danielle. Rosa was one of Perla's favorite customers. She had been in high school when her mother had first brought her to the store. Now, she was in her late twenties, married, and taking classes to become a hair stylist.

Danielle's hair was pulled back in two pigtails that glistened wet. She wore faded denim overalls and a red-and-yellow-checkered undershirt. She held out three wild clovers to Perla.

"We came from the park," Rosa said. "When I told her we were coming to visit you, she picked them."

Perla stepped around the counter and bent down to hug Danielle. She took the clovers and gave her a kiss on the cheek. "They're pretty," Perla said. "Thank you."

She put them in a mug and set them next to the statue of Santa Bárbara to the right of the front door. The statue stood on a square pedestal, holding a gold scepter in one hand, a chalice in the other. Long curls of her brown hair rested in folds on her shoulders. Perla turned to Danielle and pointed at the saint. "I think she'll like them, too, no?"

The girl smiled and pressed her face against her mother's thigh.

"I need something to keep me calm. To help me focus. I have a big test coming up." Rosa pointed to the incense sticks by the herbs and teas. "Can I get cinnamon?"

Perla took the pack, then walked over to the register to ring her up. "How's school?"

"Good. Just a lot of things to memorize, you know?" She sighed, unzipping her purse. "Who knew studying cosmetology would be so hard?"

"It's worth it, though." Perla put the incense in a paper bag and handed it to Rosa. "You'll see."

"I hope so." She took Danielle's hand, and they turned toward the door. "We'll come by your house tomorrow. After my test. I'll let you know how it went."

Hayley Garrett burst through the door, nearly knocking Rosa and Danielle down.

"Envy," Hayley said, tucking back strands of blond hair and shoving her keys in her back pocket. "Someone has that envy thing for me. What you told this one man last time I was in here."

"Envidia?" Perla asked. "The Evil Eye?"

"That's what I mean. I was in the bathroom at work, in one of the stalls. I overheard this girl, Iris Camacho, tell someone else she hated skinny white girls. She said my name. She said 'I want 'em all to go away. They're so stupid.' Something like that. I didn't catch the rest because somebody flushed."

Perla thought a moment. "How have you been feeling? Tired? Anxious?"

"Well, I always feel that way."

"Has your period come on time?"

"Yeah." The girl smirked.

"Stomach feeling okay? No heartburn?"

"Nope," Hayley said. "I've been too freaked out to eat. Working two jobs is a lot. I lost ten pounds. Everything fits me baggy." She laughed. "This Evil Eye, isn't it like a curse? Maybe she cursed me, and that's why I'm not eating. That possible?"

Perla said, "Well, yes."

"Yeah. I think that's what she did. She cursed me." Hayley paused, then laughed again. "Maybe it's a blessing. I'm starting to look good."

"Losing weight quickly like that could do bad things to your body and your system."

Hayley touched her stomach. "Well, I guess it's not worth it then. All right, all right. What do I do?"

The white wood chips of the cuasia rattled inside the plastic bag when Perla reached for it on the peg and handed it to Hayley. Cuasia, Perla explained, worked to strengthen the body and restore balance.

"I want you to soak these wood chips," Perla said. "Use one teaspoon of the chips for each cup of cold water. Steep this for twelve hours, then strain it. Drink one cup in the morning on an empty stomach and a second cup at night. Understand?"

The girl nodded.

Perla also sold her a bottle of "Repel Evil" bath salts and a "Hex Removing" veladora. "Here," she said. "Bathe with the 'Repel Evil' salts in the morning before work. It'll protect you from the girl's envidia. Light the candle at night when you're alone."

Hayley ran her finger across the pictures on the front of the candle.

"Horseshoes," Perla said. "Rabbit's feet. Crosses. Lucky symbols. Positivity."

"I hope this works," Hayley said. "Even though I might gain back all that weight I lost."

*   *   *

It was time to close. Perla began where she always did, dusting the figure of San Antonio, who stood guard on the wooden table by the front window. She took a bottle of ammonia and, using a crumpled-up sheet of newspaper, wiped down the window's glass. She straightened the statues displayed on the right-hand wall and made sure they all faced forward. She organized the shelves of soaps and oils, bath salts, and incense sticks. Some of the pegs on the wall were empty, so she grabbed some herbs from the back to fill in the gaps. She rearranged the gems and crystals, the books and decks of Tarot cards, the amulets and pendants, the rosaries and crucifixes inside the glass case where the register sat. She took inventory in her binder—noting which candles were low, what packets of incense sticks had sold, what herbs and teas she was missing—and set the list next to the phone. *I'll place an order first thing tomorrow morning.*

She locked the door, then closed out the register, separating her starting fund for tomorrow and recounting it before putting it back into the drawer. She took the rest of the money and placed it in a metal cash box. Tucking the box under her arm, Perla walked to the broom closet next to the bathroom. The closet was cramped, only wide enough for one bucket and two mops. She bent down to hide the box under a loose floorboard, then pushed the bucket over the spot.

She filled a glass bowl with tap water from the sink in the kitchenette and returned to the front of the store. Perla looked at all the stones—lapis, limestone, tourmaline—inside the display case. Removing a piece of quartz, she let her fingers slide across the edge and brought it up to her nose. It carried the scent of something fossilized, of ancient oceans and extinct fishes. Quartz helped with concentration, with memory and enlightenment and insight. Perla rubbed the stone three times over each eye and pressed it against the middle of her forehead, leaving it there for a minute to see if she sensed its energy, before dropping it into the water. The stone tapped the edges of the bowl as she carried it toward the statue of Santa Bárbara and set it on the floor beside Danielle's flowers.

She took more statues from the shelves—Our Lady of Guadalupe, the

Buddha, San Simón, Vishnu—and arranged them around Santa Bárbara. She grabbed one of the fold-up chairs she kept near the door, placed it before them, and sat down. She focused hard on the statues' faces. She wanted them to say something. She wanted to witness them move or bleed from the palms of their hands and the soles of their feet. But nothing happened.

She imagined the botánica's counters and walls as outstretched arms, beaded with amulets and ankhs and silver medallions, those arms then becoming her own, gathering her customers in. She thought about wisdom that stretched on and on, beyond the sky, beyond that and into death. She closed her eyes, tried to see it, to tap it. But nothing came.

Perla could not do what they said or believed, could not float through walls and utter strange words, could not speak with the spirits of the dead. She never could, and she knew she never would.

But Darío had said she had el don, the gift. It was strong in her. He had said so. And there were times she had even believed him.

.   .   .

The iron security gate unfolded like the bellows of an accordion as Perla pulled it along the rail in front of the door. She snapped the padlock shut, turned around the corner of the building, and headed home. Her house was close, just across the empty lot next to the shopping center. Wild sage and scrub grew beside the worn path that cut through the field. Boys sometimes rode their bikes there, doing tricks and wheelies as they bumped over mounds and breaks, falling down, laughing and scraping their knees, their faces coated with grime. Their tires left thin tracks that looped around the salt cedar trees, around the soiled mattresses and old washers and sinks that were dumped here.

People told of a curse on these grounds, of a group of monks traveling through Agua Mansa in the days when California was still a part of Mexico, back before states were shapes on a map. They said a tribe of Indians massacred the monks; they skinned them and scattered their body parts around the lot for the crows. Still others said Mexican settlers had been lynched from the branches of the cedars by Anglos who stole their land for the railroads. Seeing a piece of stone, Perla wondered about the monks and those men dangling from branches. *A tooth? Part of a toe?* Empty soda cans and wrappers were caught under boulders and discarded car parts. *What would the monks think about having a tire for a headstone, a couch for a marker?* She thought of her husband, Guillermo, of his tombstone, of the thick green lawns of the cemetery where he was buried.

When she reached her house and stepped inside, the air was warm and silent. Perla put her purse down on the rocking chair near the front door and went around, pushing the lace curtains back and cracking open the windows. She breathed in the scent of wood smoke from someone's fireplace down the street, a smell that reminded her of her father toasting garbanzo beans. She went into the kitchen and looked for something to eat.

Dinner was a bowl of instant oatmeal with two slices of toast, which she took out to the patio. The night was cold, and the steam from the oatmeal rose up and fogged her glasses as she spooned it in her mouth. Police sirens wailed down the street, and dogs answered, their cries lonely and beautiful. She looked up, and in the flashing lights saw a set of glowing red eyes.

Perla flicked on the porch light. It was an opossum, its fur dingy and gray, the tips and insides of its ears bright pink. It stood motionless, behind the trunk of the organ pipe cactus, staring at her. It climbed to the top of the fence, making a low, faint jingle as it moved. Perla looked again; a small brass bell was tied to a piece of red yarn knotted around the opossum's tail. She took her spoon and threw it. When it hit the bottom of the fence, the animal darted, the clatter of the bell frantic. The opossum disappeared behind the branches of the avocado tree and down the other side of the fence into the empty lot, the ringing growing fainter and fainter.

From under the kitchen sink, behind the pile of cloths and old sponges she could never bring herself to throw away, was a bottle of rum. She poured some into a cup and took a drink. Then another. The warmth calmed her nerves.

She imagined the ghosts of the dead monks and the lynched men rising up from the ground, awakened by her thoughts. Curls of gray smoke at first, they slowly took human form. They walked in a straight line. One in front of the other. A slow procession following the opossum's tracks through the lot and back home.

She took another drink and closed her eyes. That animal. It was a messenger. It was letting her know. Something was out there. It was coming.

She sat down and waited for it.

Release

Blanca, my sister, stands in front of the mirror, rocking her hips to a song on the radio, puckering her lips and blowing kisses at herself. She tosses me a bottle of nail polish, bright red with silver bits swirling around inside. When I put it on her nightstand, Blanca says to take it, that she bought it for me. The color's too bright, I tell her. She laughs.

Pulling me off her bed, Blanca walks me over to the mirror, tells me to look at my reflection, at my pretty green eyes. Pictures of some of her boyfriends are taped along the edge of the mirror. I look past those photos to the red pimples on my face, the dark and blotchy skin, and the rolls around my belly stretching out my shirt, my jeans, the elastic band around my underwear. My body's out of control.

Blanca wants to go to school to be a makeup artist and hair stylist, so she's always trying to pretty me up, always trying to put lipstick and mascara on me. She takes clips from the drawer to fasten my hair. There's something about the way my sister moves, the way her fingers pass over my face, the way her body hums. She glides. It's like she's underwater. When I remove the hair clips, Blanca gets upset, wants to know what's with me. She doesn't get me. Says that I mope too much and that I should learn to be more confident. But it's hard to be confident when you weigh as much as I do. When your body's so big that even breathing's hard.

My mother comes into the room, holding the car keys. We're going to the botánica to buy more of the tea I've been drinking to control my appetite. Blanca shakes her head and asks if the tea's even working. I just lost five pounds, and my mother reminds her of this.

My sister rolls her eyes.

In the car, my mother lights a cigarette. She says I shouldn't pay any attention to Blanca. That five pounds is five pounds, and I shouldn't let her attitude discourage me. My mother's recently cut her hair short and bleached it because she started seeing too much gray. It's spiked on top, and she thinks this makes her look edgy. She's decked out in gold and silver anklets and a toe ring that she never takes off.

My great-grandfather used to call my mother "Gorda" because she was chubby when she was a young girl. He would pinch her cheeks and stomach. It was embarrassing, and it wasn't until after my mother gave birth to me and started exercising that she lost the weight. And it's because of her "victory over obesity" that my mother's decided to help me win my battle.

She says that, in many ways, I'm lucky that my weight's mostly around my belly because stretch marks there are easy to deal with, that you can take the sap from an aloe vera stem and rub it on them and, over time, they'll disappear. But her weight was all in her thighs, where the stretch marks almost never go away.

As we drive down the street, my mother goes on and on about self-esteem and self-perception, about men not wanting to marry fat women, and I find my mind wandering, tuning out her voice. I catch a glimpse of myself in the sideview mirror. The words *objects are closer than they appear* are stenciled along the bottom of the glass, and when I lean my head out the window, the words are tattooed across my forehead.

I began gaining weight a few years ago. It hit me fast. My mother blamed herself for not taking better care of me and regulating my diet. She decided that this summer was our chance. We needed to do something before it was too late. We needed a plan of attack. So my problem became her project. The strategy was to have me exercise from her stack of old workout tapes, the same ones that had helped her lose weight, and to begin drinking the tea we got from the botánica.

She's been going there for years to consult Perla, the owner, on everything from nerves and migraines to picking lucky lottery numbers and the whole business with my father. I was one and Blanca three when she kicked him out for gambling her life's savings away. The first place she ran to after she did that was the botánica. Perla told her what saint to petition for help in finding a husband, but aside from a few boyfriends here and there who drank or cried too much, she's never really found a man.

Since my summer vacation started, I exercise once a day for at least an hour. I drink the tea twice—once in the morning in place of breakfast and again in the afternoon. I eat a very light lunch and dinner, mainly vegetables, skinless chicken breasts, and fish. She knows I hate all this, that I feel it's not working and that we're wasting our time and money. The other day I asked her why she didn't just take me to a doctor. She said doctors don't know anything about this. Doctors would look at me and say I was fine. They'd stick me in a room, put me on a scale, poke me, give me a clean bill, and she'd be left owing all the money. No way, she said. Who needs that? We can beat this, she said. The workout tapes are the best, she said. And she believes in old Perla, her bitter teas, her store crowded with saints and Buddhas, jars of powders and vials of oils to seduce lovers and attract good fortune.

Five pounds, my mother says as we pull up to the botánica, and she stabs her cigarette butt into the ashtray. She spreads her fingers out, wiggles them. Five pounds.

      *   *   *

The botánica's air is stuffy, as if no one's opened the windows in years. It smells like a bottle of vitamins. When I was younger, Perla had display racks and bookcases in the middle of the store. Once a man in crutches came in. He couldn't make his way around the place, and she had to move some of the chairs so that he could get to the counter. I tried not to stare at him.

Perla greets me from behind the counter. She puts her glasses on and stands there looking at me for a minute like she doesn't know who I am. Sometimes I imagine what she must have looked like when she was younger, if she was the kind of girl who had a lot of boyfriends. Even though she's older, her arms are trim and lean, and they remind me of those of a British grandmother I saw once on television who was training to swim across the English Channel.

"Where's your mamá?" she asks.

I point and say she's smoking and can't come in but that she says hello.

She congratulates me when I tell her I lost five pounds. She says it's a start, a great start, and that by drinking the tea and doing my exercises, I'll probably lose more.

As she gives me the tea and I reach out to pay, the bill falls out of my hand. I bend down to pick it up and knock over a rack of prayer cards. Perla laughs when she sees me gathering them. "Don't worry," she says. "I'll get it."

She waves goodbye and tells me to say hello to my mother.

I close the door behind me and walk to the car where my mother waits.

·   ·   ·

The whole business with the job wasn't my idea. A few weeks ago my mother told me about the part-time cashier's position at Las Glorias Market. Her friend Cecilia, who is a supervisor there, had mentioned that they needed to fill the spot quickly. The exercise tapes and the tea were good, my mother thought, but what I really needed was to be on my feet, moving around more.

"It's great pay," she'd said. "They have contests and raffles for employees. Cruises and getaways to resorts in the desert."

I wasn't into the idea. I imagined myself in one of those green smocks the employees at Las Glorias wear. Pulled tight over my stomach, my body squeezed in the cashier's booth. I shook my head and told her I couldn't do it. That I had no experience.

"You're smart," she said. "They'll train."

She kept pressuring me until I gave in and went down to fill out the application and schedule an interview with Cecilia. They gave me a math test where I had to show that I could count back change and figure out percentages without using a calculator. I got all the problems right, and that same day I was told the job was mine.

The cashier's booth where Cecilia and I spent this past week training was too small for both of us, so she had me stand on the outside instead of right next to her. When I told her I was sorry she said, "We'll manage," smiling, but avoiding eye contact.

My training period is over today. Before the start of my shift, Cecilia walks me out to the front of the market, and we sit on a bench next to the twenty-five-cent merry-go-round. It's real hot, and the sunlight stings through my black pants. I wish I could wear shorts and sandals, something light and thin. Nothing dark and thick like what I always have to.

Cecilia reaches into her pocket and gives me a red star to pin on my apron. "Red is after you finish your training," she says. "On your year anniversary, you get a green one."

She points to two gold ones pinned on her apron. "Each of these represents five years I been with the company."

I ask if she ever gets sick of the whole thing.

She rubs her hands against her jeans. She wears a man's flannel shirt two sizes too large with the sleeves rolled up. A mother walks over to the merry-go-round, puts her daughter on one of the horses, and feeds a coin into the slot. The horses bob slowly up and down to the song "My Favorite Things."

"I've got a good job here," Cecilia says. "A steady paycheck. Good people to work with. Why would I leave?"

Cecilia assigns Miguel Angel to bag for me. I've never talked to him, but I'd seen him on my first day, sitting in his car out in the parking lot with the stereo blaring music. He's not much to look at, and his face is dotted with acne scars the size of thumbprints. Both his ears are pierced, and they made him take the hoops out and cover the holes with bandages.

"Hey," he says when he gets to my station.

I try to ignore him.

"Rosa." He squints at my nametag. "I'm Miguel Angel."

I shake his hand.

He points to the star. "What's that for?"

"After your training, they give you one."

"Sweet. Congratulations."

"Thanks. Didn't they give you a star?" I ask, eyeing his apron.

"No. Guess I'm a special case."

When my shift ends, I walk to the break room and collect my things. Just this morning management had put out a box to raffle off a trip to the Bahamas, and it's already filled to the top with folded pieces of paper. I take a pencil and fill out an entry form. I imagine myself thin. In a tangerine bikini. On a beach with a radio next to me, my skin shiny with lotion.

"Have you ever been there?" a voice asks from behind. I turn to see Miguel Angel standing by the bathroom door. He winks at me.

I shake my head.

He sits down on some cases of diet soda. "Could I ask you a question, Rosa?"

I shrug, folding the form up and pushing in into the box with the rest.

"What's your last name?"

"Why?"

"Just curious."

I point to my time card.

He squints. "Rodríguez. Cool," he says. "I'm Miguel Angel Cabrera."

I tell him I have to go, that my mom's waiting for me outside.

"Okay," he says. "Te watcho."

"Yeah," I say. "Later."

When I get home, I hang my apron on the coat rack near our front door, the red points of my star getting caught in one of Blanca's knit caps. I change into sweats and stand in front of the television, exercising to my mother's workout tapes.

The woman on the tape wears tights and bends and stretches and tells me to breathe, to feel my muscles working, to push and pull and lift and move, her voice keeping with the beat of the music playing in the background. When we reach the end, she sits down Indian-style on a black mat and raises both hands over her head. "Breathe in," she says. "Then out. Relax. Exhale. Exhale. And exhale."

The video stops and pops out of the VCR. I turn the television off and sit on the couch, toweling my face, breathing so hard and heavy my chest hurts. I can't even think about getting back up right now.

*   *   *

Every Saturday at noon, a mariachi band performs in the market's parking lot. They set up next to a cart that sells slices of fresh mangoes and cucumbers powdered with chili.

Miguel Angel is assigned to bag for me again.

"Hey, it was cool bagging for you yesterday," he says. "We make a good team."

I nod and continue ringing up my customer.

"Do you like this kind of music, Rosa?" He points at the lot with his chin.

"I don't know," I say.

He gives the customer her groceries and puts his hands on the counter. There's no one at my check stand. We watch the band through the store windows, the musicians in their tight gold pants and matching jackets with embroidered designs, their hats as big as buckets.

"You don't know?" he says.

"I don't know it that well," I say. He winks, flashes a smile. I smile back.

"Got a smile. Got a smile." He claps his hands. "I knew I could. Cumbia. Do you like cumbia?"

"I don't know that either." A group of people has gathered around the band, and some dance to the music.

"I got this tradition going," he says. "See, every Saturday night I listen to music in my apartment. By myself. I open the windows and crank some tunes."

"That sounds fun."

At about two, Cecilia has us take our breaks. We sit on the benches in front of the market just as the mariachi band is getting ready to leave, putting the violins and trumpets in their cases and snapping them shut.

"How old are you?" he asks.

"Sixteen."

"Do you got a boyfriend?"

"No."

"Really?"

"Really."

"That surprises me. You're way pretty."

I think about my wide thighs that remind me of tree trunks, my blouse stretched out so far that the buttons look like they're about to come undone. I think about Blanca. Always wanting to do my makeup and nails. "You should think about going to beauty school with me," she'd said as she clipped my hair up the other day when we were in her room. "We could open up a salon. Be in business together. 'Rodríguez and Sister Salon.' What do you say?"

"Maybe," I'd said. "Who knows what I'll end up doing with this life."

"Why are you so quiet for?" Miguel Angel asks, looking over at me.

"Just because."

"Hey, you should come over to my place next Saturday, and I can teach you about cumbia music."

I cross my arms. "Why?"

"It'll enrich your life."

"My life's pretty rich already," I say.

"You're missing out, girl."

"I'm sure a guy like you can find someone more exciting to spend a Saturday night with."

"What's that mean? What's with the attitude? Maybe I wanna hang out with you."

"Why?"

"Don't be that way." He laughs, his smile smoothing out his acne scars so that they dissolve into his skin. "It'll be fun. Come over next Saturday." He taps me on the shoulder with his knuckle. When he stops, I find myself hoping he'll do it again.

"Maybe."

"Maybe? Come on, Rosa. Just for a while. I promise I won't do nothing. If I do, you know where I work."

"Depends," I say. "On how I'm feeling."

"We'll play it by ear then."

"What do you want with me?"

"What do you mean? Hey, I'm cool here. Okay? I just wanna hang out."

"I don't know."

"Think about it," he says. "Consider yourself invited."

"I will. Thanks."

I look at my watch and realize our break's nearly over. We get up and walk back inside, the automatic doors sliding shut behind us, the air conditioner cooling our skin.

*   *   *

We clean the house Saturday mornings. We each have a section: Blanca gets the kitchen and one of the bathrooms; I get the living room and the second bathroom; my mother supervises, does the vacuuming, and mops the kitchen and dining room floors.

At work today, Miguel Angel will want to know if I'm going to listen to music at his place. I haven't seen him all week.

"What do I tell this guy?" I ask Blanca. She's scrubbing the stovetop with a scouring pad, her hair wrapped in a bandanna.

"What do you mean what do you tell him? You go."

"Keep it low." I peek my head down the hall, listening to my mother vacuuming.

"Is he cute?" Blanca straightens and looks over at me.

"I don't know. I guess."

"Does he go to your school?"

"He's older."

"How much older?"

"I think he's about twenty-five."

"You tramp," she says, laughing. "Go for it."

After I've showered and dressed for work, Blanca comes into my room and sits on my bed. "Let me see your hand, fool," she tells me.

"Why?"

"Sit. I'm doing your nails."

She starts by smoothing out the tips of my fingernails with a file, bringing my hands up to her face, scraping away the dirt underneath, blowing on each one before buffing it. Once that's finished, she uses the end of the file to push back my cuticles. Reaching for the bottle of polish, she shakes it a few times and paints each nail, using long and even strokes.

"Just make sure he sees your hands," she says after she's done. "He'll go crazy over this color. What are you gonna tell Mom?"

"That I'm working a long shift."

"Good one," Blanca says.

He was assigned to stock today so he didn't bag for me, but we were scheduled off at the same time. After our shifts end, we head over to his place.

He lives in an apartment building called the Agua Mansa Palms in a part of the city known as the Zoo because all the streets are named for animals—Antelope, Buffalo, Coyote. His place is on the second floor, away from the street. From the living room window, I look down onto a narrow alley where green and blue trash cans with numbers painted on their sides are lined up against the wall. He pours a soda for me into a plastic tumbler with the image of a cartoon dog, rubbed away from too much washing.

"Sorry I don't got a better glass," he says.

"It's all good. Have you lived here long?"

"Naw. Only a few months." The stereo sits on the floor. He walks over and turns it on. "I won't turn it up too loud. I don't want the people downstairs to get pissed. Listen, okay?"

"Okay." I finish my soda, and he gets me another.

The bass line travels along the floor, and I feel it through the soles of my work shoes. Accordions blend with trumpets, trombones, and a woman's high-pitched voice.

"Were you serious when you said you never heard this music before?" He walks over to the kitchen and returns with a beer in one hand, a soda in the other.

"Well, no. I've heard it. I'm just not familiar with it."

"What do you mean?" He takes a sip of his beer.

"It's not my style."

"What do you mean it's not your style?"

"It's just not." I put my hand up to my face, pretend to examine my nails. "All that music just sounds too much alike to me anyway."

"Don't say that. Listen, this is cumbia. Those guys in the parking lot, they play mariachi. Big difference."

"I get it," I say, nodding. "I think I get it."

"Check it out, let me play you some more of my favorites."

About a half-hour later, I decide to leave. "This was fun," I say. "I should go, though."

"So soon? But there's more I want you to hear."

"Sorry. I have to go."

"Did I at least get you interested in cumbia?"

"A little," I say. "I can see myself getting to like it. Learning more about it."

"Cool," he says. "Let me give you a ride." He reaches for his keys and sunglasses.

"I'll walk."

"Don't be dumb. You've been on your feet all day. Plus it's still pretty hot out there."

I have him drop me off on the corner, so my mom doesn't see us. "Thanks for the ride."

"No problem. Wait," he says as I reach for the handle. "What you said back at the apartment, did you mean it?"

"What part?"

"The part about wanting to learn more about cumbias."

"Maybe." I get out of the car and shut the door.

He leans across the seat, rolls the passenger-side window down, and looks up at me, his arm sticking to the back of the hot vinyl car seat. "Maybe this is something we can do every Saturday after work. You can come over, and we can listen to cumbias. I can teach you about them."

"Why are you all eager to teach me this?" I sigh, pretending to examine my nails again.

"Because I think you're missing out on something meaningful."

"Not even," I say.

He slides his sunglasses down the bridge of his nose, and it excites me. I see my face in the car's window. My features look distorted. My cheeks narrow out and when I smile, the bright sunlight does something to my lips and they pucker out, soft and full and exotic.

"It's all in Spanish," I say. "I don't understand most of what they're saying anyways."

"You don't gotta listen to the words. Just the music. Come on. You can see I'm a perfect gentleman. Didn't try nothing today."

"Fine. But don't think I don't know how to take care of myself." I put my hand on my hip.

"I know you do. I'm not dumb. I'll see you at work." He pulls away from the curb, his Renault speeding off down my street.

When I walk in the house, my mother asks how work was.

"Same," I say. "The customers were rude. The break room was boiling because the air-conditioning vents broke down, so I went into the cooler."

At dinner she reminds me to do my exercises before bed.

I tell her, "What do you think I've been doing every night?" I look over at Blanca, roll my eyes, and she laughs.

"What's with you? Rosa, I'm trying to help you here," my mother says.

"Is that what you call it?" I say, thinking of the way I'd looked in the car's window today.

She puts her fork down and stares at me. "Just look at yourself. Look at that body. Do you want to go on living like that?"

"Mother, stop," Blanca tells her. "It's baby fat."

"What do you know?" she says to Blanca. "Stay out of this. Baby fat, my ass."

Later that night, after I've exercised and showered, Blanca comes into my room. I sit on the floor in my nightgown, and she climbs on my bed. She takes a few strands of my wet hair and braids them together.

"What got into you?" she says.

"I don't know," I say. "I was just tired."

"I saw you guys parked at the corner."

"You did?"

"Yeah. He's cute. He reminds me of Jacob."

Jacob, whose picture is one of those she has taped to her dresser's mirror, is a Jewish guy Blanca dated for six months until he moved with his family to Florida. On their last night together, she lit some candles, snuck him into her room, and they made out until the sun came up. They still write to each other, and Blanca plans on visiting him sometime next year. She doesn't know how she'll get there, but she will, she tells me. She will.

"What's this guy's name anyway?" she asks.

"Miguel Angel."

"Nice. Did he notice the nails?"

"No."

"Shit."

I turn to face her. "I'm hanging out with him again next Saturday, though."

She smiles. "He's so into you."

"You think so?"

"Yup. I know so."

Later that night, I lie in bed with my hair wet, my pillow dampening and smelling of conditioner. I picture Miguel Angel and me sitting on his couch, making out, touching each other all over the place. I slip my underwear off and let my finger feel the moisture gathering between my legs before I slide it in, let it tickle the walls inside. Turning my face toward the pillow, I pant into it, imagine him on top of me, in me. I tense up just before I release and my body, my whole body, melts into the mattress.

*   *   *

On the second Saturday, he tries to get me to dance with him.

He stands in front of me, his feet bare and shuffling across the hardwood floor. "Come on, Rosa."

"I don't know how to dance."

"You promised," he shouts over the music. "You told me on Wednesday that you'd dance with me today. Take off your shoes."

"I never promised you anything."

"Stop being shy. Come on." His hands beckon me.

I kick my shoes off, pull down my socks, and stand. The hardwood floor creaks under my feet.

He squeezes my hands. "You're afraid. You're trembling."

"I'm fine."

"Do you want some water or something?"

"I'm fine. Really." I let go of his hands. "I don't think I'm ready to learn this yet."

"Come on."

"I'm not good. I've got no rhythm."

"Close your eyes."

"No, I don't—"

"Just do it. Don't be afraid."

I do it, and I feel his hands press against my hips and move them back and forth. Slowly first, then quickly. The whole apartment shakes to the vibration of the music. The sound waves travel through me, right down to my muscles, my bones, breaking things up, making my skin lose its grip on my body.

"Feel that?" he says. "Feel that?"

"Yeah."

His body presses against mine. "Let it in, Rosa." He leans in and whispers it to me. "Let it in."

We take quick steps around his living room, sometimes tripping on each other, laughing as we do.

"You're pretty good," he says.

"You're just saying that." After a while, I sit down on the couch and try to catch my breath.

"Here." He hands me a glass of water. "Are you feeling okay?"

"I'm okay," I say, panting.

"Are you sure?"

"I'm fine."

"Do you need something to eat?"

"What?" I turn to look up at him.

"Do you need something to eat?"

"Nobody ever asks me that."

"Oh," he says. "I get it. Sorry."

"I wasn't always like this," I say. "I used to be thin."

"Oh yeah? Well, I wasn't always this nice. I used to get into all kinds of trouble." He sits on the couch and fans my face with his hand. "Couldn't stay out of it."

He drives me home again and parks near the same spot on the corner. Before I step out, he leans over and gives me a light kiss on the cheek.

"Next Saturday?" he says, putting the car in gear.

"Yeah."

"Good. I'll teach you to salsa."

*   *   *

On the third Saturday, we mostly talk over the music. He serves me carrots and chopped cucumbers with ranch dressing on a paper plate.

"Eat. Don't matter if you're heavy, Rosa. You gotta eat."

This morning I'd filled my thermos with some of the tea to take to work. I'd planned on drinking it during my break, but it had been too busy, and Cecilia never gave me one. I brought the thermos up with me to his apartment.

"I have to drink this first," I say, unscrewing the cap.

"What is it?"

"It's this tea to help me lose weight."

He leans over and puts his nose next to the opening. "Stinks like cat piss."

"It does." I pour the whole thing into a cup that he gives me.

"Wait," he says. "You're really gonna drink that?"

"I have to."

"You don't have to." Reaching across the table, Miguel Angel takes the cup. He pinches his nose, raises it to his mouth, and swallows the tea in three giant gulps. "I took that one for you. Now you owe me another dance."

"You didn't have to."

"I wanted to."

"I hate this. I hate myself."

"What do you mean?"

"Look at me." My hands slap my thighs. "Just look."

"I'm looking."

"And?"

"And nothing."

"I'm fat," I say.

"So you are. So what. You've got plenty to feel good about."

"Like what?"

"For one, you've got a family. More than I've ever had."

"What do you mean?"

"It's only been me and my dad. I don't talk to him a lot. Kicked me out when I started getting into trouble." He pauses and takes a deep breath. "Broke into a sporting goods store with a buddy. Did my time. I was in jail for five years. My dad never came to see me. Guess he always hoped I'd turn out different. It feels like shit coming out and having no one there to meet you, you know?"

"I'm sorry," I say.

"It's okay. I got used to it. Had this crazy guy from Oklahoma City named Tucker for a cellmate. Guy was a real trip. But jail's a bad place no matter what. A straight-up bad place."

"But you're out now," I say. "You're free."

"Yeah. Have a job at the market. A parole officer who checks up on me." His eyes scan the apartment: its bare walls, its curtainless windows, its dripping sink in the kitchen. "I'm real free now."

*   *   *

Perla had a small ice chest with fruit bars that she sold for fifty cents when I was a little girl. I can still see the faded spot in the linoleum where it stood.

"The grape ones were your favorites. Turning your tongue so dark purple it almost looked black." Perla watches me stare at the empty spot as she gets another box of the tea.

"They were so good. Especially during the summer," I say. "On days like this." I'm running low on tea again. My mother was going to drive me, but I told her it would be better if I walked, that I could burn extra calories.

Perla gives me my tea and as I head out the door, I turn back around. "Why don't I feel this tea is working?" My question catches her by surprise.

"You lost five pounds, didn't you?"

"I gained some of it back. Then I lost another eight."

"Some people are like that. Their weight fluctuates."

"What do I do?"

"What you're doing now. Just keep drinking your tea. Eat right. Exercise. Focus. Do everything you can to keep the weight off."

"It's frustrating. I'm losing it. But it doesn't feel like it's enough."

"I know. But I've helped other women lose weight with this. Remember that it takes time. You'll see. You'll start to notice yourself change."

"It doesn't make sense to me. Maybe I was meant to be this way."

"You haven't been doing this very long. You have to be patient."

"Why am I doing this?"

"Many reasons," she says. "Health. Self-esteem. Happiness. Your family doesn't want to see you hurting."

My eyes fall on the spot on the floor again. I remember the cooler's hum, the old box of baking soda underneath the fruit pops, the smell of damp cardboard. "I'm not," I say. "I'm not hurting."

She's quiet for a long time. She steps forward. Reaching across the counter, she takes the box of tea back. "If you think you don't need this, tell me." She points to the shelves and candles, the herbs and incense sticks. "Tell me, Rosita."

"I don't," I say in a low voice. "I don't need this right now."

"Fine." She opens the register and pulls out the bill I paid with. She folds it in half and presses it in my hand. "But come back to me when you do need this. You. No one else. I'll be here. Waiting."

*   *   *

"I want to talk to you about this new friend of yours." My mother comes up to me in the kitchen as I drink the last of my tea. It's early Friday morning, and I'm scheduled to be in at eleven. Blanca's standing against the kitchen counter reading the newspaper, taking bites from a piece of toast.

"What new friend?" I ask.

"This Miguel Angel guy," she says.

"What about him?"

"Yeah, what about him?" Blanca says.

"Cecilia called me earlier," my mother says. "She talked to me about him. Says she's been seeing you two leaving together after your shifts on Saturday. Is that true?"

"Yeah. It's fine. We're just friends."

"Friends? Well, did you know your friend is on parole?"

"Parole!" Blanca shouts. "Get out of here. No way."

My mother turns to her. "Blanca, please." She shakes her head.

"Yeah. So he's on parole," I say. "So what?"

"So what? Tell me," my mother says. "What do you think he wants with you?"

"Let it go, Mom," I tell her. "Are you driving me to work or not?"

"Men like him are always up to something. You better watch it," she responds.

"You're thinking that just because I'm fat a guy can't like me, right? That a guy like him can't find me attractive?"

"I didn't say that. But just take a moment. Look at yourself."

"I'm over that, Mom. He taught me how to dance. That's all." I walk over to the sink and pour what's left of my tea down the drain.

"He's bad news, Rosa," she says.

"So what if he is. I don't care. I don't need any of this."

"Fine," she says. "It's your life. Mess it up. Live however you want."

I walk out the front door. From inside I hear Blanca shouting, "Go on. You go to that man." She's clapping and cheering, her bare feet slapping against the kitchen floor.

*   *   *

I get all the way to his street before I realize I'm dressed in my green apron and hat with the market's logo on the front. The city's repaving his block, and I make my way down the sidewalk, smeared in spots with black streaks of asphalt. Miguel Angel doesn't work on Fridays. He isn't home when I get there, so I sit out on the front stoop and wait. About an hour later I see him strolling up.

"Hey," he says.

"What's up?"

"What are you doing here? Didn't expect to see you till tomorrow."

"Are you pissed I came? I can go."

"Not pissed. Just surprised. What's happening?"

"My mom."

"Your mom?"

"Cecilia called and told her you're on parole. Thinks you're a bad element. Doesn't want me seeing you."

"Maybe your mom's right." He looks out across the street.

"Maybe people should stop telling me what to do."

"What's wrong with that? Shows they care for you."

"Shows they think I'm not smart enough to do things for myself. That I'm helpless and should be grateful for every bit of good attention I get because I'm so fat."

"No one's saying that. You're thinking it."

"What? So now you know what I'm thinking?"

"Don't get pissed at me. I'm on your side, remember?"

I untie my apron and toss in on the ground. "I didn't mean to get mad."

"It's cool. I understand. No worries."

"You've been a good friend. A good listener."

"It's the least I could do," he says. "Someone did the same for me when I was in jail."

"Yeah?"

"Yeah. This girl named Wendy." He walks over and sits next to me on the stoop. "A friend of Tucker's sister. We used to write to each other. I'd draw these sketches for her—birds, clouds, a cliff with trees I'd seen in a book.

Her letters helped me so much, you know? Helped me get by. I couldn't wait to get them. I thought about going to see her once I was out. To thank her in person."

"Why haven't you?"

"Don't know. Guess I'm chickenshit. Guess it's enough to know that there's someone out there that's got my letters. It's enough to know that my words and sketches, my thoughts, are out there roaming free without me. Floating around."

I try to imagine her, this Wendy. A housewife with a husband and kids. An ex-con's letters pressed between her mattresses. I see her taking them out and reading them when she's alone. I think about the thrill they give her. See her living with that feeling for the rest of the day as she bathes her kids and makes her husband dinner.

Around us everything's still, and the temperature's starting to rise. The sun beats down on us, and the cheap polyester of my uniform makes it feel ten degrees hotter. Torn scraps of paper and fast food wrappers are stuck to the melted asphalt out in the street. The smell reminds me of the field trip my fourth grade class took to the La Brea Tar Pits. A tour guide explained to us that prehistoric mammoths and birds wandered into the dark pools and got trapped there. The tar worked like quicksand. The more they struggled to free themselves, the deeper they were dragged in. These creatures died, and their bones lay buried for millions of years without anyone ever knowing they'd lived.

Feast of
Saint Valentine

Priest and Martyr

Patron of love, lovers, engaged couples,

happy marriages,

greeting card manufacturers,

and beekeepers.

Invoked against fainting, plague, and epilepsy.

Even though the bed was warm, the sheets soft against her skin, Perla forced herself up and got ready. She used a pail and clippers and cut the flowers from the backyard, laid each one out on the dining table, and arranged them there. A piece of twine held the stems, the bouquet wrapped in aluminum foil to keep it together and make it easier to carry. It was getting late, and she hurried. She wanted to stop off at San Salvador's first to light a candle before taking the flowers to the cemetery

When she arrived, the church was empty. She thought about Guillermo's funeral Mass—the people crowded inside to pay their respects, the heavy organ music, the mahogany wood of the coffin polished and gleaming under the church's lights.

Smoke stained the feet of the statue of Christ near the front entrance. Perla knelt before the statue, picked a flower from the bouquet, and placed it at the foot of the railing. She lit a candle and prayed an Our Father. From behind her came the sound of a door closing. She turned to see Father Madrid making his way down the aisle, and she rose to meet him.

Father Madrid was from Nicaragua. Once during a service he had told the congregants about the war he had lived through and how he had watched as his family was killed by the guerrillas who came and destroyed his village. He told how he fled, hiding inside a cave deep within the jungle, fearing for his life.

He smiled. "¿Cómo está, señora?"

"I'm good," Perla responded.

"How is everything over at the store? I tell many people here about you," he said. "I tell them to go see you for novenas and scapulars. I tell the mothers you sell the baptismal candles. Not to go to the indoor swap meet. I tell them your prices are better. I try to give you business."

"Thank you, Father."

"What pretty flowers you have there," he said. "Such a beautiful bouquet."

"They're for my parents and my husband. I'm going to the cemetery."

"Oh." He extended his arm and put his hand on her shoulder. "I didn't know you had lost your husband. I always see you alone. I just assumed he practiced another faith."

"No, he was Catholic," Perla said. "We were married in this church years ago."

"Yes? I imagine it looked different in those days."

"It was smaller. They remodeled it in the seventies. Did you know that?"

"I saw pictures. Was your husband's Mass held here?"

"Yes," Perla said. "And my parents' funerals, also."

"I see," he said. "I'm sorry for your losses. All of them. I'm glad to see you are still here."

"Yes. I'm still here."

"Remember that the church is yours. It's here for you." He pointed to the bouquet. "You want me to bless them?"

Perla offered up the flowers. Father Madrid raised his right hand and bent his index finger so that it touched his thumb. He whispered in Latin, and Perla caught words here and there that she recognized. When he finished, she thanked him and left.

*   *   *

The stone trail that curved past the cemetery gates was wet from the sprinklers. Across the lawn, plastic pinwheels and balloons twirled in the breeze. Bouquets of flowers sprouted up from vases buried in the soil.

Perla set her sweater on the ground and knelt. She took the scissors from inside her purse and trimmed around the edges of Guillermo's marker, removing tangled roots and dry blades of grass. She rose and walked to the curb with his vase. She filled it with water and went back to him. Nesting the bouquet in the vase, Perla wondered about all those other arrangements she'd left, the miniature Christmas trees, the birthday party hat she had secured to the stone with a strip of duct tape, and the cards and noisemakers. They were all probably lost in a heap of dried flowers, crunching and yellow, among stuffed animals and Easter bunnies with stained fur and missing eyes.

She picked the sweater off the ground, shook away ants, and put it on. She tucked the scissors back inside her purse and walked across the lawn to her parents' markers. She arranged their flowers before tossing the aluminum foil in a trash can. She sat on a bench near a statue of Jesus. He stood on a tall pedestal, his outstretched arms receiving the souls of the dead gathered around him. The shadow of the figure's hand fell across Perla's face, his head resting on her lap.

*   *   *

The Prospect Shopping Center was a narrow building whose white stucco exterior had flaked off in sections over the years. The bright blue trim running along the edges of the flat roof and the storefronts that faced Rancho Boulevard had faded away long ago. A sign at the edge of the parking lot stood perched on two rusted posts, and the neon bands spelling out the center's name zapped on every day at six in the evening. There were only three businesses in the strip mall—Best Donuts, Everything Ninety-Nine Cents, and the Botánica Oshún at the very end of the row.

Today a boy sat at a table in the parking lot. He was selling decorative balloons with stuffed animals floating inside, heart-shaped boxes of chocolates with white and pink ribbons, and arrangements of silk flowers. Inside Best Donuts, the owners had hung crepe hearts and silhouettes of small Cupids. Donuts with white frosting and red and pink sprinkles filled the pastry racks. Agua Mansa was drained of its blues and greens, of the yellows of school buses, of the rusted browns of trucks hauling gravel from the quarry in Colton. Everything today was red and pink.

She ordered a medium coffee and two donuts. Old Vithu counted the change back and folded the bills neatly for her, then went over to help someone else. His granddaughter Alice walked around the store with the phone pressed against her shoulder. She was speaking Cambodian, her words loud and fast, and giggling every now and again. She lit an incense stick and set it next to a gold Buddha statue sitting on top of the smoothie machine. Perla sat at the table nearest the door with her coffee and donuts; she had a few minutes to spare before it was time to open the botánica.

A radio played behind the counter. A woman's voice spoke softly. "My name is Deborah. I'm calling from Agua Mansa. I'd like to dedicate 'We've Only Just Begun' by the Carpenters," she said. "For my fiancé, Juan."

Perla sat there, taking small bites of her donuts and quick sips of coffee. Paper hearts swayed above her head, and faceless Cupids aimed their arrows at her.

*　　*　　*

The botánica was always busy on Saint Valentine's Day. When she helped the young women who came to buy candles and love potions, it was hard not to feel jealous. Perla could hear the passion in their voices. They glowed. She thought hard, tried to recall if she had ever looked that way, if her voice had ever carried the same pitch, if she had glowed. At moments, she caught quick glimpses of herself in their reflections as they leaned over the glass and peered into the cases, tucking strands of their hair back, pointing with lacquered nails, some in suits and dark slacks, others in stirrup pants and baggy sweatshirts, pushing baby carriages. Throughout the day, the customers kept coming. They bought red velas and stones, amulets and oils, Kama Sutra candles and incense sticks. The day passed quickly, and when Perla stopped to rest, she saw that it was already late in the afternoon.

Alfonso walked in a little after five. "Buenas," he said, smiling. He held out a one-hundred-dollar bill. "Could you break this?"

"You're lucky I was busy." Perla took the register key out of her pocket and opened the drawer. "You can count it out if you want." She handed him a bundle of twenties held together with a paper clip.

"No. I trust you."

His store, Everything Ninety-Nine Cents, was larger than the botánica; it had six aisles, two cash registers, four shopping carts, and a stack of wire baskets for customers to use. A cooler stocked cans of soda and bars of ice cream. They sold bottles of hair spray, toilet bowl deodorizers, sponges, plastic picture frames, combs, bars of bath soap, quarts of motor oil, teddy bears, dolls, hammers, plungers, and rubber mallets. All of this and more for only ninety-nine cents.

Alfonso had taken over the store a few years ago when his father retired.

Perla liked having him as a neighbor. He ran an honest business and took care of maintenance around the shopping center. He made sure to call the landlord right away if any of the lights in the parking lot were out or if there were potholes that needed to be patched.

"What are you doing for Valentine's Day?" Perla asked him.

"We're going dancing. That's why I'm closing early. I want us to be at the club before eight, and I still need to go home and get handsome." He winked. "And you? Don't tell me you're just going to sit at home alone."

Perla laughed and closed the register's drawer. "I'm too old for dates. I haven't danced in years."

He smiled. "Don't give me that." He rested his elbows on the glass countertop. "Why don't you come? We can cumbia. Just us two."

"And how would your wife feel about that?"

Alfonso was married, and there were times his wife, Carmen, came and helped around their shop. Carmen was a college graduate with a degree in marketing. She would sit behind the counter and ring customers up or supervise the employees. She also kept track of the store's finances, recording losses and profits in a ledger they kept in their office.

"Maybe I want it to only be you and me," he said.

"Stop that. I'm old enough to be your aunt, tonto." Perla laughed again, and slapped his hand.

She turned and looked over in the direction of his truck. Perla saw herself wearing an elegant dress, a shawl draped over her shoulders. Not in a thick purple knitted sweater with crumpled napkins and bobby pins stuffed in the pockets, not in a pair of simple black pants and worn sneakers. Her hair would be styled and beautiful, not an uncombed mass of dyed brown hair. Her body would be thin. Like it had once been. *Hadn't it been that way?* Alfonso would hold the door to the truck open. The two of them would ride off, the chrome horns on the hood like arrows guiding them to a nightclub where women twirled around in ruffled skirts and men wore cowboy hats and boots and were always brave and handsome.

Perla looked down at her hands, her thinning skin, her jagged green veins, then at the gold band of her wedding ring. In the gleam, she heard Guillermo's voice again, felt him rubbing the small brown mole on her neck that he liked to kiss.

"Be good," she told Alfonso. "There'll be sobriety checkpoints. No drinking and driving."

"No, ma'am," he said and left.

His truck backed out and disappeared down Rancho. A few minutes later, Teresa Martínez walked in, her keys bunched up in her hand. She said, "I need some tea. It's my turn to be the patient."

Teresa had been her doctor since before Guillermo's death, before Teresa moved her practice out of Agua Mansa to a modern five-story building in Rialto less than two years ago. In the months after her husband died, Perla had suffered from insomnia and had fallen into a deep depression. One afternoon, Teresa showed up on her doorstep.

"I've never known you to miss an appointment," she'd said. She sat with Perla through the evening, listening to her reminisce about Guillermo and the life they'd shared.

"I hope I'm lucky enough to have what you did," Teresa had said. "Someone worth building something that strong with. Believe me, it would make my mom happy. She keeps pressuring me to get married and have kids. 'Settle down,' she says. 'You're thirty-seven. You should be thinking about a family. Look at your brothers and sisters. All of them have kids. But you? Your father and I want to see our baby a mother before we die.' What's wrong with having a career? I have choices. This isn't Mexico. This isn't the rancho anymore. I'm happy with my life. I'm a pretty successful doctor. My job demands a lot of focus. So what if I'm single?"

That was almost five years ago. Teresa was now forty-two and still not married.

"Guess what?" Teresa said today. "I met someone. This new doctor who works in the building. He's a pediatrician."

"That's good." Perla smiled.

"He's great," Teresa told her, taking a deep breath. "He's nice and funny and successful. You should have heard my mom on the phone when I told her. I think she's started planning the wedding already."

"It's not too late," Perla said, pointing to Teresa's stomach. "For babies."

"Oh, God." She set her keys down on the counter. "You sound like my mom. Craig and I, we've only been going out for three months. It's too soon for all of that. And my life's hectic as it is, what with work."

"Is that why you're stressed?"

"Yeah." Teresa sighed. "I have so much to do. It's hard keeping up. I never thought this change was going to be so drastic."

"You regret it? The move? This new building?"

"Sometimes I do. But I couldn't stay. It was time to move on. Besides, if I hadn't I probably wouldn't have met Craig."

Teresa bought a box of valeriana tea. "And you?" she asked. "Are you feeling okay? Everything still good?"

"Yes," Perla said. "I'm fine. I'm eating right. I'm walking."

"Good," Teresa said. "I know I have all these new patients, but I still want to take care of my oldest and dearest." Teresa reached into her pocket. She pulled out a business card. She took a pen from the cup by the register and wrote down a phone number.

"This is my new cell number," she said, handing the card to Perla. "You call me anytime. If there's an emergency or whatever. Doesn't matter what time. Keep it in a safe place."

Perla tucked it behind her ID card in her wallet.

"When will I see you?" Teresa asked, grabbing her keys.

"In May," Perla said. "My checkup is in May."

"Okay. If I don't come by before that, I'll see you in May." She leaned over the counter and kissed Perla on the cheek.

"Good luck with your boyfriend," Perla told her.

"Light a vela for me." She walked out the door, her fingers crossed.

Perla dressed the candle the way Darío had taught her. She reached for the screwdriver she kept in the coffee mug packed with pens near the register. She took the last red candle from the shelf and stabbed the screwdriver into the top, making a hole in the wax deep enough to pour in some rose and lavender oil. On a scrap of paper she wrote *Teresa* and *Craig*. She drew a heart around both names, placed the paper underneath the candle, and kept it lit while she balanced the register and closed up for the day.

Perla was in the middle of untangling some scapulars when she heard a soft tap. A young boy stood in front of the door, his hands pressed against the glass pane.

"Closed," she shouted.

But the boy stood there, nervously looking over his shoulder every now and again.

"Cerrado." Perla backed away slowly. She reached for the screwdriver—red shavings from the candle still stuck to the metal—and gripped the handle. "Closed," she said again. "Come back tomorrow. Mañana."

When a car pulled into the parking lot, he turned and ran off. The sides of his fists left impressions like a baby's footprints on the window glass. She waited for thirty minutes before leaving. The air outside was cold. She buttoned up her jacket and clutched her purse. When she looked back to make sure no one was following, Perla saw only the Virgen de Guadalupe painted on the wall of the botánica facing the empty lot, the bright orange flames around Our Lady's body fading to thin black lines in the vanishing February sun.

Relics

I didn't cry when my father died. Emphysema took his life. He was a two-pack-a-day smoker. In the end, it got so bad that he had to wheel around a tank to help him breathe. We'd sit out back together listening to Dodgers games on the radio, and he'd shove a ten-dollar bill in my hand, urge me to go down to the store for one last pack of menthols, one last drag. I almost went once. But the sight of that green tank beside him and the way his body would cave in and collapse every time he coughed stopped me. I couldn't contribute to his demise. He left us six months ago.

It was just after five this afternoon, and I was sitting in my office going through some last-minute things when my girlfriend Deborah called to tell me she was canceling our date for the night.

"Don't you want to know what's wrong?" she asked when I remained quiet.

"Okay," I said. "What's wrong?"

"You. Ever since your dad died, you've been off."

I sat back in my chair. "What do you mean? Off how?"

"The Juan Sandoval that I met last year was different. He used to take me to flea markets. He'd take me out dancing and to the movies. He wouldn't mope around in his robe all weekend. He exercised. You're quiet and sulky all the time now. When I try and get you to talk to me, you clam up."

"Okay. No more silent treatment. Let's talk. What do you want to hear?"

"I want to hear that you're hurting. That you miss him. That you *feel* something. You didn't cry at his funeral. It's been six months, and you haven't."

"It's a guy thing, you know?" I explained, a little irritated, not understanding where any of this was coming from.

"No, I don't know. Look," she said, "there's no other way to put this, so I'm just going to say it: I think it's best that we back up, okay? Slow things down."

"What do you mean? Are you dumping me?"

"No. But you need some time alone right now. I've been giving this a lot of thought, and I've come to the conclusion that you have unresolved issues to work out."

"What does that mean? Don't tell me I've got 'unresolved issues.' I *know* what I'm feeling, okay? Right now, I'm feeling pissed at you."

"Don't be angry. I'm doing this because I care," she said. "I need to stay out of your hair for a while. I don't want to become a nag. I love you too much. You have to figure this out on your own. The last thing you need is me sticking around and further complicating this whole situation."

I calmed down. "Listen," I said, in my most rational-sounding voice. "I'm about to leave here. Meet me at home, and we can talk about this. I want to see you. I need to see you."

"You need space," Deborah said. "You need to be alone with yourself. I'll lay low for now." And she hung up.

I sat there with the receiver pressed against my ear until the line went dead. She's overreacting, I told myself. By the time I get home, there'll be a message on the recorder. She'll apologize. She'll laugh and say she wasn't thinking. She'll drive over, we'll hug and kiss and have sex. Everything will be fine. I grabbed my things and left the office.

I did love my father, very much. He was good to us. When I was a kid we built model airplanes and classic cars together. The cars were his favorites. Somewhere in my mother's attic, there's a box filled with '57 Chevys, T-Birds, and a 1964 Ford Mustang that we never got around to painting. He let me drive the station wagon down the street once when I was thirteen, my feet barely reaching the pedals. My senior year in college, he took me on a two-day camping trip in the mountains. We spent a good part of that trip roasting marshmallows and knocking back bottles of beer. I decided that when it came time for me to get married, I would ask my father to be my best man.

When I get home, there are no messages. I sit down on the couch, reach for a pair of my girlfriend's sunglasses on the floor near my feet, and toss them aside. A month after we started dating, I suggested she bring some things over. She arrived with two duffel bags stuffed with blouses, blue jeans, nylons, running shoes, high heels, and a second alarm clock for "her side" of the bed. She filled the bathroom counter with jars of creams and moisturizers, a light-up hand mirror, and a box of tampons.

"Are you leaving anything at your place?" I'd said.

She laughed. "Sure. Plenty."

"You wouldn't know it."

A stack of fashion magazines sits on top of the coffee table near one of her house plants. In the sink, there are coffee mugs with red lipstick marks along the edges. Scattered about the floor of the bedroom are her balled-up socks, a pair of her panties, and an old college sweatshirt of mine that she likes to sleep in.

I haven't changed out of my suit when the phone rings, but it's only my mother.

"Juan? I just got off the phone with Deborah. She told me. How are you?"

"Jesus," I say. "She called and told you she broke up with me?"

"She's not breaking up with you," my mother reports. "She's just giving you space."

"Right. Space."

"You should come over. I made empanadas for the meeting today, but no one ate them."

Back when I was a kid, my mother helped found the Agua Mansa chapter of the official Elvis Presley fan club. The five members spend afternoons snacking on peanut butter and banana sandwiches and cookies. They sit around in a circle listening to his records and planning bake sales to help fund their trip to Graceland. The meeting was at my mother's house this month. There's music playing in the background. I make out Elvis singing "Jailhouse Rock."

"I have some food left," she continues. "Come over. Don't be alone. I'm going to watch *Love Me Tender*. Come watch it with me."

"What happened with everyone wanting to give me space? Look at me. Sitting around my apartment. Enjoying all this space."

"Don't be rude," my mother says. "Come over."

"I'm fine," I tell her. "Seriously. I just want to hang out here. I'm tired. I have a meeting tomorrow at work. And my girlfriend decided that I need to cry."

"Do you have food there?"

"There's something. I'll eat a sandwich."

"You're not that far. It won't take you long to drive over."

After five minutes of her pleas, I give in. "Only for a bit. A little Elvis goes a long way."

I change into my jeans and a T-shirt and head out the door.

·   ·   ·

We'd gone shopping for a birthday gift for my father the day my mother lost me in the department store. Somewhere down an aisle of racks crammed with dressy men's slacks and blazers, she turned to check the size of a shirt. I must have wandered off, must have seen something that caught my eye because what I remember next is looking up and not seeing my mother.

The place was a maze. I ran around looking for her, but the more I ran, the more lost I became. I bumped into displays, knocked things down. I ended up in the gardening section clear across the other side of the store. The shelves looked taller here, the aisles wider and threateningly lonely. A nun in a black habit stood by a group of wooden Adirondack chairs. As I approached her, she smiled. I stood there until she stopped considering the chairs in front of us and shifted her attention to me. She called me "young man" and kept asking if everything was okay. I looked down at my shoes, looked in the direction I came from.

"Are you lost?" she asked.

"No," I said. "My mom lets me do what I want."

"Is that so?" She raised an eyebrow. "Well, you look lost to me." She grabbed my arm. "Come on."

She said her name was Sister Raphael. As we walked down the aisles, she told me a story about Jesus getting separated from his parents in a temple. It was meant to make me feel better, but given that I wasn't Jesus and this wasn't a temple, I gave up trying to understand her point. We made our way past bins full of flip-flops and slippers and through the maternity section. At the front where the check stands were stood a security guard who led us into an office.

"I'll leave you here," said the nun.

Inside the room, rows of black and white screens showed different sections of the store. One monitoring the entrance lobby blinked intermittently, distorting the images of the men and women walking through the automatic doors. Another showed the spot where my mother and I had just been. A camera panned to the other end of the department, and when it returned, a man in a motorized wheelchair maneuvered around the racks of slacks and shirts my mother had rummaged through.

When my mother burst into the room, she was frantic, tears welling up in her eyes. Tucked under her arm was a silly-looking ceramic bust of Elvis Presley. I pouted as we finished shopping, made up a lie about a strange-looking man lurking behind a display of ski jackets. I told her someone could have kidnapped me or that I could have been locked inside after closing and been stranded overnight. The store was out of the style of coat my father had been eyeing all year. Instead, we bought him a package of boxer shorts and a set of drill bits.

"Those are stupid presents," I said.

"Then you pick something else out. I'll pay, and we can say it's from you."

Up front near the register there was a display case with some inexpensive gold lighters.

"That," I said.

"You sure?"

I nodded.

"Bueno."

When we were standing in line, I pointed to the Elvis head. "Is that for you?" I asked.

She nodded.

"His ears are pointy," I said. "He looks like an elf."

"Ay tú," my mother said. "He looks like the King."

It was wrapped in a shopping bag. She'd placed it on the floor of the car so it wouldn't roll around. All I wanted was to take a hammer or my shoe or my fist and smash that head into a million tiny pieces.

•   •   •

I'm standing in the kitchen watching my mother serve me empanadas on a plate. She's complaining that Mary Jane Polanco eats everything but hardly ever brings snacks to the meetings.

"So tell her something," I say.

"What do you mean? Have you *seen* Mary Jane?"

"Which one's Mary Jane?" I ask. "I have trouble keeping track of your friends."

"The hefty one."

"You mean the fat one?"

"Yes. Her. Well, they're all—"

"Fat?" I say again. "Yes, they are."

She stops what she's doing. "What's with you?"

I walk over to the table and sit in the chair my father always took. He would be there for hours—checking his stocks in the newspaper, squinting over strands of numbers, jotting down figures on the backs of envelopes and sale circulars, a lit cigarette dangling from his lips.

"You're being a brat," my mother says. "Relax."

I take my glasses off and clean them with a napkin. "My girlfriend left me today, Mom. She's gone. I'm alone. You're alone. She's alone. We're all alone."

"I didn't think you wanted to talk about it." She points to the top cabinet. "Get the television trays out. We'll miss the movie."

"How can we? It's on tape."

Deborah had found a set of four trays at a flea market one Sunday afternoon. They depict Elvis in the different stages of his career: young Elvis as he'd appeared on *The Ed Sullivan Show*; Elvis in skintight black leather; Elvis from the *Aloha from Hawaii* special; and chubby Elvis from the *Viva Las Vegas* concert. On each of them he's either snarling or pouting, his eyes seducing invisible fans.

"She'll flip," Deborah had said that day. "She'll absolutely flip." It was the first time she held my hand. She'd worn a pair of denim overalls and a hat to keep the sun out of her eyes. We'd brought bottles of water and sliced celery sticks and carrots that we carried in a backpack in case we got hungry. Deborah bought a *Partridge Family* lunch pail that still had its thermos, and she found a *Six Million Dollar Man* action figure in a red jumpsuit just like the one Lee Majors wore in the opening credits of the show. We walked around the flea market imitating the sound Steve Austin's bionic legs made whenever he ran fast or jumped high.

"You know, Mom, I can't stay. I was busy at the office today. I'm worn out," I say, handing her the trays.

"What are you going to do? Sit up in that stuffy apartment all alone? Don't be dumb. Stay. Have an empanada."

"Space, Mom. Remember? According to everyone, I need space. Or maybe I need a hobby. Like you and your Elvis thing."

"This isn't a *thing*," she says.

"Then what is it exactly, Mom?"

"You don't understand."

"You're right," I say. "I don't. What I understand is that, right now, I'm irritated and I want to go home."

"Fine. Go," she says. "But take some empanadas." She places four of them in a plastic bag and hands them to me.

"I'll call you tomorrow," I say, taking the bag from her. "Enjoy your movie."

•　　　•　　　•

After my mother's, I stop off at the Excelsior Liquor Store. Behind the clerk are rows of bottles of rum, gin, and tequila, but I'm here for vodka. There's a brand with crude Cyrillic letters that comes in two proofs. There's another one in a sleek blue bottle that looks like a vase. I stand there for a while debating. The clerk glares at me.

"Is this a stickup or what, bro?"

"No," I say, pointing from bottle to bottle. "I can't figure out what I need."

I have the cash to buy the expensive blue bottle but opt for one at the very end, the plastic bottle. It looks unassuming and potent. That's what I want tonight: something potent.

I mix screwdrivers using the orange juice Deborah bought last week. There isn't much left, and when I run out, I substitute some Tang. I drink and flip through the stations, switching between a program about the engineering feats of the Egyptians and a show about pets performing miraculous rescues, before settling on a countdown of the greatest love ballads of all time. They're only on number eighty. Somewhere between numbers fifty and forty, I feel the alcohol really kicking in. I stumble into my kitchen, fill another glass with Tang and the last of the vodka. I sit back down, tell myself I'll stay up until they get to our love song. But do we even *have* a love song? The last thing I remember hearing is Karen Carpenter singing, "We've Only Just Begun."

"That's it," I slur. And I pass out.

I wake up this morning, feeling my way to the shower. My head's splitting, and I'm nauseated. Deborah's lotions and bottles of nail polish fall as I reach over the counter for my watch and rings. My stomach is doing a serious number on me. Remembering my father's advice about eating bread to help cure a hangover, I grab the empanadas my mother gave me. I bite into a strawberry-filled one and drink a glass of water.

I arrive at work late and unprepared for my meeting. The office is decorated for Halloween. Small cardboard tombstones are arranged around the water cooler, fake cobwebs cling to the walls and the corners of windows and across computer screens, a skeleton wearing a silly top hat and bow tie is pinned to the back of a door.

"My proposal's going through some revisions, and we'll need to reschedule the meeting," I tell my assistant. "I'll be in here." I point to my office. "Revising." And I close my office door behind me. Between the throbbing headache and upset stomach, it's hard to concentrate on anything. I give up after a while and just sit at my desk, shuffling papers around, clicking random files on my computer. At around eleven-thirty, Deborah calls me.

"You're at work," is the first thing she says to me.

"Why wouldn't I be?" I say. "Where else would I be?"

"That was stupid of me to say."

"How was your night?" I ask.

"Lonely. I missed sleeping with your arm around my waist. Yours?"

"I went to see my mom. I made screwdrivers and watched a countdown of love ballads. I heard ours."

"We never had one, Juan."

"Oh. Come over, okay? This is stupid, Deb."

She lets out a long sigh and clears her throat.

"Jesus, this is impossible," I say. "What do you want me to do here?"

"Give this some time. Juan, this is all so much for me. We both need some distance."

"Bullshit!" I shout. "Distance. Distance from *what*?"

"I just think that us getting serious, your father dying, it all happened so quickly. You're still processing it, sorting through it. It's disconnected you. We need some space from each other right now."

"Then why'd you call?"

"Because I care."

"I worry," I say. "Worry you won't come back to me."

"Don't think that way."

"How long will this take?"

"I'm not sure, honey. We'll take it slow. We'll figure that out when we get to it. Hey, I'm not disappearing here. I'll be in touch."

She hangs up.

The room spins around me. The floor rocks. I get up slowly and leave the office early.

Back at the apartment, I go around looking at the things she left behind. There's a book she was reading with the corner of page 117 folded over. There are notes in the margins, and some passages are highlighted in yellow. I take a pair of her nylons and pull them over my knuckles, wrap them tightly around my hand.

We met at this place across the street from my office called Red's Tavern. I'd gone with a co-worker to grab a drink. She stood with a group of girls at the bar and kept turning around to look at me. She wore a blouse with the word *oui* written across her chest, and she was the only one among the group of five who was drinking beer.

I tapped her on the shoulder. "That means 'yes,' " I shouted, pointing to her blouse.

"Are you hitting on me?" She laughed.

"Oui," I responded.

"Good," she said. "Because you're cute."

"Oui?" I asked.

She laughed again. "What does a girl have to do to get a guy like you to ask her out?" She leaned forward, gripping her pint with both hands.

The beers I'd had were making me feel loose, confident. "Stand up on this," I said, slapping the counter. "And dance."

"That's it?" She handed her glass to her friend and used the stool I'd been sitting on to hop up on the bar. She strutted around to a song playing on the jukebox, her feet stepping between half-empty pints of beer and baskets full of pretzels and nuts. People around the bar cheered. She balled up napkins and tossed them at me. When a guy in a baseball hat made a lewd comment, she grabbed a handful of peanuts and hurled them at him. The whole room broke out in laughter.

"Never dare me," she said. "I'll always do it."

After our third date, I told her about my father. He'd been back in the hospital that week. "You can meet him once he's home again," I said. "Hospitals are odd meeting places. Too sterile."

"They're not odd to me."

She took him some balloons, a bouquet of flowers, and the latest issue of *Car and Driver*. They talked about hot rods, Deborah's love for spicy foods, and my father's desire to visit the Vatican someday. She told him how we'd met, how she'd danced for me at a crowded bar, and how, despite her bravado, she had actually been terrified.

They also talked about my mother. She was home that afternoon, cleaning and preparing for his homecoming. My father adjusted himself in his hospital bed, fiddled with the tubes leading into his nose.

"My wife can be a handful," he explained.

"Señor," Deborah said, "I met her last week. She's not bad."

"She means well. She loves her Elvis Presley."

"She showed me her collection of records and her scrapbook. Does it make you jealous?" Deborah teased.

He laughed, rocked his head slowly, the tubes tapping against my arm. "No. She's liked him ever since she was a teenager. But he's dead. Once I get to wherever he is, I'll make sure to let him know who really had her heart."

When Deborah went to grab a soda from the vending machine out in the hallway, my father beckoned me. Rolling the magazine up and tapping me on the shoulder with it, he urged me to lean in closer, much closer.

"Don't lose her, Juan," he said. "Whatever you do, don't. That girl's got vida."

"No, señor," I said. "I sure won't."

"And don't forget about your ma," he said, his eyes welling up. "In case I don't—"

"Ya," I said. "Don't think that way, hombre. You're going to be just fine." I turned to see Deborah standing in the doorway.

"I'm sorry. I didn't mean to walk in then," she said as we left the hospital.

"You didn't know," I responded.

One of my last memories of him is that day in the hospital. The way he'd smiled as Deborah recounted our first meeting, how he'd lifted his hand to show her how small I was when he taught me the difference between a good Cuban cigar and a bad one. How he went on and on about my mother and her love for all things Elvis. The way he looked at both of us as we stood over his bed. He nodded a lot, kept saying we were good. We were a good set.

*   *   *

Today the dead are set free. They wander. They follow, mimicking your movements. They knock over dishes, slide chairs across floors, crack mirrors, slam doors. They shift and morph. They take the forms of stray dogs and owls and moths beating their wings against porch lights. They become the dust kicked up by the Santa Ana winds. They become the wind itself. You breathe them in.

The Day of the Dead falls on a Saturday this year. I take my mother to the farmer's market held in the parking lot of my old high school. She buys a few dozen bouquets of orange and yellow marigolds and some bananas. From there I drive her to the Botánica Oshún to pick up the sugar skull she had ordered two weeks ago. When we walk into the store, the woman behind the counter reaches for a package near the register. She unwraps it slowly, revealing a white head made of confectioners' sugar. Bright red and green plastic jewels adorn the figure's forehead; others are set deep within its eye sockets. My mother examines the details, traces the skull's wide, eerie grin. The woman tells us that no two ever come out the same. She sells my mother packets of herbs, a bundle of incense sticks she says help attract the spirits of the dead, and a box of six candles. The idols and saints watch us from the shelves, some smiling, others with blank expressions, waiting for their chance to perform miracles, to sweat holy oil, to cry tears of blood.

Back at her home, my mother gathers her Elvis paraphernalia—teddy bears, coffee mugs with his portrait on them, small black-and-white pictures, an alarm clock that wakes to the tune of "Hound Dog," lunch pails, commemorative plates that she ordered from the television, and the bust she bought that day in the department store. She clears off the surface of the dining table and matches up and groups her souvenirs together in a strange kind of order. The tin trays and a velvet portrait Deborah had also given to her are arranged near each other.

She's been doing this ever since I was a kid. Once when I was fourteen, I brought a girl I liked to our house. The altar stood there in the middle of the dining room like a gaudy piece of jewelry. Despite the pleas to my father to convince her to take it down or to at least move it to another room, the altar stood there.

"My mom," I said to this girl. "She's kind of into Elvis."

"Yeah. *Way* into him."

We spent the rest of the afternoon hardly talking, sitting at opposite ends of the couch watching music videos.

"Why'd you let her?" I'd asked my father after the girl left.

"I don't interfere with your mother and her Elvis thing. That's a whole other part of her life she keeps to herself," he'd said, stabbing a cigarette into the grass.

She scatters the marigolds across the floor and on top of the altar, arranging them among the mementos assembled over the years. She makes peanut butter and banana sandwiches and slices them into triangles. She arranges them on a platter near a black-and-white photo on a wire easel. The sugar skull goes next to Deborah's velvet portrait.

From her purse, she pulls out a bottle of aspirin, opens the cap, and pours the pills into her hands. She organizes them in small piles near the Elvis bust. She lights the incense and sprinkles the herbs around the floor near the altar. When it's all said and done, when all the candles are lit, all the offerings positioned carefully, when the prayer to the dead is recited, my mother stops to admire her shrine.

Every inch of the table is covered. I pick up a tabloid magazine with a crude pencil sketch of Elvis just below the headline that reads: HE LIVES. I touch the small square of exposed wood, imagine us gathered around the table eating dinner. My father sits at one end, my mother at the other. I'm young again, my father still has all his hair, my mother is warm and beautiful.

"What are you doing?" she asks, taking the magazine from my hand.

I think about my father, our model T-Birds and airplanes, the ashtray I made for him in elementary school that had a mold of my hand. "Hold on," I say as I run down the hallway.

In my parents' bedroom, on top of their dresser, is a small cedar box. I find the gold lighter I picked out for him the day I got lost. I take that and a pair of his shoes and go back out to the living room.

"See? There's still some room here. Let's work some of Dad's things in." I rearrange the altar, making space.

"Wait," my mother says. "Don't."

"What do you mean 'don't'?"

"This is for Elvis. A shrine for Elvis."

"What about your husband?" I shout. "Your dead husband. What's with all this Elvis crap? Your husband died six months ago. You should be thinking of *him*." I point to the altar. "Not that."

It's not the sensation of her hand making contact with my skin. It's the sound the slap makes across the dining room that stuns me. She reaches for his shoes on the table. When she tries to snatch the lighter, I grab it and shove it in my pocket.

"Dead," I shout. "He's gone. And you're prancing around this place like some lovesick teenager. Grow up. It's embarrassing. It always has been. What are you thinking?"

My mother looks right at me. She wears the same expression I saw on her face that night when she knelt by my father's side as he took his last breath.

She says in a voice so low it's almost a whisper, "I'm thinking just how much he means to me. Just how much he's always meant."

"Who?"

But she doesn't answer. Cradling my father's shoes in her arms, my mother walks into the bedroom and slams the door.

I don't go straight home. I drive around town for hours. I bump over the railroad tracks running parallel to the 10. At Alta Vista I make a left and head down to Buffalo, passing the Agua Mansa Palms where a group of girls in baggy jackets huddle around a guy on a motorcycle and loud cumbia music blares from one of the apartments. I end up at the Excelsior Liquor Store again. This time I buy a six-pack of Rolling Rock and a carton of menthol cigarettes.

At the cemetery, an issue of *Auto Monthly* and a red hat with the words *Built Ford Tough* written across the front rest on my father's marker. I turn back, hoping to catch a glimpse of Deborah's car driving off, but there's nothing.

I arrange the carton of cigarettes and the six-pack next to the hat and magazine. I'm bad at this, I think. This arranging and rearranging. I try to envision my mother's altar, the way she grouped and organized her collectibles. But no matter how hard I try, no matter how many different ways I change things, none of this looks right to me. After a while, I give up and drive off.

I pull over next to an empty lot, put the car in park, and leave the engine running. There's a packet of ketchup Deborah had left in the cup holder one time when we were on our way home from picking up drive-thru. That night, she'd rested her foot on my dashboard and hummed a tune as we waited for our food. I trace the outline of the lighter in my pocket with my finger, recall the spark, the way the flame flickered and sputtered the first time my father used it.

At the intersection of Central and Descanso, I notice a billboard perched over the roof of a gas station. A figure wearing a white suit with shiny gold and silver buttons stands against a bright blue background. His head is down and tilting slightly to his right, completely obscuring his face. Both his arms are stretched out, his palms raised up toward the sky. The sign reads:

An Evening with the King
November 3rd
San Jacinto Indian Casino
Off I-10

* * *

The mountains off the 10 fold in and out of one another. The stereo is playing Elvis's "Burning Love," and we drive with the windows rolled all the way down. The wind kicks up dirt and gravel. When sand gets lodged in my eyes, I rub until I can see clearly, concentrating hard on the asphalt before us. My mother had still been angry with me when I phoned her. I felt bad about our fight and asked her to give me a chance to make it up. I mentioned the show and offered to take her. After all, I said, it's not every day a genuine Elvis Presley impersonator performs at an Indian casino near us.

Deborah called me earlier today saying she was coming over to pick up her things. I try hard to forget about it, forget that when I get back to the apartment later tonight, she'll be there walking out of my life.

At the casino, we sit next to a woman in leather sandals named Nora who tells us the impersonator we're about to see is really a man named Denny Jenks from Modesto. She's attended at least twenty of his performances, and she swears he's by far the best around. Nora tells my mother she's been to Graceland and visited Elvis's tomb. Hearing this, my mother smiles, and Nora takes her hand.

"No words," Nora says. "No words to describe it, honey."

There are candles lit at each table, and groups of people sit at attention waiting for the show to start. The disco globe above the room spins, casting specks of light across the dark walls. A woman up front faints before the music even begins.

Still holding hands, Nora and my mother rise in unison. They stand on their chairs, wave bar napkins, and crane their necks, looking past the rows of tables and benches, past the heads and through the mist at the figure in a powder blue jumpsuit who's just walked onstage. The spotlight falls on him. My mother and Nora scream, their faces turn red. They throw their heads back, fan themselves with the napkins they're holding.

Here's my mother, Evelyn. She's just lost her husband to emphysema.

Evelyn considers herself to be Elvis Presley's number one fan. She owns all his movies. She likes to play his records every night. Evelyn has a scrapbook with clippings she began collecting years ago when she was a girl in Mexico. It's something she's proud of and remembers taking to school one day, showing it to her friends Isela and Margarita. She didn't allow them to touch the pages. She turned them herself, smoothing out the creases and bubbles on the clippings with her palms.

Standing on a chair in an Indian casino, Evelyn's clutching the hand of a woman she's just met. Wearing a lavender poodle skirt that she pulled out from deep within her closet, Evelyn dances. Her skirt fans out, exposing the ruffled slip underneath. She wears a pair of black-and-white saddle shoes with bobby socks rolled all the way down to her ankles and an angora sweater with a furry collar. The two women close their eyes and dance. With each step, with each steady rocking of the hips, they give themselves over, releasing part of themselves, taking something new in.

Later that night, walking through the door of my apartment, I find Deborah in the bedroom. Her clothes are folded and arranged in small neat piles on the bed. Her blow dryer and alarm clock are on the floor near her high heels and tennis shoes, her socks and nylons.

My father's gold lighter taps against the loose change in my pocket. I hear his voice, feel him in the night air around us. *Vida. That girl's got vida*, he says over and over again, his voice so loud in my head now, so clear. I feel his breath on the back of my neck, his hands on my shoulders, pushing me toward her, guiding my steps. And he tells me, *This is it, mijito. ¿Entiendes? This is what we do. This is how we hold on.*

Feast of
Saint Gabriel the Archangel

Angel of the Annunciation

Patron of messengers,

diplomats, clergy, postal workers,

broadcasters, telegraphs, telephones, childbirth,

and stamp collectors.

There was no one inside the botánica. The rain was keeping the customers away. Perla lowered the volume of the television she kept on a chair behind the counter and walked over to the front window. The asphalt was slick and shiny. Parts of the street were flooded, and wide puddles had formed at the edge of the parking lot. Rain unsettled Agua Mansa. It's only a matter of time, the ones who remembered would say. The Santa Ana is too unpredictable. It will spill over the banks and flood the streets. People will be ripped away by the currents. The whole city will be washed away all over again.

Perla was one of them who remembered. So much rain had fallen that winter. She was nine and had gone with her mother and father to buy firewood from a man who sold it cheap. The wood was stacked in neat piles next to the man's shack. He smoked a pipe, the skin around his fingernails split like the wood he helped her father load onto their truck. Her father had brought a blanket to cover the logs so they would stay dry.

"Don't matter," the man had said, helping her father secure the blanket over the wood. "Water'll soak through."

"We're not going far," said her father.

The rain came down hard as they made their way back. It tapped loudly as it hit the pickup's hood. Crossing the La Cadena Bridge, Perla looked out the window, past the sheet of rain, and saw the río a few feet below. It was a mass of dark brown water, churning fast and violent. Her father stopped once they crossed the bridge, the firewood banging against one side of the pickup.

"¿Qué pasa?" Perla's mother asked.

He didn't respond. He stepped out and looked back at the bridge. Water soaked his hair and his jacket, and Perla's mother shouted at him to get back inside.

Perla turned around, her knees pressing into the bucket seat, and looked through the cab's rear window at what her father was watching. The columns cracked and gave way, and the river swallowed the road behind them. A car traveling toward the river stopped; the driver got out and ran past her father, trampling through the mud to the edge of the bank.

Pieces of lumber floated in the water like splinters, mattresses like islands. A woman's head bobbed up and down, disappearing every now and again among the waves. There was a man with his arms around the branch of a tree, fighting hard to hold on.

Her mother pressed her hand over Perla's eyes and said, "No mires."

Still, Perla heard the man screaming, the loud rush of the water, the sound of things cracking, breaking off, and washing away.

The dead were found once the rains stopped, mud caked over their bodies, limbs twisted and caught among branches and the crushed roofs of houses.

"Unos cuantos minutos," her father said once they were back home, drying his face with a handkerchief. "We could have been on that bridge. This troque could have been our tumba." He knelt on the floor of the living room and blessed himself. Her mother prayed a rosario to La Virgen that night.

It was pouring now. As she stood there watching, a figure jumped over a puddle and crossed the parking lot with a jacket held over his head. When he walked in, the boy took the jacket off and draped it over the back of one of the chairs to dry. She stepped behind the counter and made sure the cash register's drawer was shut.

Perla said, "¿Qué buscas?"

"No." He shook his head. "I looking for nothing."

He wore a long-sleeved flannel shirt and light blue jeans with a big silver belt buckle shaped like a motorcycle. His hair was cut short around the sides and back, and gold hoops dangled from his earlobes. A thick silver necklace hung around his neck with a crucifix that tapped against the pearl snap buttons of his shirt. At first he said nothing, just smiled nervously at Perla and stood there holding a book and pens.

He spoke with an accent. Perla pointed to the sign taped near the shelf above the register. "Hablo Español. Si prefieres."

"No," he said again. He hesitated and furrowed his eyebrows before speaking. "I talk a little English. I need to do the practice." He showed her the book he was holding.

Perla took it and read the title: *1,001 Big Questions.*

"I am learning how to reading this book. See?" He opened it, flipped through the pages, found one with the corner folded over, and showed it to her. It read: Have you ever done something so shameful it caused you to resent yourself?

"I found the book by where I live. I know a lot of the English words." He spoke slowly. "But I want to learn more."

He knew chill. Chill out. Chillin' like a villain. Tight. Get over it. Relax. Whatever. Disability. Okay. Food stamps. Faggot. Laid-off. Library. Fuck no. What up, dog? Buy one, get one free. Dude. Casino. Bitch. Speak English. Cell phone. Tweeker. Emergency. I'm from California. I'm in the United States Marine Corps. Nice to see you. 411. She's a ho. Are you lost? Wetback. Bro. Who's your Daddy? Call the landlord.

"Are you from here?" she asked.

"No. Michoacán," he said. "I only been here since a few months."

His name was Rodrigo. He lived in one of the small duplexes on Galena Court, he told Perla. She avoided that area. Some of her customers lived there. They told of gang fights and drug deals, of ranflas that drove around at all hours with their music blaring from speakers that rattled windows, of a baby run over by a drunk driver one night last year.

"You talk English good," he said, taking the book from her. "You teach? You teach me more, yes? I learn it from you." Rodrigo pointed.

She smiled. "I'm not a teacher. I run my botánica. I'm a businesswoman. Take a night class. At the high school." She pointed out the window.

"I can't, okay." He touched the jacket to see if it had dried yet. His gold bracelet tapped against the chair's seat. "I only come in two time since today. First time I sit here. And you remind me of my Abuela Josefa from Michoacán. I sit quiet. Like I do in her kitchen when I was small. Second time was last month. I looked through the window, but you tell me you were closed. I come here because your store is nice. You help people all the time. All the time there's people in here. You are very smart and know things books have. I think this: She can talk in both Spanish and English. I can pay you for teaching me English."

"Hijo," she said, clasping her hands and walking back to the register. "No puedo."

"Please, okay? You talk to me in English so I can learn. Teach it to me. You?"

"I can't." She leaned against the counter. "I never went to college."

"Books. I seen you. Using and reading from them."

"They're not books like that. They can't help you that way." She went to the case where the books were and Rodrigo followed.

She took one and opened it. The page showed an illustration of the palm of a hand, its lines all labeled, intersecting and breaking apart, the swirls of the fingerprints curling like smoke.

"Look," she said. "These aren't the kinds of books you need." Perla pointed to the ones lining the wall near the register, the ones with her notes in the margins. "They're different. Different books."

He studied the hardback cover of the one before him. "What does that read?" He pointed to one word.

"Palm," she said. "It's a book about palm reading."

"Reading? Like reading words for learning?"

"No," she said. "It's another kind of reading."

He flinched and shoved his hands in his pockets when Perla reached out to take them. "It's fine," she said. "Show me your palms."

He stuck his left hand out and placed it, palm up, on the counter.

She rubbed it gently. "This book teaches you to study these lines." Perla traced them with her finger.

Rodrigo took one of the pens he carried and gave it to her. "Write it. Write it here," he said, pointing to his palm.

She pressed the tip of the pen softly into his skin. The liquid gel was gold, and it dripped out slowly, freckled with bits of glitter.

"I like this feeling," he said, blowing on the gel to harden it once she finished. "I like how you write. You write more words for me? On the paper?" Rodrigo handed her a sheet from the pad tucked under his arm.

She wrote a list of words. She didn't think, just let them come to her: rain, river, water, hill, mountain, car, speed, time, statues, store, shopping, center, nice, going, trees, home, bus, learn, remember.

He watched carefully. Her wrist and hand moved gracefully over the page. The pen glided over the surface of the paper, the words shiny, the flecks of glitter sparkling under the store's light.

He shoved his hand back in his pocket when a customer walked in.

"I am going now," he said. "I learn. I learn these. And I come back here to see you. You teach me more." He grabbed his jacket and ran out the door.

          ◦   ◦   ◦

It rained all night and through the next morning. It was still coming down hard in the afternoon when Rodrigo burst through the door. He stomped on the ground a few times before walking over to the counter. From his jacket pocket, he pulled out the notepad and gel pens. He put his book of questions near the countertop display of prayer cards.

"I read the words you gave me yesterday," Rodrigo said, taking his jacket off. He cupped his hands together and put them up to his lips, blowing puffs of air to warm them.

"Sit," she told him, pointing to the chair nearest to Santa Bárbara. The candles at the statue's feet were lit. "Put your hands over the candles."

Perla bent down, reached behind the shelf under the register, and disconnected the space heater she kept there. She walked around the counter and plugged it into the outlet behind Santa Bárbara. The metal coils glowed bright orange as she positioned it close to Rodrigo's wet pant legs. She made him té de canela, and they sat for a while, watching the rain pound the pavement.

"I come for more words," he said, finishing his té.

She looked over at the notepad, the bundle of pens, then at the boy. He shivered. His hair was soaked. She left him sitting there, warming himself, and walked over to the counter. Perla smoothed the sheets of paper out, took the gold gel pen, and tried to conjure up a list of helpful words. But nothing came. She reached out for his book and flipped through the pages. She stopped at one question and read it to herself:

Who are you, exactly?

She wrote without thinking:

Who am I? Ha. That's a good question. I'm someone who is wondering why she is answering this question asking her who she is. I'm no one important. Just some vieja who lives alone in a house my husband and I bought when we got married years ago.

Who am I? Perla María Portillo. Seventy-two years of age. Born here in Agua Mansa, California, and I think I will be lucky enough (or unlucky depending on who you ask) to die here.

I am someone who is always trying to figure out who she is. When I was younger, I was a daughter. A best friend. A wife. An apprentice. Now I'm just Perla who runs the botánica.

Rodrigo rose and walked around the store. Perla put the pen down and watched him. He paced nervously, his hands gripping his elbows. He shivered, bit his fingernails, and looked around suspiciously.

"Te sientes—" she started to say, reaching out to touch him. "Are you okay?"

He nodded.

"Here." She handed him the notebook and pens. "What do you want with it?"

"For reading." He shrugged his shoulders, his voice low. "For keeping my mind away from bad things. From the bad things I think."

Rodrigo folded and unfolded the paper. He focused on the ground, his eyes resting on the tips of his cowboy boots.

"What bad things?" Perla asked.

"Just I am being silly."

Perla reached into the case. "Here," she said, handing him a book. "Take this."

He studied the bright colors on the cover and ran his hand over the title before flipping it open. There were pictures, and the pages were thick and glossy with gold-leafed edges.

"What does it say?"

"It's about saints. Their histories and their miracles."

"I will bring it back tomorrow," he said, moving to the door.

"You can stay awhile. Let the rain pass."

"I am good," he said. "I am needing to go."

"Okay," she said. "I'll see you tomorrow."

*   *   *

The rain stopped in the middle of the night, and the next day the sun came out. She could see clouds reflected in the puddles near the cars parked in front of the donut shop. It was as if the sky had shattered, the pieces scattered about the black asphalt. When Rodrigo showed up, his hair was messy and uncombed, and stubble was growing on his face.

"I forget the book," he said. "Sorry. I will bring it back tomorrow."

When she reached a hand out to touch him, the boy flinched.

"Could I make you some té?" she asked

"No. I am fine. I ate a McMuffin." He held the notepad out. "I bring only one of the pens," he said, reaching into his back pocket. "I forgot the rest, too." He sat in the same chair and closed his eyes.

"Do you want me to write you more words?" Perla asked. "Or should I answer one of the questions from your book?"

He didn't answer her. His head fell to one side, resting on his left shoulder. He began to snore quietly.

She thought about what he had said last time about thinking bad things. Maybe there was something going on at the duplexes that he was involved in. *Drugs? Gangs? Maybe he's an illegal. Maybe he's hiding out from La Migra.* She had heard about sweeps in the area. Border Patrol agents had shown up recently around Agua Mansa. Last month they'd raided Catalina's Laundry Services and Las Glorias' parking lot where the day laborers gathered waiting for work.

She reached for the book and flipped through it until she found a question: *What do you fear most?* She wrote:

Being forgotten.

The space heater's coils glowed red. Rodrigo was still, his legs stretched out before him. From behind, taped to the window, an image of a solemn-faced Jesus—his robe pulled back to reveal his Sacred Heart, thorns wrapping around it, piercing the flesh—watched over the boy. Perla flipped through the book again and decided to answer a different question: *What are you most ashamed of?* She wrote:

I am ashamed of the fact that I only agreed to do this job because it would get me out of the house. Guillermo spent all those years working, leaving me alone in the afternoons. No kids. No nothing. I felt like I had no life. Like things could have turned out differently if I'd only married someone who could give me more.

I am ashamed that I'm still angry at my husband for not being able to give me a baby and that I had once thought about leaving him because of this.

I am ashamed of so many things. I am ashamed that I can't write them down here.

She stopped only when Rodrigo stirred. It was getting colder now that the sun was going down. There were blankets on a shelf in the utility closet. Spreading one out on the floor, Perla opened a can of "Serenidad" aerosol. She got on her knees, aimed the nozzle a few inches away from the surface, and, with a slow broad motion, sprayed a fine even mist over the blanket. She picked it up and walked out front with it.

Rodrigo was snoring loudly. She noticed for the first time the long and elegant slope of his nose, a small dent shaped like a horseshoe in the middle of his forehead, and the faded remnants of a cluster of acne. She conjured up images of his mother and his father. Here was somebody's son, she thought. Alone and invisible. If she could call or write her, Perla would tell Rodrigo's mother, *He's fine. Your baby's fine. I gave him some té. He's warm. And now he sleeps.*

It wasn't until she covered him that she noticed the marks. Small round welts dotted the backs of Rodrigo's hands. They looked tender and painful, so Perla was careful as she tucked his hands under the blanket.

The rest of the day customers shuffled in and out. Yet he slept there, completely undisturbed. Hasari Gupta, who owned the Excelsior Liquor Store, showed up with his wife, Lakshmi, to buy more packages of incense sticks and a statue of the goddess Ganesh.

"The baby broke the last one we bought. He's getting to be that age. With those busy little hands." Lakshmi laughed. "Touching here and there."

"Drunk?" Hasari asked, looking at the way Rodrigo's head hung over his left shoulder, his mouth an oval. "You want me to call the police?" He pointed to the phone.

"No," Perla told them. "He's a customer. Just very tired."

"Be careful," he said. "My brother was working at a Circle K in Fontana. Second night on the job and he got robbed. Guy came in pointing a gun at his head. Good that nobody was hurt. Now my brother, he is afraid all the time."

"You make sure he doesn't sleep too much," Lakshmi said, her purple sari billowing out, sweeping over Rodrigo's feet as they walked out the door. "He'll be up all night."

He slept through the ring of the cash register, the honking of a car alarm in the parking lot, and Alfonso coming in to break a fifty-dollar bill.

"¿Y ese?" he asked.

"Nada, tú. I know him."

"I'm right next door." Alfonso used a pen clipped to a pocket of his apron to point to his store. "If he gets crazy or anything happens, I'm here. Okay?"

"Ya," she said. "I'll be fine."

He stirred a little when Rosa Cabrera walked in, excited and out of breath, waving an envelope in the air. Rosa opened it and pulled out a certificate with her name on it. "Perla, look. I'm officially a licensed hair stylist. Can you believe I did it?"

"I can," Perla said. "You worked so hard. I'm happy for you." She slipped the form back in the envelope, then reached over to hug Rosa. "What are your plans now?"

"Well, first I'm going to start cutting hair from home. I'm going to save the money so that I can rent out a station at a salon. Miguel's taking me out to celebrate tonight. Just the two of us. We got a baby-sitter for Danielle. I can't believe I'm finally done," Rosa shouted, waving the envelope around and stomping her feet. From the chair, Rodrigo mumbled something in his sleep, and Rosa turned and saw him.

"Oh, sorry."

"It's okay," Perla said.

"Is he sick?"

"No. He just needs to rest."

"Does he live nearby?"

"Yes, I think so."

Rosa said, "Tell him. If he needs a haircut or a trim. Give him and your other customers my address. I can do perms and highlights and colorings. All for real cheap."

"I'll tell them," Perla said.

She let him sleep while she balanced the day's records and counted her deposit. He only woke when Perla turned all the lights off and grabbed her purse.

"What time?" he said looking around, the shadows of the santos perched high above on the shelves watching them.

"Go home." Perla handed him the sheets of paper. "It's getting late."

"I sleep for a long time," he said, stretching and smoothing his hair back. "I wish I could sleep here all night. It's warm."

"Come back and see me, okay?" she said, thinking of the marks on his hands. "If you need anything."

"Yes," Rodrigo said. "Tomorrow."

He walked across the parking lot and down Rancho toward the Galena Court duplexes. He had stirred when Perla tucked the pouch of shells and stones into the left pocket of his jacket. She had been more careful when she slipped an estampa of El Santo Niño de Atocha into the right pocket. Watching his figure fade into the night, she thought of Elleguá, the patron Orisha of all roads, the opener of locked doors. Perla asked him to clear Rodrigo's path, to remove any of the boy's obstacles, to make him strong and wise. To help him find the way back to his mother and father, wherever or whoever they might be.

She closed the door and stepped out into the night. Perla buttoned up her sweater and tucked her purse under her arm, put gloves on to warm her hands. The air was thick with the smell of settling rainwater, of things washed clean.

*   *   *

He hadn't been back in over a week, and Perla found herself beginning to worry about him. *Something's not right,* she told herself. *I shouldn't have let him go that night.*

When she arrived at the botánica, she went straight to the reference books Darío had left. She opened them up and began her search. There were salves and ointments to diminish the appearances of deep scars and incisions. Something using fresh papaya juice. Flax oil mixed with lime water. Peeled nopal paddles placed over burns, then wrapped in gauze. She used strips of paper to mark important references in the books. One by one, they filled the main counter, stacked three and four high.

She came across a picture in one of the first-aid books. It was an arm. On it was a lesion. *Healing cigarette burn,* the caption below the picture read. *Intentionally placed on the forearm of a two year-old toddler just three days earlier.*

Had someone done this to him?

Perla continued flipping through the books, her eyes scanning the pages. They caught something in the margins of one. It was Darío's handwriting. The pencil's lead had rubbed into the paper, and the words were blurred and fuzzy.

He'd know what to do. If Darío were here now, he'd know. He always knew.

·　　·　　·

His left leg was shorter than the right. Both his ears were pierced, and he wore scarves wrapped around his head and adorned his wrists with bracelets made of shark teeth. He pulled into town one day, driving a trailer with balding tires and a cracked front windshield. He parked it down by the río and washed his clothes and bathed in the water there. Soon they started seeing the trailer in the Prospect Shopping Center's parking lot, in front of the space left vacant by Lety's Flowers.

Merchandise arrived in boxes, and the man could be seen shuffling about, working furiously, hanging packets of herbs on the walls, assembling shelves and cases. Soon there were pictures in the window and on the door of the shop, images they recognized and prayed to—La Virgen María in a blue satin robe kissing a cross, San Judas holding a staff, San Miguel slaying a demon. A week later, handwritten signs printed on simple lined paper appeared stuck to light posts and telephone poles around the city:

SEÑOR DARÍO

CONSEJERO ESPIRITUAL Y CURANDERO

Leo las Cartas
Hago Limpias y Curaciones

Se Venden Todas Clases de Tés y Hierbas
Preparo Perfumes y Velas
Ayuda de Todas Clases de Problemas:

* *Trabajo*
* *Alcoholismo*
* *Enfermedades Desconocidas*
* *Problemas de Amor y de Dinero*

Botánica Oshún
Prospect Shopping Center, Agua Mansa

Nobody had ever seen anything like it around Agua Mansa. They said the name Oshún had something to do with Voodoo or witchcraft or deep dark magics and curses. Peacock feathers and amulets of animal bones and a statue of a hooded skeleton wearing a red robe and wielding a scythe could be seen through the window. They said if you stepped foot in the shop you would be hexed. No one went in the first few weeks it was opened.

Every Sunday they saw him at Mass, sitting up front, a cane tucked neatly between his legs, always the first in line to receive the Host, always first to shake the priest's hand. Perla's mother and some women at church looked at him as he passed, tipping his straw hat as he left San Salvador's.

A friend of her mother said, "I heard he's a brujo. That he reads cards and talks to the dead. Could it be true?"

"Pura mentira," the other woman standing with them added, glancing at Perla and her mother. "Te lava el coco."

"The Devil," the first woman added. "That's what he is—the Devil."

*   *   *

It was three in the afternoon. Perla was bored. She went into the kitchen and poked around inside the refrigerator, deciding what to cook her husband for dinner. Guillermo would be home from the plant in a few hours. She rummaged through the cupboards and saw that there was no more salt. She would need it, she figured. Looking at the clock above the range, she saw that there would not be enough time to take the bus to the market and be back early enough to prepare things, so she put her shoes on and walked across the lot toward the shopping center.

Perla stopped in front of the botánica before heading into Tienda Arellano. There was a statue of San Antonio in the window. A halo of stars circled his head, and he wore a simple brown robe with a gold sash. Pinned to the robe were dollar bills.

Why is everyone so afraid? she thought. *San Antonio's in the window. There's crucifixes and pictures of Mary and Joseph by the door.*

Tienda Arellano was smaller than a grocery store, with only six aisles and a few shelves. They stocked some produce—tomatoes, avocados, iceberg lettuce, scallions—in wicker baskets along the floor. Old barrels by the front door stored pinto beans and rice customers scooped up with a liquid measuring cup. One cooler stocked sodas, eggs, and cheese, and gallons of milk and orange juice. She walked down the candy aisle toward the back where the condiments and spices were and took a can of salt. When she went to pay, Perla found Alfonso behind the register instead of his father. At the edge of the counter were a stack of textbooks, each covered in brown shopping bag paper. His name was written on one, "Chicano Power" and "Puro Aztlán" scrawled all over another. One had a pencil sketch of a peace sign just below the year, 1972.

The boy said, "Hi, Mrs. Portillo." His hair was long and wild, and it came down in bangs, covering his eyes.

"Hi, Alfonso. Where's your father?" Perla asked, giving him money for the salt.

"He went to drop my mom off," the boy said. He was tall and skinny with oversized feet and long arms and legs. His voice squeaked when he said, "She went shopping."

"Are you all alone in here?" she asked, taking her bag.

"First time," he said, smiling. Then he went back to reading one of his textbooks.

When she passed by the botánica, the door was open. It was empty inside. She looked at her watch. It was still early, and she didn't want to go back home just yet.

It was much cooler inside the shop. The shelves were bare, with only a few charms and amulets and scapulars of Our Lady of Mount Carmel and

Saint Jude. Nailed to the wall were pictures of San Ramón and the Holy Trinity, and the figure of a woman in a white dress with a star above her head emerging out of the sea, *Yemayá* written in black letters along the bottom. Incense sticks and bars of soap were grouped neatly on the counter near the front window where San Antonio stood. Some of the bookshelves were empty; others housed statues of saints and velas like those her mother lit. Silver medallas and rosary boxes and white Holy Communion candles were on the floor. Baptismal gowns hung from wire hooks on a string suspended over the counter.

The man came out from behind the curtain that covered the entrance to the stockroom. When his shorter leg hit the floor, his sandal made a soft slapping sound.

"¿En qué le ayudo?" he said, standing across from Perla.

She didn't say anything to him, just stood there cradling her bag of salt. "Oh," she said. "I'm only looking. That's all."

"You live around here?" he asked, looking at the bag in her hand.

"Across the field," Perla told him. "I was next door buying salt." She pointed at the bag. "I saw your store. I wanted to see what you sold."

"You've never been to a botánica before?"

"No," she said.

"I sell novenas and estampas. Religious articles. Rosaries and velas. Scapulars and statues of santos. Do you know what curanderos are?"

"Yes," Perla said. "Healers."

Her mother talked of the curanderas who lived in a shack at the foot of a mountain near their pueblo in Michoacán. They were two wise sisters, one blind and the other deaf. The deaf one was a curandera who healed with herbs and salves. The blind one divined the future using stones and chicken feet and feathers that she arranged in patterns on the ground of their hut.

"Well, I'm a curandero, too," he said. "I do limpias, and I know how to read palms and Tarot cards. People around here think I'm some evil brujo, right?"

She said nothing, remembering the suspicious whispers of her mother's friends.

He slapped his knee and laughed. "Not you, though. You're different. You're curious, aren't you?"

"Yes," Perla told him.

"And you believe."

"I guess," she said.

"Look around," Darío said, waving at Perla. "I'm still organizing things." He pointed to the piles of merchandise on the floor. "But browse."

A stone as big as a fist stood on a white plate behind the door. The stone had a necklace of red and black beads wrapped around it. Shells small as dimes were glued on its surface to form a face.

She pointed. "What's that?"

"Elegguá," he said. "Elegguá is old. Older than anything. One of the Orisha. Powerful African spirits. Elegguá is their messenger. He plays tricks on people. But he is also very strong. He protects your home from evil things."

"It's nice," she said. "Your store is nice. I'll come back in. Maybe tomorrow."

"I'm Darío," he said. "Here." He handed her an estampa of El Santo Niño de Atocha. "A gift. So that you will come back."

She said goodbye and walked home to prepare dinner.

Perla didn't go back for a few days. There was too much to do around the house: she needed to get rid of a bag of old clothes and shoes that the Salvation Army came by to pick up; there was washing and ironing to do; she helped her mother plant roses in her garden. She came home from her mother's, sat on the bed, and kicked off her sandals. The temperature had reached almost one hundred degrees, and she'd been working outside all morning. Perla poured herself a glass of water and lay on the bed, trying to nap because her head was hurting. When she pulled open her bedside table's drawer to look for the bottle of aspirin she kept there, Perla found the estampa of El Santo Niño.

She showered and dressed, then walked to the botánica. She was surprised to find a handful of people inside the shop, milling about, asking Darío questions, looking and pointing. He limped around behind the counter, asking a woman to describe her symptoms of anemia while bagging a Saint Joseph scapular for someone else.

"I thought maybe I scared you away," Darío shouted to Perla when he saw her.

"No," she shouted back. "I was just busy around my house."

She touched the merchandise this time—the stone Elegguá figure behind the door, the packets of powders and the bars of "Santísima Muerte" and "Suerte Pronto" and "Ama Me Siempre" soaps. She smelled the candles and the incense sticks, twined the scapulars and rosaries between her fingers.

She bought an estampa of San Ramón Nonato and a card with baby angels, some sleeping on clouds, others playing harps.

"What does the name mean?" she asked Darío after the other customers had gone and they were alone. "What does Oshún mean?"

He pointed to the stone face behind the door. "Like Elegguá, Oshún is an African spirit. The spirit of sweet water, of lakes and ríos. Of love and beauty and fertility. She loves dance and bells and fans and yellow flowers. She is the one you seek when you have money problems. She is beautiful and young just like my mother was when she left Cuba for Mexico. There she met my father, and they married. I was raised Católico, and when I was old enough she taught me Lucumí."

She said to Dario, "What is Lucumí?"

He leaned up against the counter and continued: "A religion. Some call it Santería. It came from Africa. In the Caribe, the monks tried to convert the slaves working in the sugarcanes to Christianity. When the slaves refused, they were beaten. They prayed in secret in the woods and worshipped their spirits by hiding them as santos so the monks would never know. They told themselves Oshún would be Nuestra Señora de la Caridad del Cobre." From a box, he took an estampa of Nuestra Señora and placed it in front of Perla. "Sometimes she's Saint Cecilia, sometimes someone else. My mamá showed me how to pray to Oshún and to see the other spirits in the santos at church. She made me promise not to tell anyone what she taught me, not even my father. We secretly made altars to Oshún and left her honey, canela, shrimp, and fresh water. We made boats from bright strips of paper and sent them out into the stream near our pueblo, just the two of us, the boats our offerings to Oshún. When I came here and saw the río, I named the botánica for her in honor of my mother."

He stopped talking and totaled up Perla's purchases. Darío used a pad and pencil to keep track of his sales until the register he had ordered arrived. He kept the money in a metal lockbox on a stool behind him. He totaled Perla's purchases and put them in a bag.

He looked at her and said, "The baby angels. On the card. The estampa of San Ramón. San Ramón you pray to for help with having babies, did you know?" He paused. He reached his hands out and touched Perla's head, her collarbone, her shoulders. "A baby," he repeated. "A baby. A baby. You want a baby."

The bag fell out of her hand onto the floor. Her knees weakened, and she gripped the counter.

"A baby," he said, his bracelet rattling. "You've been trying. Trying now for a long time." His eyelids fluttered. His face glistened with sweat. "Tell me, am I right?" He opened his eyes and looked at her. "Tell me the truth. It's the only way I can help you. And that's what you want: my help."

And it came as no surprise to Perla when she began to tell him everything—how they'd been married for fifteen years and had been trying to have a family, how they went to a doctor and found out Guillermo was sterile.

"He doesn't like talking about it," she said. "I'm getting older. And I don't think I'll ever be a mother."

She talked without stopping, without pausing to take a breath.

Darío pulled his hands away from her shoulders and said, "Tell your husband he should come in and see me. Tell him I've helped couples like you. Tell him I have teas and remedios we could try."

He walked around the counter and picked the bag off the floor. He handed it to Perla and said, "Go home. Come back here with him. We can try something."

That night, after they had dinner, she followed Guillermo into the garage. He turned the radio on and popped the hood of the Monte Carlo. He pulled the tab off a can of beer and threw it in the trash, then rested the beer on the roof of the car as he checked the oil.

He loosened the radiator cap and poured in antifreeze. "Car's temperature's running high," he said. "Don't want it overheating."

"I went to the botánica today," she said, leaning up against the washer.

"That crazy store?"

"The man there, he's nice."

"Is it true? What they say about him? Is he really a witch?" He looked up and shook his head.

"He's not. He's a curandero. A healer. He told me something. He touched my forehead and around my shoulders." She walked over to Guillermo and stood next to him. "He knew. He said he saw a baby."

Guillermo put the jug of antifreeze down and looked at her. "He saw a baby? What does that mean?"

"He said—" She paused. "He said he could help you. Us. He's helped other couples like us before. Have babies."

He took a long drink of his beer and tossed the empty tin can in the trash. "Those brujo types, they're just out to make some fast money. If a doctor couldn't help me, what makes you think his bull could?"

"We could try," she said.

"For what?" Guillermo shouted.

"We need to try everything."

"Is he going to put a spell on us?" Guillermo laughed. "Is he going to make me kill a goat and drink its blood? All that stuff doesn't mean anything." He waved his hand. "I'm not doing it."

"Please. We need to try everything."

"Hey, I'm fine here. We don't need to try anything. Why do we need kids?" he said. "I've gotten used to it just being us. We don't need any of that. We got the two of us."

"I want it," she shouted, hitting the car's fender with both hands. "I have nothing. I feel like I'm suffocating here. All day I'm alone."

He slammed the car's hood and walked back into the house. He went to bed that night without saying a word to her.

The next day, she found Darío helping an old man who was complaining about a pain in his elbow. There was another woman waiting to talk with him.

"My baby had a diaper rash," she told Perla. "The doctor gave me some cream, but the cream's been irritating his skin."

"My mom used to use sábila," Perla said. "On me. When I was a baby. Have you tried that?"

"Aloe?" the lady asked. "I didn't know you could use that."

Perla wrote everything down on a piece of paper for the lady. When she and the customer Darío had been helping left, Perla said to him, "My husband. He doesn't want to come in and see you."

"I thought he wouldn't." He laughed. "Most men don't like to. They don't like admitting there's something wrong with them. Makes them feel weak. They get embarrassed."

"Is there something you could give *me*?" Perla asked. "To help him through me?"

"Something, maybe," he said. "What I really need is him. Here. He's the problem. Not you."

"I guess I wasn't meant to be a mother," Perla said, looking over at the statue of the Virgen María in the middle of the glass case.

"No, you weren't."

She looked up at him, confused.

"That customer. I saw how you helped her. Listened to what you said. You have el don, the gift of healing."

"We were just talking, and I told her what to do. It wasn't anything big. I don't have powers."

"It hides. Gets buried. I felt it the first time you came in. But power like yours, like mine, like the woman I learned from, it doesn't come without a price."

He walked around the counter and pulled his pant leg up. The skin of his left leg was shriveled and pale and scarred just above the ankle. "Polio," Darío said. "It shrunk my leg. It was my price. The woman I learned from, she was burned in a fire. Another man I knew, he was blind in one eye, but his gift of prophecy and his healing powers were strong. You"—he pointed to Perla, to her stomach—"you'll never have children. It's the price you pay. But you do have power. I saw it when you walked in. Shining blue around your whole body. Why don't you let me help you? Teach you to make it stronger? You could be my apprentice. Think about it," he said. "I know it sounds crazy. And I know it's not what you want."

"I want a family," she said, starting to cry. "Not power."

She grabbed her purse and ran from the store. At home, she sat cross-legged on the floor of the spare bedroom. She imagined it furnished with a crib and a rocking chair. The walls painted a pastel blue or rose. Lace curtains covering the windows. Picturebooks and stuffed animals and a wooden toy chest. Bottles warming in hot water on the stove. Guillermo pacing, rocking their baby in his arms. She cried all afternoon, alone in her house, frustrated and angry at Darío for saying what he did, at her husband for being so stubborn, for not being able to give her the family she deserved.

When Guillermo came home from the factory that evening, they walked to her parents' house for dinner. Guillermo joined her father in front of the television, while Perla went to the kitchen to help her mother. She was peeling potatoes. Long strands of her hair fell down one side of her face. She pushed them back with the palm of her hand and looked at Perla standing near the stove.

"Ahora te enseño," her mother said. "None of this is written down. So memorize it all. Because once I die, you'll be left. Then you'll give these recipes to your babies."

"I'm never going to have kids, Mamá. I'm getting old." She didn't say anything about Darío, what he'd told her. She still didn't know how much of it she believed.

"You still can," her mother said. "You're still young."

"I wasn't meant for it. I don't know what I was put here to do."

"¿De qué hablas?" Her mother stopped peeling and looked over at her daughter. She cleaned her hands on her apron and walked over, placing her hand on Perla's forehead. "Are you feeling okay?"

She thought about Darío, his hands passing over her face.

She went down the hallway into the bathroom and locked the door. She turned the faucet on, watched water spill out, filling the green porcelain sink. In the mirror she conjured up a different face looking back, a different reflection. Not one with skin starting to tire and arms and hands that would never hold a baby. She imagined herself young. Starting everything over again.

She sat at the edge of the tub and looked down at the floor, the shaggy bath mats, her sandals. When had this happened? When had she become this woman? Did she take a wrong turn somewhere? *I could walk away. Leave him.* The sound of the television came through the walls. Guillermo and her father were talking about the game. She heard her mother drop a pan in the kitchen.

Maybe he's right. Maybe I do have it. Maybe he can teach me. Maybe he should.

She gripped her knees and cried, her shoulders shaking, her head dizzy and light.

She walked home with Guillermo in silence. When he tried to take her hand, she refused to give it to him.

"What's with you?"

She said nothing. Passing the empty field, Perla looked past the trees and saw the wall of the botánica painted with graffiti.

"The man at the botánica offered me a job," she said to Guillermo.

"Doing what?"

"Helping around the store. He'll pay me."

"You don't need money. You don't need to work."

"What if I want to?"

They stopped in front of their house. He opened the door to the chain link fence, and they both stepped into the yard and walked to the porch steps.

"You don't need to. We have enough money."

"I'm not doing it for that," she said. "I'm doing it because I'm empty."

He fiddled with the house keys. The sun was setting. Burnt orange light spilled onto the sidewalk, erasing the cracks and chips in the concrete.

She took his keys and threw them across the lawn. "I want more. Something else to do besides sitting at home all day cooking and cleaning. If I can't have kids, I can have a job. I don't care what you want. I didn't have a say in any of it, of us not having kids. So you can't have a say in me getting a job."

He stayed quiet. He shrugged his shoulders. "Do what you want." He fetched the keys and went inside.

The next morning Guillermo said nothing when he left for work. He walked down the driveway, slammed the car door shut, and pulled out, the tires skidding as he drove away.

She dressed modestly—a green pleated skirt, a plain tan cotton blouse with red buttons, and a pair of low flats. Perla grabbed her purse and went to see Darío.

"Señor," she said, closing the door. "Where do we start?"

Darío smiled. "I think we begin at the beginning." He turned the television off and had her sit down in one of the chairs. He closed the front door, flipped the sign, and sat next to Perla. "I want to tell you about how I got started doing this."

He had been taught by a woman who lived in Mexico. "She was a Fidencista," Darío said. "They're disciples of El Niño Fidencio, Mexico's most famous curandero, a man many said was blessed by God himself. This teacher of mine, her name was Agripina. When she was a child, she had been caught in a church fire and was the only one to survive. The flames burned one side of her face. Skin melted over her eye. It was hard to look at her. But that woman liked to joke around and laugh. She had the best sense of humor. Not serious at all. That fire, she said, gave her powers. Made her see things. Sicknesses and diseases. So she started helping people with remedios and petitions. She delivered many babies. Many of them were named for her."

He stopped and handed her a notepad and a pencil. "First," he said, "I will show you how this place is laid out, how I've decided to set everything."

Perla followed him around the store, jotting down the names of santos and herbs. Candles and crystals. Spirits and talismans. By the time they were finished, she had filled up seven sheets of paper. Her hand cramped up, and when a customer came in and asked for something to help with her loss of appetite, Perla was relieved.

"Now go home," he said. "Read those notes. We'll continue tomorrow."

She and Darío spent a good part of the next week arranging the store—stocking the candles and sorting through the piles of merchandise. Once the botánica was set up, Darío had her follow and observe him. She watched how he handled cases of empacho, susto, and low sex drive. Preparing for limpias, Darío had her gather the necessary items—the romero, the cigars and rum, the feather and the egg, which he said would absorb the malas vibras—and arrange them to his specifications.

Darío talked about santos like Jesús Malverde, San Simón, and La Santísima Muerte, ones she'd never heard the priests at church mention. He showed her astrology charts and books on palmistry and auras. She learned the tenets of Buddhism, Judaism, Hinduism, Voodoo, Candomblé, and the Lucumí of Darío's mother. He taught her about some of the other spirits—the many guises they assumed, the many roles they served. There was Changó the lord of lightning, thunder, drums, and dancing. Orunlá, the spirit of wisdom and divination. Oggún, who liked offerings of smoked fish and oak leaves. Obatalá, the wise father of all the spirits. Yemayá, the daughter of the seas, whose colors are sky blue and white. Elleguá, the energy of the universe, Elegguá who opens roads and possibilities.

The day the cash register arrived Darío made her learn to use it first.

"I don't like those things," he said. "You learn, then you teach it to me."

Guillermo hardly spoke to her that first week. He turned the other way in bed while she sat up and studied from her notes. In them there were treatments for anemia, gout, diabetes, and kidney stones. There were remedies for tapeworms, susto, and choque de nervios. She concentrated, memorizing her scribbles, sought patterns and connections, quizzing herself well into the night, her husband's snores keeping her company.

She came home one afternoon and found him in the bedroom, just sitting there.

"You get off early?" she asked, putting her stacks of books on the bedside table.

He said, "I lied. I said I wasn't feeling good."

"Are you hungry?"

"No." Guillermo took her hand in his and squeezed it. "I know it's too quiet in here for you," he said. "I can tell this work makes you happy. I'm glad to see you this way. I'm sorry I can't give you what you want."

Five years passed quickly, then one day Darío called from a phone booth to tell Perla he was leaving.

"I have to go," he said. "For good, Perlita."

"Why?"

"Because. When I came here, it wasn't to stay forever. It was just to open the store. To find someone to run it. Now I have to go again. Move to another town somewhere and start the whole thing over again. Perlita, I want you to take over the store."

"But how? I can't."

"You have to. Trust me, Perlita," he said. "I know what I'm doing."

*   *   *

Darío always knew what he was doing.

She reshelved the books. It had been so long now. And in that time, her parents had died. Guillermo had gone quietly in his sleep. Three years ago, Darío's daughter Sylvia had called. Her father's cancer had been too much, had ravaged his body. In his notebook he'd written, "Call my Perlita when I go. She was my favorite. My best pupil."

Perla remembered those early days when the store had first opened. She remembered the piles of boxes and merchandise on the floor, remembered climbing the ladders and stocking things, getting the store ready, exactly to Darío's specifications.

It was still like that today. The only thing that had changed over the years was the amount of merchandise on the sales floor and in the stockroom. It had grown. There was more of everything. Cluttered and busy. But it was all still exactly where he'd wanted it to be.

None of it, she thought, telling Darío. *I haven't changed it. It's all still just like you told me.*

On the shelves nearest the door were the statues—the Divine Eyes, the Money Frogs, and clay Pancho Villa courage heads, white witches and black spirits of good luck, bronze Buddhas of good health and happy homes, Vishnu and elephant-headed Ganesh and Shiva the Destroyer with his many arms, the wood-carved Kachina dolls covered in feathers and beads, Santísima Muertes in red and black shrouds, Santa Teresa, San Simón sitting in his chair with his black suit and bolero hat, the Infant of Prague, Our Lady of San Juan, San Antonio, and the little Holy Spirit doves perched on terra-cotta tree branches.

Then there were the veladoras. The colored seven-day candles—blue for serenity, red for love, white to end curses, green to attract prosperity. There was Santa Bárbara, patrona of prisoners and invoked against evil; San Judas Tadeo of lost and desperate causes; La Virgen de Guadalupe, madre de México; El Santo Niño de Atocha, who keeps lawsuits away; Nuestra Señora de la Caridad del Cobre, patrona of Cuba, who protects travelers at sea; San Martín de Porres, the patron of African-Americans and the poor; San Martín Caballero, who draws customers to your business; La Mano Poderosa, the holy hand of the crucified Christ; and Las Siete Potencias Africanas—Elegguá, Orunlá, Obatalá, Oggún, Changó, Yemayá, Oshún in the guises of Catholic saints. There were the mystical spell velas—Ven Aquí, Indian Spirit, Justo Juez, King Solomon, Shut Up, Evil Away, Break-Up, Do As I Say, Trabajo, Víbora, Quédate, Road Opener. Below them were candles shaped like crosses and snakes, skulls and mummies.

Then there were the soaps and cleansing bath waters—Gemini, Conquer Everything, Black Horse, Fast Luck, Eres Mío, Cuauhtémoc, I Control

All, Quetzalcóatl, Si Puedo, San Simón, Bring Me Everything, Enemigo Retírate, I See Everything. There were glass vials of rose and tea and patchouli oils and aerosol sprays—Hex Removing, Mariposa, San Judas, Osiris. There were the Holy Helper and Good Spirit floor washes, and beside the strawberry-, frankincense-, vanilla-, and cinnamon-scented packs were the Lotería, Paul Bunyan, Mother of Clarity, and Mother Teresa incense sticks.

The herbs and teas hung on short metal pegs—anís de estrella, cuasia, huizache, boldo, manzanilla, valeriana, epazote, uña del gato for diaper rashes and body aches, cola de caballo for kidney stones and skin problems, damiana for hangovers and bed-wetting, yerba buena—spearmint—good for colic and uncontrollable flatulence, romero—rosemary—for rheumatism, canela—cinnamon—to reduce fever and aid indigestion.

There were the silver medallas stored in a plastic tackle box sitting on a shelf behind the register, Egyptian ankhs and pendants in wooden boxes lining the countertops near the booklets and novenas, the estampas and rabbit's feet, the Tarot cards and numerology charts. In the glass cases were satchels filled with stones and gems—quartz, hematite, coral, geode, pyrite, turquoise, jade. There were necklaces of cowrie shells, rosaries, scapulars, menorahs, and Stars of David.

She took it all in and concentrated, then walked over to the books she had shelved and rubbed her hands over their spines—*Interpreting Dreams, The Zodiac, Candle Magics and Rituals, Essential Yoga, Palmistry, The Mystery of the Tarot, La Santa Biblia Católica*. Perla grabbed one, not bothering to note its title, and flipped through the pages until her eyes rested on a particular passage:

It is a universal truth that all manner of belief stems from an inherent human desire to know what occurs beyond our own plane of existence. With the help of the candles and stones, chants and offerings, the lines of communication between our world and the Other Side open up. These roads widen and expand, clearing a path where knowledge is shared in order to help us feel a part of a greater consciousness. Much like a mechanic who utilizes wrenches and other implements to aid him in his task of "fixing" whatever is broken, so

do the candles and amulets and deities described herein help to ful-
fill the task of alleviating and uncrossing, healing and enlightening.

She read the passage over and over. She read it to the audience of Buddha
and Shiva statues gathered next to the plastic display of prayer cards on the
counter. She whispered it to the Kachina dolls and the glass unicorn. They
offered up no insights. No knowledge. She imagined copying the passage
down in Rodrigo's notebook, imagined him reading it to himself, searching
for meaning in the words.

"What should I do now?" she said out loud, her words desperate. Then
she heard Darío, his voice in her head, clear and strong. *Feel it, Perlita,* he said.
*All of it. Use it. This santo here for this. That yerba there for that. Don't waste any part.
All of it is precious and powerful. Like you, Perlita. Like you.*

Así Like Magic

I don't know how to dress for this. Everything I have is either too tight or too bright. Or too shiny and skimpy. My shoes are too high, too silver and gold and red, the straps that wrap around my ankles too flimsy. Everything about the way I dress is too much. I have nada to wear. Nothing fits right anymore.

The last time I worked with Beatrice she'd gone home early complaining of a headache. I was off the next day, and that was when she died. Something got clogged in her brain, a blood vessel popped. Y como nada my only friend up and died on me.

"We didn't think to call everyone," Steven, the front office manager, said to me when I got to the clínica. "I'm sorry. We're taking donations to get a wreath."

I gave him ten dollars.

"You can go home today if you're not up to working," he said. "Come back next week."

I left and went straight to the club. I knew Bibi would be there, balancing the books like she does every Friday morning and getting ready for the weekend shows.

"What do I wear?" I asked her. Bibi sat behind a desk, her face rubbed raw and pale without mascara and lipstick.

"Something somber. A dark gray or black dress," she said. "You can find one at the indoor swap meet in San Bernardino. They should be open right now." She punched the adding machine's keys; a long receipt spilled over the edge of the desk like a waterfall. "Don't stress about it."

I didn't want to tell her I had no money to spend. That I'd been saving up for the operation. That I was more determined than ever to go through with it. She'd think it was stupid. What's the point? she'd say. Me with my wild ideas. It was a big step. And I was too young to make those kinds of decisions. It's been slow going because I don't get paid very much, but every month I've been putting away a little, saving the tips I get when the men toss dollar bills onstage while I dance. I keep the money in an envelope taped to the bottom of my nightstand. I have a lot. But it's still not enough.

So I left the club and took the bus home. I spent all of Saturday crying, unable to go out shopping for a dress. It's now almost ten on Sunday, and I've been going through my things all morning. The funeral's at noon.

The closet's almost empty. All my clothes are piled up on the bed. As I go through what's left, I find my black skirt, the first one I bought when I moved here to California, hiding behind a gold-sequined dress and a pair of imitation Guess jeans. I have a top. It's dark brown with a fur collar muy fluffy and warm. The blouse has shiny white buttons, but some have fallen off. It'll have to do. I'll use small safety pins to close up the gaps.

And shoes? I'll wear the low flats. The dark blue ones that almost look black. No one will be able to tell. You would have to squint to notice that they're not quite what they seem to be.

*   *   *

I needed to make more money. La Lola, who dances with me, said they posted new jobs every day at the unemployment office.

"Look for the little cork board," she'd told me as we dressed before the show one night. "They pin the cards there. But if you want something that'll pay you under the table, right outside there's a telephone booth where people stick flyers looking for all kinds of help. My sister got a job as a babysitter. One hundred bucks a week it pays. Cash."

I met Beatrice at the bus stop the day I went downtown to find some work. While I waited, I decided to do my nails. I'd bought this new color called "Temptation" and had just started to paint my pinky when Beatrice showed up, wearing a green smock and pants with white shoes.

"That's such a pretty color." She pulled out the most recent copy of *Tú* from her purse.

"Thank you. Got it at Las Glorias," I told her. "It's on sale right now. They have them in those plastic clearance bins in the cosmetics aisle."

"I like anything that's red. It's such a sweet color. So alive—you know?" She smiled.

I moved over so that she could sit on the bench. "I know what you mean."

"I'm Beatrice."

"Azúcar."

"Azúcar. I like that."

I'd already read the magazine Beatrice was holding. It had this recipe for an ointment to rid your thighs of cellulite. You could make it at home using olive oil and fresh lime juice. I'd made it and had been using the stuff every night even though my legs were trim from all the dancing and walking I do.

"Does it work? I need to lose some weight," Beatrice said, massaging her own thighs. "Just look at me. I've got to do something about my figure."

"I've seen some results. But when I'm done, I smell so much like a salad that it gets me thinking about food again."

We swapped beauty tips. She gave me a recipe for a hair conditioner made of egg and honey. I told her how every morning I apply a facial mask made from a sábila plant I was growing in a coffee can.

"Just slice a stem in half and massage the gel into your face," I explained. "Leave it there for a half-hour before rinsing it away with warm water, then pat your skin dry."

I'm not sure how long we waited there that first day. But it was nice to have someone to talk to and right away this girl seemed special to me. Call it intuition. She was taking the number 4 also, and when the bus pulled up to the curb, we boarded and took seats next to each other.

"Are you a nurse?" I asked.

"No. I work at the Clínica Mujer."

"The one on Alta Vista?"

"Yes. Are you a patient? You don't look familiar to me."

"No." I smiled. "I've never been in there."

I make a good woman. You would never know standing next to me in line at the market or the bank. The hair's all mine, no wig here, no extensions. It took me years to grow it this long, and I'm proud of it. I can braid it, tease it, wear it curled up, or blow-dry it straight.

My eyelashes. So thick, and they flutter up and down like a bird's wings. My face is smooth, my cheeks so kissable that a man once stopped me on the street and said I had the complexion of an angel. That's because every night I rub creams and lotions into my skin, especially around my eyes to prevent wrinkles. I keep up on the latest beauty treatments the stars use. I buy the magazines, clip those articles out, and pin them to my dresser and next to the bathroom mirror. I follow them exactly like they're written, and it pays.

I've seen the way some women stare at me while I wait with them at the bus stop, the way they roll their eyes, hiding their mouths behind their hands and whispering in Spanish because they think I don't speak it. Until I snap back at them, and they shut up right away. It's because I do myself up, because I take the time to make myself look this good that they're jealous.

It's the way I walk in high heels, the way my legs look in nylons. It's my curves, too. So round and tight. It's all about confidence. The way I hold my shoulders, keep my back straight, never slouching, always crossing my legs, says to people that I know I'm a woman. A real chingona.

So, you see, it wasn't unusual that Beatrice didn't notice. I convince most people.

"What do you do there?" I asked. "At the clínica?"

"I just answer the phones and schedule patients. I've been there for a few years."

"You must really like it."

"I do. We give these women someplace safe to come," she said. "Sometimes it's hard because you see some sad things. Women strung out and pregnant or beaten up. The county comes and takes the babies away from them. Sticks them in foster homes where they end up getting abused. I wish I could save just one of those babies. Break that cycle." She sighed, shook her head. "And what do you do?"

"I dance," I said. "I'm a dancer. But I don't strip or nothing like that."

"Like cabaret? With music and costumes?"

"Yes," I told her.

"How glamorous." She looked down at her shoes, then over at my high heels. "I'd fall and break my neck if I ever had to dance around in those. Are you going to work now?"

"No."

"A rehearsal or something?"

"Actually, I'm on my way to the unemployment office. I need a second job. I'm saving up money for something big."

We traveled down the street, houses and intersections whizzing by real fast. The windows on the bus were amber and scratched up with graffiti, and I could see my reflection looking back at me, transparent, the branches of a tree melting into my hair, the letters of a street sign floating across my face.

La Beatrice, she took my hand and said, "I've got an idea. The clinic is looking for someone to come in mornings to clean up around the office. I know it might be beneath you compared to your dancing career. But it's something."

"True. It is a little menial. Nothing like the show." I went along. "It needs to be under the table, though. My other job can't find out."

"I can work it out with the office manager. Leave it to me. I'll put in a good word."

A few days after, once Beatrice had cleared everything with Steven, she gave me a tour of the clínica and got me ready to start. There was a checklist of things I had to do every morning, and when I completed them, Beatrice would sign off so that I could get paid.

We'd get to the clínica at seven, two hours before it opened. Beatrice had a set of keys to the front door and the supply cabinets. She always carried them with her, stuffed in the deep pockets of her smock. While she organized folders and scheduled appointments, I'd go around with my list. I'd empty the wastepaper baskets and polish the furniture. I'd collect the toys that were scattered around the floor in the waiting room and put them back in the buckets. I'd stack the magazines on the coffee table and make sure the floors were swept and mopped clean. I'd scrub the toilet and the sink the patients used.

Across the street is Tom's Original Burgers #2. We'd sneak over before the clínica opened, have a cup of coffee each, and split a blueberry muffin.

We gossiped about everything: our families, our futures, our dream husbands. When I'd tell her about my dancing, the costumes, the applause I'd
get from the crowds, she'd sit there with elbows resting on the table, all
wide-eyed and smiling.

In high school, she'd been in a play. A small part. Just a few lines. She re-
hearsed day and night for weeks in front of a mirror. For a while, she'd
wanted to become an actress, but instead went to trade school and took
classes in office management.

There were so many moments when I could have told her, so many
times when we were on our knees reaching under the waiting room chairs
for blocks or as I swept around the front desk where she shuffled papers and
printed out reports. But I stayed quiet. On the morning I finally worked up
the nerve to tell her, I walked into the clínica and found her sitting in the
chair, her hand over her eyes. When Steven showed up at nine, she took off
because she couldn't stand the headache. She wanted to lie down.

"I'll see you next time," she said, handing me the keys to the clínica.
"Here. In case I can't make it in tomorrow morning."

Y fue todo.

·   ”   ·

I bought a bouquet of red roses from a woman on the corner. The flowers
fall right in the middle of the pile on top of her casket when I toss them. I sit
on one of the folding chairs and grip my knees, my eyes looking down at the
grass.

"Te tengo algo que contar," I say. "Me llamaban Andrés Contreras. Nací
niño. In Arizona. I never knew my father. He split when I was a kid. My
mother, Josephine, raised me solita. When I was thirteen, I stole a pair of
panties from the Junior Miss department at Sears. I wore them every day
for a week, and it was the best feeling in the world. My mother found them
stuffed in my drawer, underneath my T-shirts and tube socks. When she
asked where they came from, I was honest. I told her I'd stolen them and
that I wanted to be a Vegas showgirl. And my mother, she didn't care.
She'd had her suspicions, she said. She grounded me for stealing. She then
put her arms around me and said that life for someone like me would be
hard."

I stop for a minute, let my breath catch up to my words.

"It has been hard. But, listen: I'm tough. Once when a boy at my middle school called me a sissy because I'd started plucking my eyebrows and filling them in with pencil, I punched him in the stomach so hard he fell over and cried. I carried rocks in my pockets, leather gloves with the fingers cut off just in case someone decided to pick on me. I came to California because there's nothing in Arizona. I took the job because I'm saving up money for the surgery. The doctors put you on hormones first and after that you can have the breast implants. You go through counseling to make sure you're ready for the operation. To become a woman. It's long, I know. And expensive. But I'll get there.

"I dance at La Chuparosa. I do Madonna, but only songs from her first two albums. Sometimes I catch myself getting sick of doing the same routine. Maybe I should try something different. What do you think?"

Only the wind answers me back. Stirring up leaves that get caught in my hair. I shake them out and walk down the path toward home.

.   .   .

I've decided to be Pat Benatar tonight. La Lola thinks it's a mistake. Maybe it is. Tonight I'm just not thinking straight. It's hard enough for me to pull myself together to do a routine. But I have to. This time of the month is always good for money. It's always packed, and everyone's just gotten paid. The men come to the club to drink and tip big.

"Pat Benatar? What brought this on?" La Lola stands before the mirror in boxer shorts and a stuffed bra. She hasn't shaved her legs and stubble is starting to grow on them, the tips of the hairs like millions of tiny black needles. "You've only been doing Madonna forever. *For-ev-er!*" Her face is caked with foundation, filling in the deep creases around her cheeks and forehead.

"It's gotten muy tired," I say. "I want something different."

"Career suicide, Azúcar. Did you see the crowd out there? Pat's so second-rate. At least you could have chosen Stevie Nicks or Annie Lennox. But Pat?" She adjusts her red wig, straightens her fake tetas. "Please."

"And Cyndi Lauper isn't just an eighties babosa?" I shake my head.

"She's not Pat. That's for sure."

"What song are you doing?"

" 'She Bop.' " She pulls a pair of panties on and squeezes into her bright orange dress, taking three deep breaths before she has me zip her up.

" 'She Bop'?" I say. "Why are you doing that one and not 'Girls Just Want to Have Fun'? That's everyone's favorite."

"What do you know, *Pat*?" She smirks. The fishnets La Lola wears have tears she made with a razor blade, and she puts them on slowly, careful not to rip them more. She laces up her black boots. " 'She Bop' is better to dance to."

" 'She Bop' is about masturbation."

"Qué what?" She laughs. "It's *so* not."

"Haven't you listened to the words?"

"I lip-sync it, don't I?"

"But have you listened to the words? What they're saying?"

"I lip-sync it," she says again. "*Lip-sync* it. What do you think that means?"

"That you're not paying attention to the lyrics," I say. "You should pay attention to the words to help you pick up cues to work into your act." A few weeks ago, Bibi asked me to give La Lola pointers on how to finesse her performance. Bibi hadn't been happy with what she'd been seeing. As she put it, "That girl's a whole lot of attitude and nothing else. Too wrapped up in her own drama."

Lola asks, "What song are you doing?"

" 'Love Is a Battlefield,' " I say.

"Why *that* one?"

"Because I like the lyrics. And, in the video, a bunch of women get sick and tired of being ignored. They fight back."

La Lola rolls her eyes. "It's just a stupid video, Azúcar. Nothing more. It's all scripted. Make-believe. Así like magic."

"I know what it is."

"Then do your routine without the whole *mystique*. Get your head out of the clouds, mija. I know you just lost your friend, but it's time to get over it. Bibi wants you on. She's not gonna go for no tired washed-up acts." She gets up to take a smoke in the back alley before her performance.

I finish my makeup and put the black wig on, teasing it a few times until it's perfect. I put on the blue dress and tie torn strips of cloth to my waist.

After La Lola's Cyndi, the crowd is worked up, hooting and clapping, tipping like crazy. Bibi's always the MC, always dresses as Marilyn Monroe.

Tonight, she's in a black velvet dress and matching gloves with a blond wig. Bibi's voice is deep. She laughs loud and stomps around up there, ungraceful, scratching and grabbing her huevos, pretending to spit. After she announces my name, I walk onstage as the room dims. The crowd quiets down, their whistles and claps floating around me, mixing with the threads of smoke in the air.

It feels different. The lyrics to the song, the pace of the music, the way I have to position my feet when I spin. I miss a few steps here and there but cover it up by twirling and curling up my lip, pouting the way Pat did in the video. The crowd cheers.

I think of Beatrice.

*   *   *

There's a botánica that sells velas and statues of santitos. It's the only one in all of Agua Mansa, and the same old lady has been there all the times I've walked by on my way to the discount store. I've never been, never had a need. But today, after buying two bottles of Aquanet and a packet of hairclips, I stop in there for a candle and a prayer card of Nuestra Señora de Guadalupe to help guide Beatrice on her journey to Heaven, which is where I assume she'll end up because she was so good, at least to me.

Only when I get in there and tell the old cura lady that my friend died and that I want to help guide her, she tells me, "Lighting a candle won't be enough for that."

"¿Qué más?" I ask her. "What do I do?"

"Pray a rosary," she tells me. "For nine days."

"Why nine days?"

"It's the number of days it takes their spirits to wander around before they move on."

"But why nine days?

"It's written that way."

"Where?" I ask her. My questions start to irritate her.

"It just is. Trust me. Are you willing to help your friend or not?"

"Sí," I say. "What happens if we don't do it in time?"

"After that it's too late," she says. "They stay stuck in Purgatory. Or here. Ghosts haunting houses and cemeteries. Not good for them. Not good at all."

"I don't know how to pray the rosary," I tell the cura lady. "What do I do?"

So she gives me this book to read, an instruction manual. With pictures even, and it tells me what each bead stands for. I have to buy a rosary since the only one I had I tossed into the crowd one night during my performance.

"Give me that one." I point to the cheapy plastic one with pale green beads that glow in the dark. I cup my hand around the box to make sure each bead lights up.

"There are more here," the cura lady says. In a case near the register are wooden rosarios and more expensive glass ones.

"Give me that one, too," I tell the lady, pointing to a red one with beads that shine like wet pomegranate seeds.

What I have to do first, she said, is light a white candle. Then I have to pray the rosario the same time every day for nine days straight. I use the glow-in-the-dark rosario since the more expensive one I bought only for my act. I thread it between my fingers, and the beads click against my nails. I open the book, and it's all laid out there for me, all very easy to follow, all of it drawn out like a blueprint with numbers and arrows.

I can't tell off the bat if I'm doing it right, if my words are meaningless, empty puffs of air bumping up against the ceiling because I've never really believed in any of this. God probably thinks I'm just playing the part for now to get something out of him.

*　　　　*　　　　*

I must have set the alarm clock to go off at the wrong time because it wakes me an hour and a half early. Instead of sleeping in, I decide to get up and dress and go to Tom's to have coffee and a muffin before Steven gets to the office.

I sit at the booth that Beatrice and I always took, the one that looks onto the front of the clínica. It's hard, but I try not to feel lonely without her. Eight days have passed already. The vela's halfway gone, and when it's lit, bits of black ash float around the melted wax. Today will be the last time I'll pray the rosario. I've memorized it by now, know the order of the prayers. I slip into it easily—closing my eyes, caressing the beads, my voice whispering, my mouth forming each word.

Burger and breakfast special prices are airbrushed into the windows in fat letters. I look between the legs of a backward "R" and see a woman peeking through the main door of the clínica. She's holding something wrapped in a towel. The baseball cap she wears is pulled down low, her hair in a ponytail. I can't see her face.

By the time I pay and make it across the street to the clínica, all that's left is the bundle sitting on top of the newspaper near the front door. I walk up slowly, bend down low to get a better look. Something moves. I reach a hand out, peel back a layer of cloth to see a baby rubbing its eyes with its own small fists. There's a blue bag near it, full of diapers, wipes, a canister of formula. There's also a note. The words are big and crooked and wobbly.

He's a boy, the note says. She apologizes for leaving him here like this. She just can't keep him. She's sorry for doing this. She hopes he'll understand someday. Toward the bottom of the note the writing becomes bigger, the letters shakier and harder to understand until they dissolve into wavy lines and strange shapes. I stop trying to make sense of it and put the note in my purse.

His face. So red. Eyes pressed between soft skin. They're not round. They're slits. His hand reaches up. Small fingers wrap around my own. Pick him up. I have to pick him up off the ground, or he'll cry, get sick because the concrete's cold, dirty. I scoop my hand under his head, place my arm under his legs, lift slowly, and bring him up to my chest. So light. Like holding a possibility. Did she rock him in her arms while he slept? But my arms. They can't move, feel like they'll break off the rest of my body, and he'll fall to the ground and shatter.

My back is to the entrance of the clínica. I stand at the top of the stairs looking down onto the street, the passing cars, a man pushing an empty shopping cart down the sidewalk.

I hear Beatrice's voice, *I wish I could save just one of those babies. Break that cycle.*

I hold him tighter, his cheek pressing against my shoulder.

I walk to the corner. Hop on the first bus that pulls up.

●   ●   ●

His pajamas are dirty. Only three diapers are in the bag. He'll need things. The discount store has this one aisle. There are diapers there, plastic spill-proof bottles, teething rings filled with water, bibs with pictures of bears and birds with musical notes drifting out from their beaks.

By the time I get to the shopping center, the stores are opening. It'll be hard to shop with the baby in my arms. Since I don't have a stroller and I'm afraid I'll drop him if I have my other arm full, I peek into the botánica and see the cura lady standing behind her counter, a notebook and a pencil in her hand.

"Seño," I tell her. "I need your help. I'm watching this baby for a friend, and I have to run next door to buy some things. Could I leave him here with you for a minute?" ·

I pass him gently over to her. "Andale." She waves me away. "He'll be safe here. Go do your shopping."

At the discount store, I start with the diapers. Then I buy a stuffed animal that squeaks every time you pick him up. And lotion and baby powder and a few T-shirts. By the time I'm done, my basket's full. The clerk who rings me up puts everything in one bag because I tell her I'm walking and will be carrying a baby.

"I know totally how it is," she says. "I got kids, too, and I take the bus."

"Oh," I say.

"How old is your baby?"

I guess. "Three weeks," I say to the cashier.

"Congratulations. I'll double-bag. Just to be safe." She winks. "For you."

"Thank you," I say.

Back at the botánica, the cura lady holds him in her arms. "Where's his mother?" she asks.

"She left the country." I put my bag down and reach for the baby. "She'll be back next week."

"Strange," she says, stepping away, picking up her booklet and pencil.

"It's not strange for someone to leave the country."

"Yes," she says. "But strange if you've just given birth." She points to the diaper bag. "And stranger that she wouldn't leave him much."

"She left some things."

"Not a lot. I peeked into it."

"You peeked?"

"He needed to be changed. What's going on with the mother?"

"She has problems, seño," I say, toda serious. "Big problems. Drugs. And lots of other things."

"Like what?" she asks. "What other things?"

"Her husband." I point to the baby. "The father. He used to beat her. Call her and the baby all these bad names. Told her if she ever left, didn't matter where, he'd find her. And he'd make her pay."

"Qué lástima," the cura lady says. She's quiet, then says, muy seria, "You have to take care of him." Plastic cards, each with a picture of a different saint on the front, are arranged in a small rack on the counter. The cura reaches for one and hands it over to me.

"This," she says. "Nuestra Señora de la Caridad del Cobre. She'll protect you both. You make sure nothing happens to him. You do whatever it takes to make sure he grows up safe, you hear me?"

In the picture, Nuestra Señora stands on the heads of baby angels with wings sprouting from their necks. She floats above an ocean where three men sit in a paddleboat looking up at her.

I stand in the doorway, looking back at this old cura lady, her hand gripping my arm, her bottom lip curled down, defiant and tough.

"You hear me?" she whispers. "Whatever it takes."

"I'll try."

         .   .   .

He lies on my bed. Do I have to burp him? Will it make him sick if I don't? I reach back in my memory, try to picture the women sitting in the waiting room at the clínica rocking their babies, tucking their small heads under sweaters and blouses to breast-feed.

I had to bathe him in the sink because the bathtub's too big. I took all the dirty dishes out and let the water run, touching it with my elbow to make sure the temperature was just right. It was hard holding him in there. I was afraid to let go, afraid my arm would slip or get caught on something.

The formula. The formula was easy to make. You fill the bottle with warm water and pour a capful of the powder in, then screw the top on and shake it. I sat with him on my bed, propped a pillow against my back. I didn't know if my angle was off, if I was holding his head too low, and I remembered reading in a magazine that if you were to hold a baby's head wrong while feeding, milk could fill his nose and he could drown. How was I going to do this? How was I going to save him from dying?

He sleeps now. He was fed. He rests. I'm thankful.

When the time comes, I recite the last rosario. The prayers tumble out quickly and with force and, when I reach the very end, I watch the room for signs, try to feel if the temperature drops, look over to see if the candle by the window goes out. But nada pasa.

The baby kicks at something. I look over at him. Who will he grow up to be? I see him. Fifteen or twenty years from now. Body all scarred in strange places and marked up with tattoos. A troublemaker. A bandido. Stealing cars and money. Leaving his own babies behind.

I ask Beatrice, "¿Qué le doy? There's no way I can do this. You know it. Just look at what a mess my life is. This was never part of my plan."

The light coming through the window falls differently on the floor and the furniture. Shadows are sharp and menacing.

I have to go. Back to the clínica. I have to.

                    *   *   *

I wait at Tom's with the baby. Wait until Steven's Honda pulls out of the parking lot and takes off down the street.

I'm sorry, Beatrice. For using the keys you trusted me with to do this. I fill his blue bag with wipes and tubes of creams for diaper rash, bibs and pacifiers and bottles of pills to help ease the pain in his gums when his teeth start coming in. In the waiting room, I take pamphlets: *When Your Child Has Colic*, *What Is SIDS?*, *A Balanced Baby*. The bag is packed full and heavy, but I keep cramming more in, fitting things here and there, folding and pushing down. I have to. I have to. For him. I throw the keys and the note that came with him in the dumpster behind the clínica.

                    *   *   *

Agua Mansa passes by us. I watch the avenues and streetlights, hoping to see my apartment, La Chuparosa, and the rooftop of the clínica one last time.

I took all that money. I went right for the envelope. I had taped it so good and strong to the bottom of the nightstand that chips of paint and varnish peeled off and flaked my hands and arms. I paced in the kitchen, planning my next move. I thought about all those shows. All those nights I rolled around onstage, bruising my knees and legs while I did my thing up there in my tight dresses and lace halter tops. Necklaces and earrings, boots and belt buckles, all of it making me sweat, weighing me down. All those mornings I scrubbed the toilets and mopped the clínica's floors, organized the waiting room only to come back the next day to find it all a mess again.

I imagined myself finished. Reunited with the woman I should have been.

And then I touched the soft spot on the back of his head.

The rocking of the bus has lulled him to sleep now. And I let my voice fill us up with dreams.

"Don't worry," I tell my baby. We merge onto the 10, leaving the city behind. "You'll have things—clothes, toys, your own soft crib to sleep in. I'll make sure of it. The money will be enough to last us for a while until I find another job. We'll settle down. Find a small place with a yard for you to run around in and trees for you to climb.

"I'll pick a birthday for you. I'll tell you how I met your father. How we fell in love. How we held hands while we talked about a future all romántico like I'd seen on the telenovelas. People will tell me we look alike while we stand in line at a department store waiting to take our family photo. They'll believe my made-up stories—the ten hours I spent in labor, how much you weighed, the first time you rolled over on your stomach.

"When you're older, you'll go away leaving me to dance around in our empty house with the memories of my youth—of when you were young— bouncing off the walls covered with pictures: you in elementary school; you in a baseball jersey and cap with your fist stuffed inside a worn mitt; both of us smiling in front of a faded blue background with fake painted clouds that look like swan feathers. But you'll come back one day when my body is old and bending. You'll find me there in my bed asleep with my long gray hair spread out across my pillow like a spider's web. I'll be waiting for you to wake me with a kiss. Like a fairy tale. Like magic.

"After I'm gone, you'll tell them about me, won't you, hijo? You'll tell them about my dancing, the costumes I wore, the way I made the crowds cheer.

    " 'She was a class act,' you'll tell everyone while you pass around my picture. 'A real lady.'

    "They'll smile and see that I was and never doubt your word."

Feast of
Saint Bernardine of Siena

Franciscan Missionary Preacher

Patron of advertising, public relations, Italy, and
the diocese of San Bernardino, California.
Invoked against hoarseness, respiratory problems,
and compulsive gambling.

Three months had passed since Teresa had been to the botánica, so Perla brought along a box of valeriana tea to give to her. The receptionist in Teresa's office sat at her desk, writing on a piece of paper. She looked up, startled, when Perla tapped on the window that separated them.

"Appointment?" she said, handing over a clipboard.

Perla nodded. "Nine o'clock."

"Sign in and have a seat. You'll be called in shortly."

The waiting room was empty. From the window came the sound of the nurses and file clerks talking and gossiping. She had never gotten to know these new nurses very well. They always appeared to be in a hurry, rushing to get Perla into an examination room, jotting things down in her file quickly and without looking up. She missed the girls at the old clinic. She knew all their first names—Magali, Annette, Beatrice—and brought them lemons or avocados from her trees.

She didn't like this new office either. The building was too cold and impersonal. The old place was perfect. It was small and the waiting room felt more like a living room.

When the nurse called out her name and led Perla into the hallway, she saw on one wall the framed diplomas with Teresa's name, their embossed stamps, the fancy letters with thin swooping tails.

"Step on the scale," the nurse said. "Here, I'll take that." She reached for the small wire cart Perla had brought along with her.

Inside the examination room Perla sat on the table and removed her sweater.

"Don't talk or move. Uncross your legs." She took Perla's blood pressure. "What are you here for?" she asked, recording the results.

"A checkup," Perla said.

"Have their been any changes in your condition since your last visit?" She closed Perla's file and looked up.

"No," Perla said. "Nothing's changed. I feel the same."

Teresa would be in shortly, the nurse said before leaving. On the wall there was a poster with the words *The Respiratory System* written across the top in bold letters. In the diagram, plumes of air traveled down a tube labeled *trachea*. Strands of blue and red lines twisted and knotted around one another and fanned out to the arms and legs, the fingers and toes, the heart and brain.

At the botánica there were charts and books that showed how to read palms. One book contained an outline of the chakras of the human body and how and where they all lined up. Sitting there, Perla tried to remember. She envisioned a figure sitting in a lotus position. Indigo and violet and orange chakras like gems lined up and hidden behind the heart or floating just above the genitals. Perla was still gazing at the poster when Teresa walked into the room.

"Hi." She sat on the stool and wheeled herself over, her shoes skidding across the tiles. She looked over in the corner and pointed to the cart resting against the sink. "Is that yours?"

"Yes. I have some shopping to do on my way home. Heavy stuff. I don't want to carry it all back from the bus stop. How did the té work?"

"Good. It made me feel better. I'll need to get more."

"Here," Perla said, handing her the box she had brought.

"Oh, thank you so much, Perla." She set the box next to a glass jar of wooden tongue depressors on the counter. "How are things?" She opened Perla's file.

"Good," Perla said.

"Okay. Let's take a listen to your heart and lungs." Teresa walked over to her.

"How are you?" Perla asked. "How is everything with that doctor? What's his name?"

"Craig." Teresa smiled. "Very good. I'm taking him to meet my parents this weekend." Teresa pressed the stethoscope over Perla's heart. She listened carefully, squinting her eyes. She placed it on her back, slid it around, and instructed Perla to take deep breaths.

"Excellent," she said. "Everything sounds good and strong in there."

"You're nervous? About him meeting your parents?"

"A bit," Teresa said. "I wouldn't be surprised if they ask us if we've set a date for the wedding." She laughed.

She took her stethoscope off and placed it on the metal table, next to the thermometer. "It's been so long since I've brought a guy over, you know? I just want everything to go smoothly."

"It will," Perla said.

Teresa opened up Perla's file and scribbled something in a chart. "Your pressure's a little high, but that's normal. Just remember not to skip your medication. Stay away from salt and greasy food and alcohol. Watch what you eat."

"I know. I take good care of myself, Teresa. I eat right. I still walk every morning."

"I know you do," she said. "Just don't overdo it."

"All right."

Teresa sat down on the stool and rolled back over by the cart. "I sound like a broken record. If I do it's because I care. Especially about you. You've been my patient for years now. You're one of the few that came over with me from the clinic."

"What about everyone else?"

"Some stayed there. The others? HMOs. Shuffle patients around like cards." She rested the back of her head against the wall and sighed. "How's the botánica?"

"Fine," Perla said. "Nothing new." She wanted to mention Rodrigo. She wanted to ask Teresa about the marks, if there was anything to help heal cigarette burns. But she could see Teresa was tired. *She's got a lot on her mind, I'm sure,* Perla thought. *So much work, so many patients.* When she'd walked by the front office, Perla had seen files stacked on desks and cramming tall white bookcases. Office assistants were busy pulling and filing and refiling folders. Others clicked and typed on computers or scheduled appointments for patients who called on the phone. *Plus she's seeing the doctor now. Craig.*

"You seem distracted," Teresa said.

"What do you mean?"

Teresa stretched her legs out, and they touched the examination table. "Off. Your voice is off. I can tell. Far away."

"I'm just tired," Perla said.

"Do you think it could be work?"

"What do you mean?"

"Could be wearing you out. You've been running that place for, what, about thirty years now?"

"About," Perla said.

"Ever thought about getting someone to help you out around there?" Perla said, "No."

"You should. That way you could take a vacation. Relax. Travel."

"I can't right now."

Teresa hesitated before speaking. "I'm sorry. I'm just saying. It's that, well, I don't want you working too hard." She got up and placed her hand on Perla's shoulder. Perla tried to look past Teresa's layers of clothing and skin and into her body where her chakras lay, glowing like embers, warm and tranquil, nourishing her soul and heart. *If I had a daughter, this would be her.*

Teresa said, squeezing Perla's shoulder, "I'm here to help. Look out for you."

"Are you worried about something?" Perla asked. "Did you see something in the tests we took last time?"

"No. I'm sorry. I didn't mean to scare you. You're in great shape for someone your age. You're alert and sharp. Your heart's as strong as a horse's. You've got lungs of iron, and your blood's rich. You'll probably outlive me. Take it easy. That's all I meant. Take it easy. Step away. Clear your mind."

∘   ∘   ∘

¡JESÚS SALVA!

LOST? CONFUSED? HE IS THE WAY.
THE TRUTH. THE LIGHT.
COME FIND HIM. IGLESIA DE DIOS. AGUA MANSA.
REPENT. FOR HE IS COMING SOON!!!

The sun had faded the words on the flyer taped to the light post in front of the medical building. There was a phone number and the church's address and a map with black lines for streets. A quote from the Bible scrolled across the bottom. It was the Twenty-third Psalm, one Perla knew well. She always instructed her customers to say it when praying for a particularly serious petition to be granted or when confronting great danger. Perla turned away and recited it:

The Lord is my Shepherd; I shall not want.
He maketh me to lie down in green pastures:
He leadeth me beside the still waters—

Just then the bus pulled up to the curb. The cart banged up the steps, and Perla set it against the handrail as she reached into her coin purse to pay the fare. She took a seat behind the driver, bracing the cart between her legs, running a list through her head of the things she needed: milk, a gallon of drinking water, a packet of dried chiles, bleach. *It's a good thing the prices at Las Glorias are low.* She looked at the cart and thought of Alfonso.

"I've got no other choice," he had told Perla when he announced he'd be packing up the business and moving to a new shopping center. "I'm in the red most of the month. My store's just not making it. They're taking my customers away."

Perla had asked, "They who?"

"Las Glorias. All modern and high-tech. I can't compete with them. They got everything cheaper. You can wire money to Mexico. Refinance your house. Get cable television. They even got this shuttle that goes and picks people up who can't drive. I can't do that. I'm dying here."

"It'll be fine. This will pass. Just wait—"

"No," he interrupted her. "We're moving. There's this new strip mall. Near the 215 in Grand Terrace. We can get in there for a little more than what we pay here. It's right off the freeway. By some new apartment complexes. It's perfect."

Perla rested her elbows on the glass counter. "Te me vas?" she'd asked.

"Yes. I have to."

"Did you tell your papá?"

"Yesterday. When I came back from checking out the new space. I took pictures of it and sent them to him over the computer. He's sad. He was here when this shopping center opened. When this botánica was a flower shop. When Mr. Finch owned the donut place." Alfonso shook his head. "I think this is right. So does my dad."

"It'll be lonely here without you."

"I'm sorry. I can't stay. I have to compete with those places."

The day after, Alfonso started packing things and hauling them away. Over the next few weeks she watched as he filled the truck's cab with boxes and crates of supplies and merchandise. The last week, they had a sidewalk sale. They put up tables in front of the shop and sold some of the clearance merchandise at half price. There were candy dishes, marbles, decks of playing cards, plastic combs and hand mirrors, hairclips and packs of assorted socks.

"How much is this cart?" Perla asked, taking some plungers out of it and setting them near the curb.

"That's ours," Alfonso said. "But if you want it, it's yours. A going-away present. For my favorite neighbor." He showed her how to collapse it, how to lock the wheels to prevent the cart from rolling away.

The bigger things—the metal shelves and cases, the two Casio registers and the coolers—were going to be moved later in the month. By the end of May they'd be out completely, Alfonso had told her.

At Descanso and Meridian, the bus stopped to pick up a woman holding a little girl by the hand.

"Aquí, Yessica," the woman said as they took the aisle seats across from Perla.

The girl held a backpack with a picture of a mermaid. The mermaid sat on a rock underwater. Rings of coral adorned her fingers, and she wore a tiara made of scallop shells. She thought about the pouch she'd placed in Rodrigo's pocket that last night. He hadn't been back since. She tried hard to blink away the memory of those marks. The way he'd trembled when she reached out to touch him.

He knows where I'm at. Burns or not. I've got other customers. I've got other things to worry about. If he needs me, I'm right here. I'm not going anywhere. Alfonso is. But I'm not.

*   *   *

The banners flapped in the wind that came down from the passes, and the windshields of cars gleamed in the sun. The bus dropped her off on the corner of Valley and Pepper, and Perla made her way through the crosswalk, the cart trailing behind. She walked across the bridge over the freeway. The billboards along the westbound lanes of the I-10 hovered above a veil of exhaust. *Familia Medical: Para Tu Salud* read one showing a woman cradling a naked baby. A family of five wearing 3-D sunglasses posed together on one ad that read *Summer Fun Passes at Universal Studios, Hollywood.* A girl blew kisses at passing cars and semis. *I'm Reina,* was written above her head. *I'm at the Fantasy. Exit Pepper Avenue. South.* Next to the freeway a green road sign marked the miles to cities: Fontana, 10; Ontario, 17; Los Angeles, 53.

Inside Las Glorias, posters announcing sales on toilet paper and ground beef hung from the ceiling on transparent wires. Murals covered the walls: Pancho Villa riding a horse; Vicente Fernández singing to a woman in a red dress; Benito Juárez holding a scroll; an Aztec sun calendar; Indians in feathered headdresses climbing a pyramid; La Virgen de Guadalupe looking down onto the farmacia's counter. Near the last of the check stands, a man stood behind a glass window, speaking to a customer through a round hole. *Giros a México y Latinoamérica,* read the sign above him.

Perla bought some bolillo and two pieces of pan dulce from the racks beside the pastry cases. In the produce section, she picked up vegetables—cabbage and carrots, celery and squash to boil. Down the dairy aisle, she grabbed a half gallon of milk before heading to the household supplies for the bleach.

She walked up Aisle 14 where the veladoras were. They had expanded the section. There were so many now. She picked one up, the price "$1.25" stickered on its side. Perla did some calculating in her head as she pushed her cart to the check stand. *I could ask my wholesaler to cut me a break on the price. That way I could compete.*

She had finished putting all her groceries on the conveyor belt and was reaching for her wallet when she looked up and saw Rosa Cabrera behind the counter.

"You're working here again?" Perla asked.

"Yeah. Just temporary. For extra cash to save up for my station." Rosa punched some numbers on the register and passed the groceries over the scanner's red lasers. "But don't worry. I'm still cutting hair from home. So come by, okay?"

A bag boy wheeled the cart back around and set it besides Perla. "I will."

Rosa flicked a switch near the phone, and the light above her check stand turned off. She placed a sign at the end of the conveyor belt. "You're my last customer. I have to go and pick Danielle up. A lady who works the night shift is watching her."

She took the phone and dialed a number. "I'm closing out," Rosa told someone on the other line, then hung up. She pulled out the register's drawer and said, "About a week ago one of the cashiers was going to the manager's office with her till when she was dragged into the bathroom and robbed. Now when we have a lot of money a security guard has to escort us." When he arrived, Rosa handed the security guard her till, then walked around the counter. "I'll see you soon," she said, hugging Perla.

"Okay. I'll see you."

The sun was higher now. Heat rose from the concrete. Perla pushed the cart across the parking lot toward Pepper, walking under the shade of the ash trees lining the street, the shadows of their leaves like ghost hands patting her arms and shoulders and face.

·   ·   ·

Perla decided not to stop off at home before opening. She could place the milk and the vegetables in the mini-fridge at the botánica. Everything else would be fine.

The shopping center was quiet when she arrived. The moving van was gone, and so was Alfonso's car. Yesterday he and the men he had hired had worked all day without stopping. She cupped her hands around her eyes and looked in. The shelves were gone. The counter where the registers had been was pulled out. Only blond strips of wood from its foundation remained, dry caulk and glue drizzled over them.

The slip of paper fell on the ground when she pushed back the iron gate to get to the front door. Perla had stepped into the botánica and only noticed it when she turned to keep the door from hitting the cart. It was no bigger than a business card. Her name was written in block letters. She unfolded it and read the note:

Senora I come to looking for you but you are gone I come back soon. I am needing your help. I am afraid. The cops they wont help me and not even a church because I have feeling they will call the migra.

Please be here.
Rodrigo Zamora

She walked out into the parking lot and used the note to shield her eyes. Maybe she had just missed him. But there was no sign.

Aftershocks

I normally sleep in on Sundays, but when my husband, Darrell, woke up early this morning and went out for a run, I couldn't go back to bed. I've been sitting in my pajamas all morning, watching the news and sipping coffee, waiting for him to get back home. As I'm about to turn off the television and get dressed, the phone rings.

"How are you?" I hear my mother's voice ask.

"Fine," I tell her. "What's up? How are you?"

"Not good. It's your dad."

"Oh?"

"Your father." She sighs. "Cabezón. He hasn't been taking care of himself. Every time I try and remind him to make an appointment or watch his diet, all he does is get mad at me."

My father has diabetes. When it first developed, he was always thirsty. My mother complained that she couldn't sleep because he kept getting up in the middle of the night to go to the bathroom. He was tired all the time and became moody and irritable. He began losing weight.

She says he's been smoking and drinking despite his illness, despite the pamphlets from the doctor that she tries to get him to read. They explain in detail the complications that will develop if a person suffering from diabetes doesn't watch his diet or exercise daily.

He developed a cyst on his right heel that she noticed one morning when she bent down to pick the remote control off the floor. His bare feet were hanging over the edge of the mattress. "It was about the size of a quarter," she says. "Now it's infected. Who knows how long he's had it?"

Gangrene has set in, and they'll be amputating his foot.

"No blood was flowing there," she explains. "No feeling. He didn't even know he had it. We caught it too late. They have to take care of it before the infection spreads."

I stay quiet. From where I sit in the kitchen, I can see a pair of Darrell's old sneakers near the front door. I try to imagine my father hopping around on one foot. Will he need a cane? Can he be fitted for a prosthetic?

"I need you to go down and see Perla at the botánica," my mother says. "Find out if there's anything I can give him. A tea or something, I don't know. He's not taking his pills, so find out if there's anything I can sneak in his food."

"If the doctors can't help, what makes you think something from there can?"

"I have to try, Nancy. Your father doesn't care. You know him."

Apparently my father's taking this whole thing in stride, his usual fashion when faced with tough news. He told my mom he was going to take all the shoes and socks that he owns and donate just the left ones, not the complete pairs, to the Salvation Army.

I imagine him slapping his hand on his thigh, saying to my mother, "Lorena, vieja, wouldn't that be too much? Just too much. One shoe. One red sock. One of each."

The last time I saw him was just over two years ago. He wasn't cracking jokes, though. He was angry, shouting at me and Darrell, shaking his fists at us.

* * *

Growing up, I was the troublemaker of the family. My kid brother, Jesse, and I are four years apart. As teenagers, we were the opposite of one another. I was loud and rebellious. Jesse was quiet and shy, perfectly content to stay at home with my parents on Saturday night instead of partying with his friends. I pissed my father off back then, questioned his authority and challenged his will. It wasn't deliberate. I didn't do it because I hated him. I was born with this defiant streak in me, something I could never suppress. I can say that now. But what mattered to me when it came to my parents, especially my father, was that I got *my* way. Our arguments became a part of our relationship. It was the way we were wired, I suppose. He enforced and tried to dictate. I revolted and fought back. We argued and would go weeks, even months, without speaking while my mom would act as liaison between the two of us. Eventually we would come around and things would smooth themselves out just in time for another confrontation.

Like any good parent, he lectured and punished and threatened me. I stayed out past curfew and hung out with a group of "questionable" girls. I went through this punk rock phase where I wore green lipstick and safety pin earrings. My mother was always more tolerant.

"You take after him," I remember her saying once, after my father and I had gotten into an argument over a hickey on my neck. "Both of you are as stubborn as bulls. Always butting heads with one another."

After I graduated from high school, my father wanted me to attend a college nearby so that I could still live at home and he could "keep me on his radar." But I was eighteen and told him that wasn't going to be the case. That I would be leaving. After it was clear to him that I wasn't going to bend to his will, he said, "Fine. At least let me help. I don't want you living like some homeless person." He promised to pay part of my tuition and told me he'd be sending a check every month. He was proud of me, I could tell. Proud that I had made it all the way to college. We hugged and apologized to one another for all the arguments throughout the years. We promised to learn to understand each other. I packed my things, and he drove me all the way to Santa Barbara.

My senior year in college, I met Darrell. I was sitting out in the courtyard reading a magazine when he came up to me. He was tall and his shaved head shone smooth and waxy under the sun. He had the most beautiful black skin I'd ever seen. I dropped my magazine, and he bent down to pick it up.

"Nancy Pérez, right?" A pen jutted out from the side of his mouth.

"Yeah."

"We have Español," he said, in a heavy accent. "Soy Darrell."

I tried not to wince at his rough pronunciations. "Hi."

"Hola. Mucho gusto. Práctica," he said. "I try to practice as often as I can."

"It helps."

Our textbook was in his hand, the page turned to the lesson on the seasons and temperatures. "Can you help me translate this?" He sat down next to me on the bench and pointed to a sentence: A Juanita le gusta el verano.

Every day after class, we'd go to the library. I'd help him conjugate verbs, count, and recite the months of the year. As a way to practice rolling his R's, I would have him repeat the word "ferrocarril" over and over.

Our first real date was a week after we'd gotten our grades.

"Una A," he told me over the phone. "Let's celebrate."

María Candelaria with Dolores del Rio was playing at a small theater downtown. After the movie, we went for a walk along the beach. We took our shoes off and left them in his car. I don't really remember now how it happened. It just did. Somehow, we ended up sitting down on the beach, our bare feet burying into the sand, our toes wiggling up against each other's. His stroked my cheek, then he put his lips to mine and we kissed.

After long debates with my parents about graduation and the commencement ceremony, I decided not to walk. They had moved to Las Vegas that same year—into a master-planned community that had its own man-made lake complete with paddleboats and swans. Since my father had been diagnosed with diabetes just that year, I told them the last thing we needed was for them to hop in a car and drive all the way out to Santa Barbara. No, I said. What my father needed was rest.

"It's just a stupid ceremony," I said to them over the phone. "All that matters to me is that I get the damn piece of paper." I said I would save them the trip and go out there to spend a few weeks.

Darrell and I had been going out for about ten months. He wasn't going to walk either. His family was in Louisiana, and he had no money to fly back and spend the summer with them, so we were going to be with each other the whole time. I asked him if he wanted to come with me.

"I want them to meet you," I said.

"I'd like that. If it's cool with your folks."

A few days before, I called home. "Can I bring someone?" I asked my mom.

"Of course," she said. "Your father can't wait to see you. That's all he's been talking about for the past few weeks. His daughter, the college graduate."

We drove there in Darrell's car. When we were about an hour outside Santa Barbara, he said, "I've been having some real fun with you the last year, you know that?"

"Fun?" I turned to him. "Is that all it's been for you?"

"I didn't mean it's only been fun. I mean, well, it's been fun and really great."

I began to worry he was breaking up with me.

"I *hope* what we have is more than just *fun*," I said.

He cleared his throat and drummed his fingers against his leg.

"You're having more than just fun when you're in love with someone," I said and smiled.

"You in love with me?"

"Like you couldn't tell?"

He shrugged his shoulders, relaxed, and tried to play it nice and cool. "Maybe. Maybe not. Maybe I just wanted to hear you say it."

A few hours later, we stopped for gas at an AM/PM in Victorville. From the car, I watched as he stood in line with bottles of water, bags of Doritos, and soft serve ice cream drizzled with chocolate jimmies. He walked over and handed me the food. When the tank was full, Darrell came around the car to my side and opened the door. My fingertips were coated with fake nacho cheese when he kissed them.

"Mi amor." He said it perfectly, and it made me proud. From his pants pocket he produced a small box. Round oil stains coated the concrete but he still got down on one knee. A Youth Authority van full of boys with crew cuts and in baggy orange jumpsuits pulled up to the gas pump next to us. A guard in a uniform got out. "I'll be damned," he said and gave Darrell an approving nod.

He proposed in Spanish. The boys in the van slapped each other on the back and cheered. One of them said I was *fine*.

A woman knows these things. She knows it's right. When she sees a man, on his knees, the grime coating his legs, his skin, the scent of petroleum and popcorn on his clothes, she can't help it. She loses herself, thinks about that moment just before the doors to the church open as the wedding march begins and her relatives and gray-haired tías sit in the pews wearing funny hats, balls of tissue paper pressed against their noses. I saw Darrell there and the desert behind him opened up, vast and wide and untamed and the sky was so purple. Everything stopped like it did that night at the beach when we first kissed. And all I could think of was how much I loved this man.

"What do you say?" For a minute, I could see the hesitation in his eyes, a moment when he questioned what he had done. "I bought the ring just before we left. Been carrying it this whole time. My brother said I was fucking nuts. It feels good. I almost chickened out back there, you know? Before you said you loved me."

Inside the store, the man in the uniform was at the counter. He said something to the attendant and the people behind him in line. Everyone looked over at us. A woman scooping relish onto her hot dog stopped. People leafing through magazines put them down and stood still.

Darrell held the ring up.

I closed my eyes and took a deep breath. "Sí," I said. "Sí."

When he slipped the ring on and kissed me, the people in the store cheered, the boys clapped and hooted, pressing their hands against the iron bars of the van's windows. The hot dog woman walked over to the car. "You're going to make a darling bride, sugar," she told me.

We drove through miles of flattened desert, and everything looked different the rest of the trip. I had graduated and would be starting a teaching credential program in the fall. Darrell had graduated with high honors. We were young and in love and engaged. I twirled the ring around on my finger, imagined my dress, Darrell's family flying in from Louisiana and meeting my relatives.

"We won't tell them right away," I said. "I mean, not the minute we walk through the door. We don't want to shock them."

"Sounds fine," he said. "You know them better than I do."

I took my engagement ring off and placed it back in the box.

It was after nine by the time we pulled up to the driveway of my parents' house. The front porch light came on, and my father stood in the doorway. Even though it was night, I could hear the hum of air conditioners up and down the block. My parents kissed and hugged me. When I introduced them to Darrell, my father said hello, then turned and went back into the house. My mother shook his hand and led us both into the living room.

When we sat down, I noticed how much weight my father had lost since the last time I saw him, how pale and gaunt his face appeared. He moved more slowly, staggering. When he walked into the kitchen, he almost tripped.

"Is that really you?" Darrell said, pointing to a high school picture of me hanging above the fireplace.

"Hard to believe, isn't it?" I smiled, feeling embarrassed. In the picture, one side of my hair was dyed red and the other blue.

"She got this crazy idea," my mother said. "She looked like a snow cone."

My father came back into the living room and sat in his recliner. "Your drive good?" he said to me.

"Fine."

"Good," he said. "That's good." His raised his voice and shot a glace at Darrell. "Is he your friend from school?"

"We took Spanish together," Darrell said. He leaned forward. "She was a real help. We studied together."

"I see," my father said. He looked over at me and at Darrell again. An awkward silence filled the room.

I was glad when my kid brother, Jesse, came downstairs. "Hey," he said to me. We hugged, and I introduced him to Darrell.

I reached out to touch the side of Jesse's head. Tattooed there was the number thirteen.

"Did that hurt?" I asked.

"Like hell," he said.

"And he doesn't think I know the reference," my father said. "But I do."

Jesse got up and walked over to the sliding glass door that led out to the backyard. My parents hadn't planted grass out there yet, and there were no trees. He turned the light on and went out.

"Pot," my father said. "It has something to do with pot."

"I hear some kids call it 420. Write it on their folders and get the numbers embroidered on jackets or write it on the bills of baseball caps with markers," Darrell said to him.

My father didn't respond. He just rocked in his recliner. After a while, he excused himself and went upstairs to sleep.

In the kitchen, my mother told me about his prognosis, how he needed to watch what he ate, how he needed to stop drinking and smoking.

"But your father," she said, shaking her head slowly. "None of that matters to him. Doesn't take care of himself at all. I get so frustrated sometimes. And he and Jesse are always fighting."

"It's him," Jesse muttered. "You should see the way he gets, Nancy. Soon as I'm old enough, I'm out of here."

"Quiet," my mother said to him. "This sickness, it's serious. The doctor said if he doesn't take care of himself, he could die."

I slept in the room my mother had designated as mine even though I had never actually lived in the house. All my things were there, though. From my old bed, I listened to the desert wind, blowing sand against the window. I heard the sound of the bathroom door opening. The fan went on. Without having seen who'd gone in, I knew it was my father. I crept down the stairs into the den. Darrell was sitting up on the roll-away cot that my mother had pulled out from the closet.

"Hey." He was in his pajamas and a T-shirt.

"You're not sleeping," I said.

"Too much wind." He got up and walked over to the glass door. "The whistling noise is keeping me up." I heard the hiss of the toilet upstairs. A few seconds later came the click of my parents' bedroom door closing.

"Let me ask you a question," Darrell said. "Is your dad okay with this?"

"What do you mean?"

"He was throwing me some shade. Didn't shake my hand. Didn't acknowledge me all that much. He okay with me?"

"Why wouldn't he be?"

"Don't know," he said. "How much you tell them about us? They know we're dating?"

I stayed quiet.

"Shit," he said and walked over to me. We sat down on the bed. "They don't know we've been dating? You didn't tell them?"

"They know," I said. "I just haven't *told* them."

"You embarrassed of me or something? You afraid they won't approve of me?"

"That's dumb," I said. "I'm not afraid. I love you. That's what counts. I'm not afraid of them."

I turned and went back to my bedroom.

It was eight-forty when I woke the next morning. Darrell was right. It was time. I slipped on the engagement ring and went downstairs. My parents were sitting at the kitchen table. My father had his bottles of pills rowed up next to each other. Darrell sat next to him, and I went over to the refrigerator. I took a carton of orange juice and poured some into the glass in front of my mother, keeping the engagement ring in full view. She didn't notice.

I pointed to the pills. "Have you even been taking them?"

"What's this? Is everyone turning into my damn doctor?" My father slapped his hand on the table. Darrell's eyes fell to the floor.

"Can we have a few days of peace and calm before the two of you start?" my mother said. "Or do I need to put you both in boxing gloves all the time?"

"Sorry," I said. "Just looking out for you, Dad." I sat on the opposite end of the table from him, pressed both hands on the surface. After a short silence, I cleared my throat and said, "Here's the thing: Darrell and I have something to say."

Darrell shifted uncomfortably in his seat, then got up and walked over to the counter.

"He proposed." I looked over at Darrell. "Yesterday. On the way here. I said yes."

At first my father said nothing. He simply shook his head a few times and cleared his throat. "Well," he finally said. "That's something, isn't it?"

"I said yes," I said again. "I hope I have your blessing." I looked over at my mother, who remained quiet. She watched my father, then made the Sign of the Cross.

"I don't want to tell you what to do, Nancy," he said. "Because every time I've tried, you just ignore me anyway. Disrespect me. But, I don't like this. Don't like this one bit."

I walked over and held Darrell's hand. He was sweating.

"Octavio," my mother said. "Let's go upstairs."

"No," he said, pounding his fist on the table.

"I knew this was a bad idea," Darrell said to me in a low voice.

My father looked at him. "Then why'd you do it? Huh?" He then turned to me and said, "Is this what you've been doing in school? Going out with black boys? Having sex with them? Being a tramp?"

"Octavio," my mother said. "Con calma." She turned to Darrell. "My husband, he's sick. He's not racist or anything. His blood sugar level's off. That's it." She turned to my father. "Just take your stupid pills, and stop making an ass out of yourself."

My father clenched his fists. "Don't make excuses for me, Lorena."

"We should go," Darrell said. He told my father, "Look, señor, I can understand why you're upset. I mean, I can imagine. Nancy and me, we got something good here. We want to share it with you. And you," he said to my mother.

When he tried to get up, my father stumbled and held on to the wall. "Don't come in here trying to win me over. You're no good."

"What the hell is that supposed to mean?" I said.

My mother helped ease him back down into the chair. When she tried to place her hands on his shoulders, my father recoiled.

"Tell me," I said. I crossed my arms, widened my stance.

Darrell grabbed my arm. "Let it go," he whispered. "Come on."

"Let them do what they want," my mother pleaded. "You should be worrying about taking care of yourself. Not going out of your way to pick fights with her."

"Fine," I said to my father. "Be that way."

In the hallway, my mom tried to calm me down, tried to convince us to just let my father rest and think about the whole thing. "News like this, it's natural that it would upset him. He gets mood swings. Stay," she said. "I want you to. Just wait a while. He'll be better."

"Sorry, Mom," I said. "I knew this would happen. Doesn't matter what I do, it's never good enough. He always has to find something to hassle me about. I'm sick of this."

I kissed her, and we grabbed our bags and left.

On the drive back, I slid close to Darrell, put my head on his shoulder, and watched the cars traveling in the opposite direction. This was it, I thought. If my father wouldn't accept Darrell as my husband, if he wasn't going to give us his blessing, I would never speak to him again. What he needed, I felt, was for me to show him that this time the little games of tug-of-war we'd been playing since I was a girl weren't going to work. We were no longer living under the same roof. I didn't have to abide by his rules. I was going to show him that this time he'd done it. He's pushed me too far, I told myself. All he wants is to make my life difficult, to make it so that we would never have a normal relationship where we both understood and loved and respected each other like we'd promised to do.

"Does he think I'm going to give in?" I said to Darrell. "Well, he's wrong. If he doesn't care about what makes me happy, I don't care about him. He's gone to me."

When we returned to Santa Barbara, we were married. I wore a white dress with spaghetti straps. Darrell wore a dark suit with a silver tie and a carnation pinned to his lapel. He looked so handsome. We said our wedding vows in Spanish, and Darrell was so proud of himself for not having mispronounced any of the words.

We stayed in Santa Barbara for another year while I earned my teaching credential. The only contact I had with my family during that time was the phone calls from my mother. She always made a point to call me when my father was around. She would say in a loud voice, "You sound *so good*, mija. So happy" or "Wonderful. It looks like things are coming together for both of you over there" when I told her Darrell and I bought a coffeepot that was on sale. Darrell had been interning for a local councilman "until something else popped up." That something else finally came when he was offered a job working for the city of San Bernardino.

"Where to?" he said. "That's your neck of the woods." He unfolded a map of the area on the floor of our apartment.

I sighed when I saw my hometown. "Here, I guess." I pointed to Agua Mansa.

I looked in the newspaper for a place. There was a small two-bedroom house with a detached garage for rent. Darrell and I took a drive down there one weekend and checked it out. We signed a lease and packed up everything we owned. Whatever didn't fit in our cars, we just donated or gave away.

         .   .   .

Agua Mansa had changed since I had left for college. The freeway had been widened, the mounds of dirt the tractors gathered pushed back and held up by tall concrete walls with engravings of speeding locomotives and mountains etched into their surfaces. An apartment building near the house I grew up in burned down one night and in its place a Baptist church called the Holy Nazarene was built. On Descanso, a Salvadoran restaurant that sells pupusas now occupies a building that used to be a Taco Bell. Even though I recognized streets and locations, I had a hard time getting around. I got a job teaching second grade at Wyatt Elementary. Despite knowing exactly where it was, and even though I left early enough to give myself plenty of time, I took a wrong turn and got there a few minutes late, frazzled and embarrassed.

One of the few places that looks exactly the way it did when I was a kid is the Botánica Oshún. The botánica was the place my mother came to only when other measures had failed. She believes in the power of the unknown, in the intangible strength and magic of rocks and stones and amulets. There's a thing to be said, I remember her saying once, about something as unassuming as a lucky coin or a medalla someone wears around their neck, the way these things absorb the hopes and desires of the owner, the way they act to harness, to stockpile, so much life energy that even the simplest and most ordinary of articles can retain so much strength, can have the ability to make great and wonderful things happen.

"Sure," I had said. "Sure, Mom."

Today, women hover around the counter in polyester skirts, their faces shiny from the liquid foundation they dab onto their cheeks with cotton wedges. They peer at the talismans in the cases, pointing and muttering, wondering which is good to help a sick baby or a dying parent.

I take a seat by the window, drumming my fingers against the back of my chair.

"I'll be with you soon," Perla says to me as she walks over to a woman about my age in a pair of cotton stirrup pants and red sneakers.

"I'd appreciate that," I say. "I'm kind of in a rush."

The woman she's helping asks Perla, "And this will help with the rash? The doctor said it was from the diapers. I've started using the cloth ones."

"Make sure you put it on him every day," Perla tells her customer as she rings her up.

The woman pays and leaves. Perla tucks the twenty-dollar bill in the register and shuts it. "You're the Pérez girl, aren't you?" she says to me once we're alone.

"Yes," I say. "Nancy."

"How are your parents? Do they still live out there in Vegas?"

"Yes."

"I miss seeing your mother at Mass and in here. How is she?"

"Good," I say. "Except she doesn't like that there isn't one of these places out near her. At least not that she knows of."

"And your father? How's his diabetes?"

"Not good. My mom called this morning. He got a cyst that became infected. They're going to amputate his foot."

She sighs, shakes her head again.

"He's stubborn, you know. Hates taking his pills. My mom's afraid. So, she asked me to come by and talk with you. To see if there was something you could recommend. Some herbal remedy."

"Nopales," she says. She reaches for a small plastic sack and opens it up.

"Nopales?" I furrow my eyebrows. "That's it? Cactus?"

"Have her take a patty and remove the thorns." From the sack, she pulls out a few packages of instant horchata drink mix. "When she's removed the thorns and washed the patty, have her blend it until it turns to pulp. Mix that with some water and stir it with a spoon. She can use flavoring to make it taste better." She hands me a few of the packets of horchata powder. "Like horchata or tamarindo. Whatever he likes. It has to be sugar-free, though. Have him drink it daily."

"Okay. How much?" I take some money out of my pocket to pay for the packets.

She shakes her head. "It's nothing. I bought those for me. They were on sale. Buy two get one free. I have more."

"Thanks."

"And tell her to give him massages." She makes small circles with her hand in front of my face. "On his good foot. To keep his blood flowing."

"I'll tell her," I say, putting my sunglasses on.

*   *   *

It's early Monday morning. When I get out of the shower, Darrell says my mom called.

"They're getting ready to do this thing with your dad. What are you going to do?" He's reading a section of the newspaper and doesn't look at me when he talks.

"What do you mean?"

"I mean she says it's pretty serious. They're getting rid of his foot, but they think the infection's spreading. You should go."

I put my jacket on and lean up against the door frame.

"Well?" he says.

"Not until he apologizes."

He laughs, shakes his head. "Whatever."

"I know. You think it's stupid. You think I'm acting like a brat," I say. "Are you forgetting that I didn't have anyone to give me away at my own wedding? Are you forgetting how shitty, how completely shitty I felt after that whole incident?"

"Nope," he says. "I haven't forgotten. She says your dad says you owe him an apology."

"Oh, I see." I shake my head. "He insults the man I love, then expects me to apologize. That sounds fair."

"I'm not sure who's to blame for what," he says. "I can't wrap my head around any of this."

"That's easy," I say. "He made an ass out of himself in front of the man I love."

"This whole thing, it's not just about me." Darrell walks over to the sink and washes his hands. "The two of you have been at each other since you were a kid. I'm just saying you may have to be the one to give first if you ever want this relationship to work again. You may have to be the bigger person and go see him and let the apology slide."

I step away from the door frame and stand in the middle of the kitchen. "I don't want to give first," I say. "He made it clear: He doesn't care about me. About us. I don't care about him."

Darrell's silent. "'Course not," he says, drying his hands. "You ended the whole thing."

"Right."

"Man's not your father anymore. You're not his daughter."

"He did it to himself. He asked for it. Could have handled things differently. I don't care. I just don't."

"Yeah," Darrell says. He reaches for his car keys on the counter, near the packets of the horchata powder I got from the botánica yesterday. "I can see that."

He kisses me on the cheek and leaves for work.

I take the long way to school this morning, passing the car wash where my dad used to take our Chrysler. What Jesse and I liked the most was sitting inside with the windows rolled up. We'd watch as the automatic hoses sprayed water on the car. The bristles would descend from the ceiling. They'd pass over the car and swirls of white soap would drip down, coating the windows. I remember once looking through the wet glass, seeing my father standing at the end of the car wash, waving at Jesse and me as we sat there listening to the strong jets of water rinsing the soap and wax away.

Inside the classroom, my students are shuffling about, hanging their jackets in the coat closet, getting settled in their desks. I prepared a lesson on earthquakes for today, and I tell them we'll be having a mock earthquake drill.

I stand in front of my classroom, talking to them about plate tectonics, about the Ring of Fire, and pressure points. We talk about Richter scales and magnitudes and epicenters. We talk about the fault lines our school and homes rest on. I go over what to do after the shaking stops, how to shut off the gas, and the essentials every first-aid kit should have.

"Is California sinking?" April Lugo asks. "My mom says she wants to win the lottery before it happens, then move to Texas with my grandparents. But it can't sink before she wins the jackpot. She says it's not fair that old people always win it."

"It's moving," I tell April. "Not sinking. The piece we're on is drifting north."

My students look at me confused.

Lily Sánchez says, "My dad says when the Big One hits, California will become an island."

"Will people get hurt?" Jimmy Phuc asks.

"If they're not prepared they will. So, we must be ready. Have an earthquake kit. Wear heavy shoes in case there's broken glass on the floor. Expect aftershocks."

April asks, "Will people die?"

I think about my father lying on a bed in a hospital. I imagine him hopping around on his one good foot, urging me to dance with him like we used to when I was little, bracing himself against my mother and Jesse, trying not to fall over, as they lead him to the recliner where he likes to sit.

We end with the earthquake drill. I watch the clock near the door, shout "Now" when the second hand reaches the twelve. My students duck under their desks and lock their hands together behind their heads. Their faces are pressed against their knees.

"Everything around you is shaking," I shout to them. "Whatever you do, don't unlock yourselves. Stay in your position. Glass is falling to the ground and breaking. Bookshelves are toppling over. Stay put. Don't move. Stay right where you are."

I know that beneath us the ground is rumbling. Oceans of magma are hardening to form layers of rocks that the earth's restless temper will break apart. We float on giant plates that crash and buckle into one another, and straight roads bend into elbows, rivers rechannel, mountains sprout up. We separate, then collide and try to hold on to one another. Because we know it's only a matter of time before we're pulled apart again.

I turn off the lights and run around my classroom. A few students shout and giggle. Someone screams. I toss books on the floor, take coats and hats and throw them up in the air where they get caught on the light fixtures hanging above.

Tired and out of breath, I stomp on the ground and continue running up and down the aisles. I shout and throw a clipboard against the wall. I pound the tops of the desks, feeling the sting and vibration throughout the palms of my hands, running all the way up to my elbows, my shoulders, my neck.

"This is it," I shout, my hands turning red now, throbbing. "The Big One. It's here. This is it. This is it."

Feast of
San Juan Soldado

Martyr

Patron of illegal immigrants,

the poor, the helpless, and those unjustly accused.

Invoked against political and civic corruption.

Alfonso had been gone a few weeks now. Today the construction workers arrived. They unloaded sheets of drywall and pieces of lumber, toolboxes, sanders, drills, and band saws with sharp steel blades. Things crashed and fell against the floor of the shop as they tore down walls and rerouted the wiring. Hammers pounded, power tools turned off and on, the voices of the men laughing, cracking jokes, cursing, made their way through the wall and into the botánica where Perla stood watching. The few customers that came in didn't seem to mind all that banging and noise. Still, she turned the volume of the television up to cover it.

"Are you expanding?" a woman buying a Virgen de Guadalupe prayer card and a can of Lucky Bingo aerosol spray asked.

"No," Perla said. "The store moved."

"Do you know what's coming in?"

"No."

"I hope it's a check-cashing place. One where I can pay my utilities."

That afternoon, the workers gathered up their tools and supplies. Metal boxes and cans of plaster and paint rattled around the beds of their trucks as the men pulled out of the parking lot and sped down the street.

Everything was quiet again after the last of them left. It was past four. Outside the sun burned bright white against the trees, singeing the tips of their leaves and turning their barks ash gray. Since she had come across Rodrigo's note, she had stayed late just in case he came by. The note was taped to the register now. *He'll be back. If he really needs me, he'll show up. It can't be that bad if he hasn't showed up since he left the note.*

She flipped the television to channel 34 and caught the last half of *Primera Voz.* It ran a report about people disappearing along the border, women coming home late at night from maquiladoras near Ciudad Juárez. They assembled circuit boards for radios and computers, all for low wages, the report explained, only to end up mugged and raped in dark callejones, under blurred streetlights, their bodies dumped in shallow ravines. The camera showed a pair of legs dangling over the edge of a dirt mound, feet stuffed into white heels with gold clasps, the edge of a skirt torn and bloodied.

Más desapareciones en Tijuana, a voice said.

Images of a wall covered with pictures of boys and girls flashed across the screen: *Antonio Macías; Josefina Peña, hija; Olga de la Cruz, Su familia la busca.* Staples stitched their faces to street signs and wooden beams. *Babies ripped from the arms of their mothers to be sold on the black market,* the reporter mentioned. *Sex trade. Young girls sold into slavery. Satanic cults that practice cannibalism and human sacrifices.* A reenactment showed a sleek silver car, an arm with a gold wristwatch reaching out to grab a girl selling gum to tourists along the border. A hotel sign blinking off and on. There was a bedroom with bare white walls and a pair of hands passing over the girl's body. The images on the screen blurred and faded out slowly. Then hooded figures holding hands and chanting around a group of red candles passed before the screen. There was a pentagram drawn in white chalk on a floor and the number 666 written in blood on a woman's forehead.

Perla turned the television off once the program ended, then locked the front door. From the shelves behind the register, she took a candle of Juan Soldado and lit it. The image on his veladora was neither a drawing nor a painting, but a photograph. El soldadito's boyish face, his round eyes, looked back at Perla as she lit the vela and set it on a plate. Juan Castillo Morales had been a soldier stationed in Tijuana in 1938 when the body of eight-year-old Olga Camacho was discovered in an abandoned garage. She had been raped and killed. The police arrested five suspects, but, by morning, had fixed upon Morales as the murderer. He confessed, was tried, and was publicly executed by a firing squad. Soon after, doubts arose about his guilt. Word spread that corrupt generals and town officials were responsible, that the confession was false, and that Juan was innocent of the crime. People said blood oozed up from the soil of his grave and claimed to hear his voice crying out for justice. And so in death, Juan Morales became Juan Soldado, invoked against corruption and injustice, protector of ilegales, patron of the downtrodden and poor.

Perla looked at her register and shook her head. *I barely have enough for someone to buy something to eat.* She counted out her small deposit and thought about Rosa at the market, the thick wads of bills in the slots of her register.

She locked up and started for home. Children played in the yard of a house across the street, swimming in an inflatable pool in the shade of a tamarisk tree. Instead of cutting through the lot, Perla took the sidewalk. On the corner, she tried to stretch her neck, tried to see past the telephone poles, past the plastic branches of the cell phone tower disguised as a tree where birds didn't nest, to the Italian cypresses near Galena Court.

No sign of him. I'm right here, she thought. *You need me? I'm right here. Not gone.*

⁕ ⁕ ⁕

Rosa took a plastic chair and set it on top of the newspapers she'd spread out. She draped a white towel over Perla's shoulders and tucked it tightly under her collar.

"I'm spending too much money on dye," Perla said. "Maybe I should just stop doing it."

"I think you'd look fine with white hair." Rosa arranged her scissors and combs, and filled a spray bottle with water. "Like sophisticated."

"Sophisticated?" Perla laughed as she sat in the chair.

"That's the word my sister, Blanca, always used when we were younger. 'Rosa, look. Do your hair this way. You'll look so *sophisticated*,' she would say. Always trying to give me makeovers and do my nails." Rosa smiled. "God, I miss having her around."

"And your mother?" Perla asked. "Have you talked to her?"

Rosa sighed. "Every now and then. She's still mad at me. I can tell. All this time. Ever since Miguel, things between us have never been the same. The only reason she came to our wedding was because Blanca forced her. When the baby was born, she hardly ever stopped by. Blanca says it's because she's not ready to be a grandma yet. That she still sees herself as a young woman. She turned fifty-six last week. She's got this new boyfriend, Roy, who thinks he's a musician. Carries a guitar around everywhere. A real show-off. Smooth talker."

Rosa leaned over and pointed at Perla with a comb. "That's what you need, I think. A boyfriend. Someone to take you out, to drive you around town." On top of an overturned trash can sat a portable radio. Rosa turned the volume up and adjusted the antenna. "A guy to take you dancing. That's what brought Miguel and me together, you know? Dancing."

"I'm not a girl anymore."

"Girl? You don't have to be. Look at my mom. Besides, it would be nice. So that you wouldn't be alone all the time." Rosa combed out strands of Perla's wet hair and began snipping off the tips. "I know you miss your husband."

"I forget," she said. "Sometimes I'll wake up in the middle of the night thinking I hear his snores. Or I'll feel the sheets being pulled away. All this time, and I'm still not used to it." Strands of hair tickled the back of Perla's neck.

Rosa stopped cutting when two police cars sped down the street. "Every day you see more and more of that around here," she said. "It's getting crazy. Did you hear about the break-in over on the next block?"

"No. When?"

"Last week. This girl Sandra and her husband. Their house was robbed. They were both there. Happened during the night while they slept. Could you imagine? They took their computer and television and stereo and everything. Good thing no one got hurt."

"They just walked in?"

"Through a window." Rosa stopped to add another load of laundry to the washing machine. "I'm telling you. The other morning we come out and find bottles of beer and Night Train in the yard. Over there." She pointed toward the street. "We're thinking about getting a dog. In case they ever try and rob us."

Around Rosa's garage, boxes with "Navidad," "Baby Clothes," and "Hats and Sweaters" written on their sides sat on the shelves. Trash bags full of crushed aluminum cans and plastic bottles waited for Miguel to haul them to the recycling center in Las Glorias' parking lot.

"You're lucky," Perla said. "You have Miguel and your daughter. You don't live alone like I do." Turning to the street, she imagined Guillermo jogging up and down the sidewalk the way he used to, each hand holding barbells, sweat covering his face. "He was old when he died, but Guillermo, he was very strong. He was my company."

"If you need anything, you come here," Rosa said. "If you hear a noise or someone breaking in, you jump out of your bed, and you run down the street over here to us. Don't matter what time or anything."

When she finished, Rosa plugged her blow dryer into an outlet, then combed and styled Perla's hair, fluffing it up to add volume. She brushed the clippings from her shoulders and back and behind her ears with a clean paintbrush. She untied the towel and walked Perla over to the full-length mirror nailed to the back door that led into their kitchen.

"Wait," Rosa said, reaching behind an overturned trash can. She held out an aluminum baseball bat. "Here. Take this."

"What? Why?"

"Protection," Rosa said. "For the night."

Perla took the bat and turned to look at herself in the mirror's reflection. She could see the street—the cars parked along the curb, the crooked wooden posts of a fence, thick iron bars over a window screen.

She held the bat tightly and widened her stance.

∘   ∘   ∘

By mid-June, fireworks stands had gone up in the parking lots and fields around Agua Mansa. They had already started selling sparklers and rockets. People stood out in their front yards or in driveways lighting firecrackers, tossing them up into the trees or shoving them in empty soda cans.

Perla leaned the bat against the couch. She turned on the shower in the bathroom, then went into the bedroom. She removed her underwear and bra and stood looking at herself naked in front of the dresser. On it were pictures: her high school graduation photo; she and Guillermo at their wedding; the two of them standing in front of a boat when they took a trip out to Catalina Island a few years before he died. She tried to find remnants of herself in the face that looked back at her, smiling. She remembered being soft and tall and always laughing like her mother. She looked down at her hands. The brown spots dotting their backs appeared foreign, and she couldn't recall when they had first formed. Her arms were thin, so thin. *What had they looked like before?* Her breasts were flattened and wrinkled, and the skin by her knees and around the soles of her feet was dry and split like an elephant's.

She thought about Rosa's garage, about those boxes stuffed with old clothes and Christmas tree ornaments, about the dog they wanted to get. Maybe she could get one, too, or bars on the windows. She looked around the room. Was there anything they would want? This was all she had now.

Old photos. Couches covered with blankets and sheets to keep them clean. A television with two large knobs and wood-paneled doors to cover the screen. Lamps with heavy bases, their shades ruffled along the edges like old-fashioned petticoats.

After showering, she changed into her nightgown and walked out to the living room. She squeezed the bat over and over again, massaging the neck until it was warm.

She stood in the middle of the living room and widened her stance, bending her knees, bracing herself. The night air boomed and hissed from the fireworks her neighbors lit. Smoke drifted across the front window in thin ribbons. She pictured it: a figure standing a few feet away near the kitchen. He towered over her so high that his head scraped against the roof of the house, banging the chandelier, as he made his way across the room. He knocked over the desk, spilling sheets of white paper and pens. His long arm reached out. Smoke fingers wrapped around her neck, scratching her arms. Perla swung at the figure again and again, the bat cutting through the black mist of his body. The figure bled back into the walls and floors. The bat rolled across the floor and under the coffee table where a pair of Guillermo's shoes still sat, the laces neatly knotted.

*   *   *

The dollar bills pinned to the statue's robe weren't even real. It was play money from a game for children. The notes were green with fuzzy letters and numbers printed on fluorescent paper. Anyone standing in front of the display window that faced the parking lot could see that it was fake.

The statue had always been there. Darío had placed it there and pinned the ofrendas to Saint Anthony's robe.

"Take it out if you want," he'd said the day he left for good. "The window's due for a change."

But she had decided to leave him there even though the statue's robe was fading, the soft velvet so worn away that white netting could be seen in spots along the back.

She noticed the shards first, the way they sparkled on the concrete walkway. *One of the construction workers probably dropped something.*

She had her key in the lock and was turning the knob when she stopped and saw a piece of glass jutting out from one side of the front window. Saint Anthony was gone. There was a rock on the floor beside the display table, which had been toppled over.

Perla didn't go inside. She turned around, walked through the lot, and went back to the house. She found the baseball bat, under the coffee table, grabbed it, and walked back to the botánica. She inched open the door, gripping the bat with both hands. Aside from the window and the things in it, everything looked fine. Nothing else was missing or broken. She went straight for the closet and removed the loose floorboard. The lockbox was there, the bills and rolls untouched.

After she put the money in the register, she took the broom and went outside to sweep up the glass. A truck pulled up and parked a few feet away. It was one of the construction workers. He stepped out, a leather tool belt draped over his left shoulder, black hair pulled back in a ponytail. He flicked a lit cigarette on the asphalt and ground it in with his boot sole. He took his sunglasses off and watched her.

"You all right?" he asked, pointing to the window. "Everything cool?"

Perla stayed quiet.

He pointed to the window again. "Ventana? That's how you say it, right? Somebody break? Quebró? Ventana?" he said again, pointing. "Policía come?"

"I speak English," she said.

"Oh. Were you robbed?" He walked up to the window. He looked at it, then picked up the rock. "Are you okay?"

"I'm fine. They only took my statue. It was here. In the window." She showed him the outline of the base. "Saint Anthony."

He wore a backward baseball cap. A patch of hair covered the tip of his chin, braided and thick as a root. *Domínguez* was written in marker across the thermos he toted. He said, "I got some extra sheets of plywood in the truck. Give me a sec, and I can patch it up for you."

He measured the window and the sheet of plywood. He made small marks like X's in the wood and cut it with a saw he pulled out of a toolbox. He pointed with his chin to the bat near the front door. "That your weapon?"

"Someone gave it to me," she said.

"You could do some damage with a bat like that." Sweat beads collected on his forehead, dampening his eyebrows. "If I were a crook I wouldn't mess with you." He rose and said, "There. That should hold up for now. We'll wanna get it fixed soon. I'll call the landlord. Tell 'em what happened. We'll need to place an order for some glass."

He grabbed a pad and a pencil and took some measurements. Perla looked at the rock that he'd set on one of the chairs before putting up the plywood.

He said, "You want me to take that? I'll toss it for you."

"Thank you."

He put it in the front seat beside him and drove away.

She turned the fan on and stood there looking at the empty window, at the bent heads of the silver nails the construction worker had hammered. *A statue*, she thought. *Who would want a statue? Saint Anthony. Rodrigo? Did he come back? Did I miss him again?*

The note was still taped to the register. She stopped to light the candle of Juan Soldado again and placed it at the foot of the statue of Santa Bárbara.

She busied herself the rest of the day by rearranging the statues on the shelves. She brought out some incense sticks and candles and tried to arrange them in a different order, making sure they were all visibly priced, that each peg looked full and organized.

She closed early, locking up at three. The construction worker had taken down the SPACE FOR LEASE sign from the window of Alfonso's shop. In its place was a new sign:

COMING SOON

Stigmata

Body Piercing and Tattoos

Perla gripped the bat as she made her way home. She tried not to think about any of it. Alfonso. Rodrigo. If he would come back or not. The rock. The missing statue. Walking through the lot, she stepped cautiously to avoid killing any of the beetles that darted across the path. They dashed around in a panic, hiding under the leaves and shrubs below.

Taking Stock

I took my first hit of speed the same night I popped Nancy Pérez's cherry. My friend Beady's parents were away that weekend, and the party was his idea. He got this bug up his ass and started spreading the word around school that week. Had some flyers made in printing class and passed them out. Wild party at my pad, he told everyone. Keg and DJ. Party until everyone passes out or the neighbors call the cops. We called him Beady because his eyes were always low and red from smoking weed. You'd see him walking around campus with a bottle of Visine. Allergies, he'd tell the teachers.

His older brother, Ramón, got the keg. The DJ was this puny dude who called himself Chaos. Showed up with a milk crate full of records. Set up the turntables out on the patio, spinning and mixing all night. Everyone huddled around the keg, drinking beer from plastic cups. All the girls were dancing together, waving their arms in the air, hooting to the beat of the music, taking turns stepping into the circle they'd formed.

Nancy had it for me. Beady said she would hit him up for information.

"What's his deal?" she'd say. "Ask him if he thinks I'm cute. He seeing anyone?"

She wasn't my type, I won't lie. But she still looked fine in those tight denim skirts, the outline of her panties showing through. I intrigued her, she told Beady. I liked that. That I intrigued her.

So she's there at the party, sitting on a lawn chair with her friend when I stroll up. And I can tell she's checking me out. I'm getting myself some beer, shooting it with Beady and this other fool, when I turn around and catch her eyeing me.

I go over and we get to bullshitting about school. Next thing I know we're both feeling good from the beer, and we end up in Beady's parents' bedroom. Music's thumping downstairs. I hear the girls dancing, clapping their hands, calling one another out. We're getting it going nice and heavy. She's letting me do everything. So I'm touching her here and there and she's moaning, saying, Oh yeah. Um. I like that there. She's taking my hands and putting them where she wants. We end up on each other. Going at it while the party's happening downstairs, and the DJ's flashing strobe light's turning the bedroom red then blue then white. Beady's parents watching us the whole time from framed pictures on the wall.

When we finished I told her, "I'll see you around."

"Yeah," she said. "Anytime. You know where I'm at."

After everyone split we got high. Ramón had this friend of his there, some dude from around San Bernardino named Smoky. The speed was cooked good and strong, he told us. Made fun of me and Beady when we said we'd never done none.

So we crouched around the coffee table. Empty blue cups tossed over the top. Bags of chips. Cigarette butts jammed into an ashtray shaped like a sombrero from the vacation Beady's parents took to Acapulco.

Here's what it felt like and why I'm still doing it. It felt electric. Like volts of energy making my blood boil, turning everything inside me on all at once. I punched a hole in the wall of Beady's bedroom. And I didn't feel no pain or nothing. I felt invincible. All this shit got pushed aside. I'm talking pushed way aside. I know I'm not doing it no justice. So there's no point in even trying to describe it except to say it's good. I came to life that night, and I didn't wanna die no time soon.

                               ·   ·   ·

Me and Beady rent a two-bedroom apartment at the Agua Mansa Palms. We got nothing. No furniture except for a couch with the stuffing coming out of the arm that Beady got from his aunt, and a freestanding lamp in the corner next to a wax plant I took from my mom's garage. The only thing we spent money on was the television. Sleek black and real modern. Beady says it looks like we can contact the *Enterprise* with the remote because it's all high-tech. A twenty-seven-inch Panasonic with stereo sound. I got it on an employee discount from my job. I work in an electronics store. Selling television antennas and power strips, cable wires and connectors. Have to wear a nametag and vest. The pay sucks, and the only reason I stay is because I need the cash. That's why I'm real dependable. I'm never late. Never take longer than a thirty-minute break to eat. Never call in sick. This one time I was running a fever of one hundred and five. Dragged my ass out of bed to work a morning shift. Those are the best shifts because it's nice and slow and I check out the stock, eyeball the expensive cordless phones, computer printers, monitors, and keyboards. The closing shifts are when all the fat fucks come in, the couch potatoes looking for splitters to hook up their cable to their VCRs, buying remotes, bringing in their runts who run up and down the aisles making a mess out of all the merchandise, banging on the keyboards, using the typewriters and leaving stupid messages on the sheets of paper like "Bite Me" and "Juan Loves Deborah."

Beady and me, we got this scam going. We only do it on slow nights when my manager, Bill, does the paperwork. Bill usually goes in back about eight, a half-hour before we close. Stockroom's so small the manager's desk bumps up against the door. So he leaves it cracked open, just enough for me to see his bald head when I stand by the register.

The way it goes is Beady uses some of his money to buy something real cheap like a pack of batteries. Before he comes in, though, I put some shit aside, small and not so expensive, like three universal remotes and some printer cables. When he strolls up to pay for the batteries, I ring him up, make sure Bill hears me giving the total. Real quick I stick the stash in the bag, say thank you real loud, say, "I hope that works out for you. If you have any problems hooking that up, just give us a call." Pointing to my nametag, "I'm Shawn."

You don't need a receipt to get your cash back here. Just as long as nothing's opened and our tags are still on the boxes. So Beady goes in a few days later to return some of the stuff. He never takes back too much. We spread it out. Do it little by little. We got a good thing going, so we don't wanna blow it. We keep the return amounts low because too much will make management suspicious. Play it right and we could pull about two hundred bones a month.

Tonight we're coming back from scoring some from this Vietnamese kid we know who's our source. We're going to our pad to get high and stay up all night and watch pornos since I'm off tomorrow and Beady's gonna call in sick.

"I say fuck the forty-dollar shit," Beady goes. "Let's go for one of those printers. Or those Sony monitors you guys just got in."

"Not even," I say. "Only got three or four of those in. Management watches that." They've been getting all suspicious lately, making us empty out our pockets every night before we leave and anytime we step out of the store for a smoke.

"We could take one this month. One next month. Stockpile the shit." He laughs.

I roll the window down, watch the streetlights blur as we drive past. The way light bends and the trees fly by makes me think about time travel, the speed of light, the ghosts of dead stars up in the sky right now looking down on us and laughing. How we're all just moving, just passing through and nothing's ever meant to last.

I can't wait till we're at the pad sketching. Beady's tapping his hand on the steering wheel, and it starts to get me all edgy. He's not even paying attention to how slow we're going.

"Stop driving like a grandma," I go. "Fuckin' punch it, man. Let's go."

At an intersection, he guns the engine. When the light turns green, we take off, the tires skidding on the concrete. I imagine flames trailing behind us like in the cartoons.

When we get back to the apartment Beady tells me he invited this friend from his work.

"Her name's Daisy. You'll like her. Says she's got this supplier who cooks some real good shit out in Perris."

She's standing out in the hallway when we stroll up. Daisy's got this red windbreaker on, and she's wearing red Converse high-tops with black laces. Acid-wash jeans too baggy for her skinny ass. First look and I know already I'm not gonna be liking this scab because of the way her eyes move, all hypnotic like a cat's. I get this vibe. She's too low and mellow.

We get the music going and Daisy sits on the couch, talking real slow, like she's on downers. Beady hands her a beer. I get up and take one from the fridge and pace around the dining room. She takes sips of her beer and gossips with Beady about work. She never once eyes me, never once asks me about myself. That's another thing that bugs me about this scab. How she just comes in making herself all regal in my pad like she don't care one way or another that I'm there.

She's got a runt. Two-year-old named Xavier. Says, "My mom's got him. I told her I was having a girls' night out." She laughs. I can see a big black gap where a tooth should be. Her face is pockmarked. She's got speed bumps on her face that she's tried to cover with makeup and they're dusty tan, so it looks like she's slid marbles under her cheeks.

I throw my beer across the room and say, "Fuck this." The kitchen's full of dirty paper plates on top of the stove and all over the floor because Beady and me don't own real ones. Forks we get whenever we go grab fast food. Got a drawer full of ketchup and hot sauce packets from different restaurants, individually wrapped sets of plastic utensils, and straws. When I crouch over the counter to snort my lines, I sweep my hand across it and all those paper plates and utensils fall to the ground.

Right when the speed's starting to hit me and I'm getting pumped, Beady and Daisy get up off the couch and go into the kitchen to snort. I'm pacing around, listening to music. Beady comes around, turns the television on, and changes it to the Spice Channel. Two girls, one redhead and the other a blonde, are standing under a waterfall. They're naked and feeling each other up, rubbing nipples, their lips pouty and shiny.

"Don't get too crazy," he says. And he takes that skank into his bedroom. A few minutes later I hear moaning, Beady's headboard banging up against the wall. Then it's quiet. He walks out, naked, the tattoo of Jesus on his chest looking at me. Jesus' face is tanned, hair from Beady's chest poking out of his left eye. A mole right by his nose looks like snot.

"Hey," Beady goes to me. "Want some?" He grabs my arm.

The bedroom door's open, and I can see her leg, pale and skinny. Skin's sagging like it's dripping right off the bone.

"It's cool," I say, rubbing away some drip coming out of my nose from the speed.

He turns around and goes back to her. He leaves the door open. I can see him riding her, those ugly-ass legs of hers wrapped around his waist. She laughs, says something that sounds like my name. I reach for the remote, turn the volume up on the television hoping to drown it out.

*   *   *

The only reason Beady gets me to go with him to Daisy's a few days after is because he says her supplier out in Perris gave her a break on the speed so we could try it. He says if we like it, he'll hook us up.

"Daisy says his shit's good," Beady goes. "And it's cheaper than what we pay now."

"Don't matter," I tell him. "We'll be driving out to fucking cow country and spending money on gas anyways."

"It's all good."

"Bullshit."

When we get to her pad, the runt's there, too. Running around in nothing but a saggy diaper that's got pictures of blue bears prancing around rainbows on it. He stinks like a sewer.

"Here," Daisy says. She gives the runt an empty plastic soda bottle to play with. She's got the speed sitting on the coffee table between an ashtray and an oven mitt.

Beady takes it and says, "We're going another route." They decide they're going to shoot.

"What for?" I say. "Same shit. Different hole."

"It hits you faster," she says.

I'm keeping mine the same, I tell them. "Not getting me near needles."

"Rots your nose," she says.

Like your body's not already fucked up, I wanna say to her. Just look at you. Twenty-something, and you look like a corpse. Pale and sick skinny. Eyebrows nothing but sorry-ass drawings. Cheap dye job. Dime store, I think. The runt's playing in the kitchen, and I feel sorry for the bastard. This accident's his mom.

"I got this thing," I say. "Needles freak me out."

"Aw," she says. "You afraid, güero?" She walks over and sits next to me on the couch, runs her fingers through my sideburns, rubs the stubble that's growing on my head because I haven't shaved it in a few days. "Look at you.

All mysterious with those bright blue eyes." She gives me a long-ass look. "Those cords would look real good on the floor of my room, you know that?"

Beady laughs. Goes, "Stop throwing moves."

I snort my lines, hoping the speed'll rub away that picture. I watch the runt while Beady and Daisy get to cooking their shit. They're doing it in the kitchen while that kid's banging a blue block against a cabinet door. Runts. Sometimes I think they got this instinct. Like they know just when you're thinking about them. Like some telepathy. Some Aquaman sonar shit because just as I'm watching him there on the floor while a few feet away his mom's got a man's belt tied around her arm and Beady's about to stab her with a needle, the runt turns around and sees me eyeballing him. So he gets up and walks over.

He's handing me the block. It's dripping wet from his spit. He's making these noises and grunts that almost sound like words. Pointing. His hair's a mess. Looks like it hasn't been combed in weeks. Yellow stains on his cheeks and he's smelling even more. The diaper's so loose and sagging that when he starts pissing, it runs straight down the sides of his leg and onto the carpet and he's not saying or doing nothing except pissing and grunting, pissing and grunting. What a sorry-ass situation, I think. All-around sorry.

*   *   *

"Where's your piece?" I ask Beady. It's Tuesday night, and we're out for a drive.

Bill always schedules me to open with him on Tuesdays because it's when we get a shipment from the distribution center out in Industry. We get there at six in the morning and check in merchandise and stock shit. I got off at noon. When I came home, I crashed and didn't wake up until seven at night because I'd been spinning since we got back from Daisy's the day before.

Beady was in the living room watching television when I woke up. He was still in his overalls, his hands greasy from tire grime. He'd stopped to pick up food. On the kitchen counter there was a burrito wrapped in foil for me. A few minutes later he showered. We got dressed and decided to go out for a drive.

"She couldn't get her mom to watch the kid," he says, lowering the radio.

We're doing sixty-five up Rancho. We bounce over the railroad tracks and continue up, passing the freeway. On Valley we hang a left, heading toward Fontana.

We stop at a liquor store and get a twelve-pack of Bud Lights in the can and some smokes. Beady lights one up and hums to the Beastie Boys' "Girls" on the radio. When we pass the porn shop on Valley, Beady laughs and goes, "Hey, let's scope it out. Twenty-five-cent movie arcades."

"For what? Place is full of fags cruising and cops looking to bust."

We drive past the empty Kaiser Steel plant, past the tall smokestacks like burned-out birthday candles. Off the main road, we turn down some small street that's all dark. A few minutes later, we pull over and park in front of an abandoned warehouse next to these old railroad tracks.

He uses a brick to bust the window, and we climb in through there. The warehouse is one big room. Old wooden pallets are stacked up in the middle of the floor, and the front cabin of a tractor is over by the main doors of the place. Air's stuffy and smells like oil. We take a spot near the windows. The huge gravel pyramids from the factory across the street are lit up, and we watch cement mixers haul ass around them. It's warm, so Beady and me take our shirts off and lie there with our backs against a pile of crates, smoking and drinking beers, tossing the cans behind us.

"Daisy thinks you don't like her," he says.

I sip my beer, take a drag of my smoke.

He laughs. "What's your problem with her, man?" He gets up and walks over to the windows. Unzips his pants and takes a piss.

"Didn't say I had one."

I take long puffs, watching him shake his dick before zipping his pants back up. I can tell he's already got a good buzz going nice and strong inside that head of his. He's talking all slow, almost whispering. He sits back down. Me, I'm relaxing to the hum of the cement mixers across the street.

He says last night's speed made him feel like he was superhuman. "Like it was a love potion. We were going at it for hours, man." He flicks his cigarette butt.

"Better watch it with her," I say, wiping the sweat from my forehead and down the middle of my chest. "Could be using you."

"Don't worry." He takes another beer, cracks it open, and hands it to me.

"She's too smooth," I say. "Too fly for my taste. Watch your step with that one."

* * *

I notice little things around the apartment at first—her socks tucked near the couch, a pair of heels in the hallway, a curling iron in the closet by the entrance. When I go grab a roll of toilet paper from under the bathroom sink, I scope a box of tampons.

Before I know it, Daisy's a regular at our pad, kicking it on the couch when I come home. Beady with his arm around her. All proud like she's some real find. She brings some pots and pans and tells Beady she's gonna teach him how to cook rice just like his mom's. One day she shows up with a plant in a hanger made out of twisted strips of wire. They hook it to the handle of one of the kitchen drawers. Every time I walk by, it rocks, and it makes me want to toss it out the fucking balcony.

"Where's your kid's dad?" I ask her one night.

"Chino," she says. That voice of hers rattly. "Armed robbery."

Beady's left to get more beer, and it's just her and me. He's been gone only a few minutes, and I'm already feeling weird. The way she looks at me. Those crooked pencil eyebrows making her whole face look lopsided.

I'm leaning up against the wall in the kitchen, and she's sitting on the counter. Right near the sink. Wrinkled miniskirt riding her thighs. She shifts, spreads her legs, and I get a look at her patch.

"Can I ask you something?" she goes.

I shrug my shoulders, staring her down.

"What do you got against me?" She smooths her hair back. "You're throwing me some mean looks."

I stay quiet.

"I like you. In high school I had a crush on this cute-ass white dude. Something about you reminds me of him."

I keep mad-dogging her.

She sighs, shrugs her shoulders, pushes her tube top up, trying to act decent all of a sudden. Like she just heard about shame. "Beady says you guys are tight."

"You got that right," I say. "I know him better than anybody."

She says, "I'm not here to mess with what you guys got going."

"Then why are you here?"

"He treats me real fine."

When Beady gets home, they go straight to his bedroom and close the door.

The next day, I'm doing an opening shift when the phone rings. It's Beady, and he asks if I can talk.

"Yeah," I say. "Just pricing shit."

"Can I come in today? To do a hit?"

He tells me he's hurting for cash. "Fuck. All my money's been going to wining and dining Daisy."

"Didn't I say?"

"Come on, man."

It's risky today, I tell him. Because I won't be the only one on the floor. Management's getting real suspicious, I say. Inventory's coming up off. So they're clocking people they recognize that come in a lot.

"They could recognize you," I say. "Blow your cover."

So he goes, "I'll send Daisy in. They don't know her. Then she can go later tonight to return."

I stay quiet.

"Come on, bro. I'm *begging* you."

"Fuck," I say. "Fine. Send her ass in at eleven. That's when Bill's going to the bank."

It's me and this rookie named Mark on the floor when eleven rolls around. Bill's left me in charge. When I see Daisy walking in, I tell Mark to go look for something in the back.

"A headset for a cell phone," I tell the rookie. "Special order. Customer called and said they'd be by in a few to pick it up." As soon as he goes in the back, I tell Daisy, "All right, grab some shit, and I'll throw it in a bag."

Only she's moving real slow. So I say, "Quick."

I'd stacked up the printers by the main aisle. There's only five. She goes over and picks one up. "Beady said to get one of these."

"You can't," I say. "They'll know one's missing."

"But this is what Beady told me to get," she says.

I can hear the rookie's footsteps in the back stockroom, and I know he's about to come out.

Stupid bitch is standing there in the middle of the store holding this huge box, no customers around, no employees. That stupid fucking look on her face.

"Shit," I say. "Fine. Just go. Get your ass out of here."

She walks out the front door just as Mark comes out of the stockroom.

"I couldn't find anything," he goes.

"It's cool," I go. "I'll look later."

After Bill gets back, the rookie clocks out and takes off.

Sure enough, Bill notices one of the printers gone. "So we sold one, huh?" he says.

"Guess so," I say. I tell him the rookie must have when I was out back looking for something.

"You left him on the floor alone?"

"Only for a minute. Customer called checking on an order. He was pissed."

Bill says I need to practice more floor control. "We're thinking of moving you up to key holder. But you have to prove yourself and can't be making dumb mistakes like that, Shawn."

"Sorry," I say.

Later that night, Beady and Daisy come to the apartment, a hundred bucks richer.

"We got you something," Beady says. He hands me a balloon of speed.

I snort my lines and sit on the couch to watch some television.

Daisy laughs, goes, "Oh my God. That was too easy."

Fucking great, I think. Now she's in on it. Now I'm gonna be risking it for this fool.

I go to my bedroom and slam the door shut.

*   *   *

The thing about living around so many Mexicans is that you start to pick up their ways. The streets and cities and mountains around here have Spanish names, so already, right there you learn some words. From Beady, I get all the cuss words and I can say the name of the state in Mexico his family's from without an accent. You wake up hungover and menudo suddenly sounds good. Around Christmastime, you start to crave tamales. At birthday parties, you get a piñata for the runt and stuff it with candy, break off a broom handle so that they can have something to whack it with.

In high school, I dated this girl named Beatrice. I went with her once to this store on Rancho when her parents were having money problems. Her dad was laid off, and the mom couldn't get a job because she hardly spoke English. When she finally did find something, it was janitor work. Barely enough for them to make it.

So she went to this store. Shelves with statues of saints and fat gods I didn't recognize decked out in robes and feathers with rags wrapped around their heads. Wooden idols and figures of animals I couldn't make out. Incense sticks hanging from pegs on the walls so everywhere there was this strong smell of church, of holiness.

Beatrice bought a candle called a "Road Opener" with three different colors of wax in it. The woman that worked there poured some smelly oil into it, told Beatrice to take a folded dollar bill and stick it under the candle and to light it for five days straight. She sold her a rabbit's foot and said to rub it all the time, to concentrate and pray.

I don't know if it ever worked, though, because we stopped hooking up. Last time I saw Beatrice was a while ago. She was sitting at the bus stop. Dressed in a nurse's uniform and reading a magazine.

So I'm in the shopping center, checking out this new tattoo shop that just opened up because I'm thinking about getting some new ink done on my forearm. "I got too much skin," I tell the guy there. I show him the Celtic cross tattooed on my right bicep.

"What are you thinking about?" the guy goes.

"Don't know," I go. "Maybe something religious. I'm thinking about changing my ways." I laugh.

I spend some time looking through the books they got, showing all these different pictures of tats they've done on people. I check out the stencils on the walls. But all they got are pictures of Jesus all scarred up and bleeding. I don't wanna get one of those because it'll look like I'm just biting off of Beady.

"See anything you like?" the guy says.

"Not really."

"Go next door," he says. "The old lady sells these prayer cards with all these saints. Got all these sweet religious pictures."

I step in there and that smell hits me, and I remember Beatrice and that candle. Not the one she bought. But this other one. The words "Stay Away" floating across the top. I browse around, the old lady sitting behind the counter watching television. I think it's the same lady from way back when. But my memory's hazy from the speed I did earlier today.

"What do you need?" she says, lowering the television and getting up.

"I need a candle," I say, forgetting about the tat, scanning the rows of statues and idols. "There." I point to the one I saw years ago. "I need to get rid of someone."

"Okay," she says. "Is this person doing harm?"

"Yeah," I tell her. "She's destructive."

She tells me to use something sharp like a key or a knife to carve the name of the person I'm trying to get rid of into the top of the candle. "When she leaves, all those bad vibes will go along with her."

She says it would help if I take something from the person I'm looking to chase away and put it by the candle. A piece of cloth that I can tie around it, she says. Or a picture. Keep it there while it's lit for ten days.

No one's home when I get back. Beady's room's a mess. Piles of clothes and wrappers from fast food places are all over the floor. I have to dig through some of his stuff, feeling my way through piles of his boxers and dirty socks. I'm careful, though. Because, even though it's all messy, I don't want Beady to find out I'm going through his shit. So I set his boxers aside, the elastic bands all stretched out and wasting away. He needs new ones. Every time he comes out of the shower and he's walking around the apartment, they creep down. Sometimes he holds them up with his hand. Other times he just lets them fall off and strolls around ass naked. "Don't have nothing you don't," is what he says when I tell him to cover up.

I find a pair of panties tangled around one of his muscle shirts. So I take that and head back to my room. In the closet, I put the candle on a piece of cardboard from the box I use to keep my clothes, then carve her name into the wax just like the lady said. I use my hands to tear the panties up into pieces. I tie one of the strips around the candle. When I light it, my closet glows red and spooky.

I know Beady. Know him so good I can practically get into that head of his. I know his ways and he knows mine. We're family, Beady and me. That's the way we've always seen each other. That's what this scab don't get. That

Beady and me have been doing just fine by ourselves. That we don't need someone like her coming in and messing up what we got, what we've kept for ourselves.

Around me, there's shit that's unsettled, but that's the way it's always been. Everything with me's temporary. That's what I'm used to. All the things I own are thrown all over the place. Like someone opened up this box with my name on the side of it, turned it over, and shook everything out. And my stuff, I'm talking about my clothes, my shoes, my belongings, just came tumbling down from the sky and landed here in this place. And that was it. Some voice said to me, You're here, Shawn. This is you for now.

It's the same way with Beady. Which is why we operate the way we do, why we got it good here when it's just the two of us. When we're not tied to nothing or no one. And we're moving and going and getting it done. Taking what we need to get by day by day. Fucking with our setup only makes too much bad happen.

*   *   *

After work, I decided not to go home. I knew Daisy would be there. So instead, I went to this bar Beady and I go to sometimes called the Lickety Split. They had this chick there decked out in a one-piece bathing suit, "Official Corona Girl" written on a sash draped over her tits. She went around, getting all hugged up next to the men sitting on the stools, passing out bottle openers.

"Buenas noches," she said, handing me one.

I took it and gave it back. "Don't got no use for this," I said, mad-dogging her until she walked away. I stayed there, tossing back a few beers, getting a good buzz going. I thought about the time Beady and me were here, and we sat at the back booth and I carved my initials into the wood top.

I take my time getting home and walk in pretty late. Beady's snoring in his room. In the hallway, right by his door, I see her sandals. The impressions of her crooked toes in the padding make me gag.

My back's gotten used to lying on top of a bunch of blankets I use as a bed. So I'm there, wearing nothing, smoking a cigarette. I left my bedroom door open. From the hallway, I can see the moonlight coming from the living room, the shadows of the blinds making sharp lines going across the walls.

A few minutes later, I hear Beady's bedroom door squeak open. Daisy's standing in the hallway in one of his old football jerseys.

"Hey," she whispers, leaning up against the door frame. The shadows from the blinds are falling on her face, and I'm wishing they were razors or knives. "You awake in there?"

"I'm awake." I grab a shirt to cover myself. I offer her a cigarette.

"I don't smoke," she says.

Crazy bitch, I think. She shoots up speed, but she don't smoke? "Suit yourself," I say.

"Why are you sneaking in all quiet and late?" She walks over and sits on the floor near where I'm lying. When Beady's jersey hikes up a few inches, I can see she's got nothing else on underneath. She takes a good look at me lying there, my T-shirt covering my dick.

"Felt like it," I say. "What are you, my warden?"

She laughs. "No. Just that I was hoping to see you tonight, Shawn."

"Why?"

"You're fun to be around. To look at." She gives me another long sweep. She pulls the jersey off and straddles me. "Do I make you nervous?"

I stay quiet. She traces the outline of the Irish flag tattooed across my chest, then tickles my nipple. I don't even get a little hard. When I look away, she takes her hand and moves my face so that I'm looking right at her.

"I do, don't I?" she goes. "I make you nervous."

And I'm thinking how could Beady find this face attractive? How could he find this body sexy, enough to be giving it to her almost every night since she started showing herself around here?

"You make me sick, to be honest," I say.

I let the cigarette drop and burn the carpet when I take my hands and push her off of me. The shirt falls off, and I'm standing there naked. I grab her and shove her hard against the wall.

"Here's what I want," I say to her. "I want you to leave me alone."

She doesn't look scared or shocked or nothing. Her eyebrows are rubbed away, and without them she looks like an iguana. I'm expecting a forked tongue to come whipping out of that mouth of hers.

I take Beady's jersey and throw it at her. "Leave us alone, puta."

When I hear the door slam shut, I go over to my closet and light the candle. With my head propped up on a pillow, I smoke and watch the flame, hoping she's feeling the hate.

I don't think she told Beady what happened in my bedroom last night. He's going around acting lovesick, saying Daisy makes him feel "real." Beady says the scab told him she understands me. That sometimes people just don't see eye to eye.

I tell Beady, "What? She think she's fuckin' Oprah now?"

*   *   *

I'm scheduled to work a mid-shift today. When I get to the store, Bill and the assistant manager, Karen, are both there, standing by the register. As I'm heading for the stockroom door, I see Mark leaning up against a computer desk we use to display shit.

"Don't clock in, Shawn," Bill says. "I want to go over some things with you."

He leads me out to the parking lot. A few minutes later, Karen and Mark follow us out.

"Tell me about that printer you said Mark sold," he says.

I lean up against the hood of a Toyota, watching the other employees running around the sales floor. The rookie's standing there, his arms crossed. He's trying to mad-dog me. Like he's a real bad-ass. I laugh and shake my head at him.

"What?" I say, getting up in his face.

He backs away.

Karen's got a clipboard with some notes on it, and she's holding the yellow copy of the journal tape management pulls out every night to check stock and balance the books.

"You said Mark sold it," Karen says, taking her glasses off and biting the left tip.

I say nothing.

"Mark says he heard someone come in that day, the day you said you went to the back to check on an order. He also doesn't remember hearing the register door pop open," Bill says.

Karen puts her glasses back on, says, "Printer wasn't sold that day. I checked." She holds that clipboard and the journal tape up. "But someone returned one later that night. Got cash back."

"You can tell us now what really happened," Bill says. "Because I think we already know."

So they make me sign this paper saying I'm guilty of gross misconduct, and they hand me my last paycheck. Bill says that, by law, they have to give me my pay.

"But if it were up to me," he says, "I'd keep it and call things even."

Karen starts saying how they know I'm behind all the shit that's been missing and how, because of what I did, the rest of the employees are gonna have to pay.

"Your actions only end up hurting innocent people," she tells me.

Rookie Mark says, "Yeah. Don't implicate me in your schemes."

"Suck my dick," I go to him.

Karen shakes her head. The rookie turns around and heads back in the store.

"I'm disappointed," Bill says. "Shawn, I liked you. You were hardworking, and you knew this job. We wanted to promote you."

"Yeah, well . . . sorry," I say. "Sorry about all this, Bill."

I hand him my vest. But I keep the nametag.

At the liquor store, I cash my last paycheck. I buy five lottery tickets and a twelve-pack of beer. The thing is I'm not even that mad at the stupid bitch for blowing our cover. I almost saw it coming, and that's the thing that gets me about all this. When she was standing there hugging that big box, I said to myself, This ain't good. I think I'm fucking pissed at myself for letting it go on without doing anything to stop or change it.

At home, I pound some beers, turn the radio up, try to imagine myself doing something else. I sit out on the balcony and settle in, take my shoes off, kick my feet up on the railing. It feels good right now, I think. This not having to work, not having to be anywhere. It's nice and quiet. I got a good buzz going. Later I'll go score some speed. Get to spinning nice and early. Don't matter if it's by myself. I can take Beady's car while he's in the bedroom fucking the scab. Maybe take a cruise out to the desert until I run out of gas.

I head back in and grab another beer. I turn the radio up, and I stand there in the living room. There's shit everywhere—pizza boxes and empty soda cups with the straws still poking out of the tops, Beady's dirty sock and shirts, a pair of my Dickies with the underwear still in them from when I was passed out drunk and Beady stripped my ass and dragged me to my room, junk mail, one of Beady's rubbers. There's more of her shit. Blouses with the armpits stained white. A box of shoes. A statue of a unicorn on the kitchen counter. When I stumble to the bathroom to take a piss I see strands of hair stuck to the side of the toilet.

I walk between my room and his, hugging the wall to keep myself from falling over. He'll be coming home soon, I know. He'll find me here like this. All passed out and broken and messed up. He'll lift me up by the shoulders, my feet dragging on the carpet, and put me to bed so I can sleep heavy and deep and long for once in my life.

Feast of
Saint Francis of Assisi

Founder of the Franciscan Order

Patron of the poor, peace, animals, birds, ecology,

families, tailors, needle workers, and merchants.

Invoked against fire and dying alone.

Rodrigo Abel Zamora was born in Michoacán, the youngest of four children. His brothers, Leonardo and Moisés, were both in the United States. Leonardo was a waiter in a restaurant in Buffalo. Moisés worked construction and was always moving around—Tacoma, Chicago, Nashville. It was hard to keep track of where he was, and months went by without any word from him. His sister, Noemi, had moved with her husband to Veracruz, where they owned a small business that rebuilt motors for farm equipment.

Just before his fifteenth birthday, Rodrigo told his parents he was moving to Tijuana. He hoped to cross into the United States like his brothers.

"I'm going to California," he said. "There's nothing here." Things in San Miguel were hopeless. Every day someone left the pueblo. Houses had emptied out, and there was no work.

His mother gave him an address. Her comadre Margarita's daughter Araceli and her husband had left San Miguel the year before for Tijuana. "Araceli said she'd be there for us if we needed," his mother said. "Go there. Stay with them."

His father tucked a roll of bills in the boy's pocket. "Be careful," he said. "That city, it's dangerous." He patted his son on the back and watched him board the bus from the terminal lobby.

The bus to Tijuana traveled all day, along narrow roads that curved around mountainsides. Looking out the window, he saw deep ravines, the charred hulls of cars lying below like old bones. White crosses staked into the ground floated past, and he made a game of keeping count of how many he saw.

Tijuana was nothing like San Miguel. There were cars and buses everywhere. Wild dogs with bloated stomachs roamed the streets. Houses stood stacked on top of one another on hillsides that crumbled when the rains came.

"Aquí," Rodrigo said to the taxista, giving him the address his mother had written down.

The house had a yard surrounded by a fence made of chicken wire, and geraniums grew inside plastic tubs on the steps leading up to the front door. "They left," the lady that answered said, barricading the door with her legs. Five pairs of hands poked out from behind her.

"Where?" he asked.

"I don't know. Everyone comes and goes around here. Are you a relative?"

"Yes," he said. "I need a place to stay. And work."

"El dompe," she said. "There's work in the dompe. You can't stay here. We're seven. The house, it's small. We're piled up."

That first day at the dompe, Rodrigo met Félix. He was older with callused hands that lifted old tires and wood planks with ease. When he saw Rodrigo, Félix winked at him and stuck his hand out.

"¿Qué onda?" he said. "I'm Félix."

"Rodrigo."

He held Rodrigo's hand, felt his arm. "You're strong," he said. "That's good. How old are you?"

"Fifteen," Rodrigo said.

"Are you all alone?"

Rodrigo nodded.

"Watch me," he said, pointing to his eyes with two fingers. "I'll take care of you. I'll help you."

He showed Rodrigo what to look for in the trash—rubber, plastic, anything shiny or made of glass, clothes and shoes.

Rodrigo found shelter in a ditch. He slept on scraps of cardboard and ate very little. He made sure not to spend the money his father gave him too quickly, and he hid it in his shoe. That week he was beaten and robbed, the pesos gone.

"I'll give you money," Félix said to Rodrigo when the boy told him what had happened. "But you have to give *me* something back." He grabbed Rodrigo's hand and placed it between his legs. From his pocket, Félix pulled out a wad of crumpled bills. "Andale," he whispered. "Just touch me. That's it." He pointed to an abandoned building with dark windows. "I told you. I'll take care of you."

Rodrigo looked around. People with soot-covered faces hauled piles of trash and combed through the smoldering rubble. He thought of his mother and father back home, waiting for money. He knew coyotes were expensive; his brothers had written this in their letters. Sifting through all this it would take years to raise so much.

He heard voices in the rafters of the abandoned building that night and watched birds nesting on the metal beams supporting the roof. Félix took his shirt off and asked the boy to do the same. He only wanted Rodrigo to touch him. His chest. Between his legs. That was all.

"Ya," Felix said when they finished. He gave the boy some money, enough for him to buy something to eat. "Don't tell anyone," he said. "The men. They'll make fun of me. Beat me up. And you."

A week later, he saw a young woman with long tangled hair wearing leather huaraches by Felix's side. She was pregnant, her blouse tight against her stomach, her belly button a round nub.

"Meet me," Félix said, when the woman left his side to go to the bathroom behind a stack of crates. He pointed to the building.

Rodrigo went that night and found Félix kneeling on the floor, crying and shaking.

"Perdóname, señor," he said and kissed the crucifix around his neck. "I'm sick," he told Rodrigo. "The girl. She's my wife. And I love her. She's having my baby. I don't want to burn in hell."

He handed Rodrigo a bundle of pesos tied together with an oily piece of string. "Leave," he said. "You'll tempt me if you stay here. I can't look at you anymore. Watch yourself. The callejones. They're dangerous." He swept his arm over the lights of the city gleaming through the windows. "Leave. I don't want to see you."

"But I can't," the boy said. "I don't know anyone here. I'm alone. What will I do?"

"You're young. You'll find work. Go." He grabbed a fistful of dirt and threw it at the boy. He cried out and said, "It wasn't my fault. It was you, Diablo. You came here. Tempted me. I was here first. Go." He got up and chased the boy out of the building, throwing rocks and bottles at him until Rodrigo was far away.

He thought about going back to San Miguel. To the emptying streets and the desolate homes. But Félix and the things they'd done were too fresh in Rodrigo's mind.

I can't go back. I can't face them.

What Félix gave him was only enough to last a few days. He bought a bottle of glass cleaner and found sheets of newspapers near a bus stop. He stood at busy intersections, cleaning the windshields of passing cars. Many of them just drove off without paying. Some drivers shouted curses and threatened him. Cops chased him away. Sometimes he had to buy them off, losing everything he'd earned in that day.

He was standing near the entrance to a store one morning gathering scraps of paper and old newspapers when a boy reached over and pressed several pesos into Rodrigo's hand. The boy smelled good. He was clean. He wore nice pants with white shoes. Sunglasses covered his eyes. He studied Rodrigo for a long time, then whispered, "Do you need work? Do you need to make money?"

Rodrigo nodded.

"Vamos."

Rodrigo followed him.

His name was Chino, and he led him to a bar called Estrellitas. There were boys there, all of them skinny, all of them in tight shirts and red shorts. There were older men there, too, watching a boy on a platform dancing naked. Rodrigo saw doors high above the dance floor behind a metal railing that circled the perimeter of the room. Each door had a different number painted on it, and white light bulbs burned beside them like eerie full moons.

Rodrigo followed Chino into a booth below the stairs to the second floor. The man sitting there was the owner, Ignacio. He instructed Rodrigo to sit.

"You're looking for work?" he asked. "Looking to make money?"

Rodrigo nodded.

"Good," he said. "You're very handsome. You could make money here. If you are good and my clients like you."

Chino led Rodrigo up to one of the rooms and told him to shower and change and comb his hair. Chino said their job was to entertain the customers. Some of them were powerful and rich.

"A lot of them come from los Estados Unidos," Chino said. "You have to keep this a secret. You can't tell anyone about these men. If you leave here and don't come back, Ignacio will find you and kill you. Wherever you go, he'll find you. I've seen him do it. Entiendes?"

"Sí," Rodrigo said.

"Have you ever done this before? Been with men?"

He thought of Félix. The abandoned warehouse. His wife's belly. A baby kicking around inside. "No," he said.

"Don't be nervous," Chino said. "The nice ones, they treat you real good. They just want to be with you. There are some, though. They will ask you to do things."

"What kinds of things?"

"Things, okay? You can't say no. If you do, Ignacio will kick you out. He'll go after you and kill you. You're lucky. He likes you. I can tell. I've worked here for four years. Since I was twelve. You can make good money. You're safe here. From all that caca out there. The police, they don't bother us. Ignacio pays them. Where are you from?"

Chino smoked a cigarette and blew out through the shutters of the room. When he saw the smoke, Rodrigo thought of the ribbons of mist hovering around the green hills that surrounded San Miguel.

"Michoacán," Rodrigo said.

"You haven't been in Tijuana long, right?"

"No," he said.

"If you go back out there, they'll eat you up. You don't matter out there." Chino lifted his shirt, revealing a scar like a pink worm burrowing beneath his skin. He wiggled his fingers and Rodrigo saw a stump, round and soft. "In here, you'll be safe. There's food. You'll make money. And Ignacio knows people. He can even help you cross the frontera. Get you papers."

Rodrigo thought of his mother patting tortillas, his father wandering through the dead fields of San Miguel. *I'll stay for now. I'll make some money. Save up.*

Rodrigo and the others were free to leave Estrellitas during the day as

long as they were back by nine at night. Chino took Rodrigo shopping. He
bought two pairs of pants with his first few earnings. Then a pair of boots.
Nice button-down shirts with the next. And bracelets and a chain. Chino
showed him where to wire money. Rodrigo wrote letters and told his
mother and father not to worry. The city was being good to him, he wrote.
Very good. *And I hope to cross over soon with the help of a coyote. A very well-known*
one. Very safe. My boss knows many people. My job here, it's good. Still, every night,
he returned to the club, sad, missing his mother and father. Estrellitas was
his home for now. He was safe. He was free to come and go as he pleased, as
long as he came back on time.

Some of Rodrigo's clients were kind. They hugged him and petted his
hands. Some taught him English words and told him about the United
States. But there were others who wanted Rodrigo to do more than just talk
and lie close. One made the boy urinate on his face. A man named Eric
brought a thick braided belt and spanked Rodrigo with it. *But the money,* Rodrigo reminded himself every time. *It's good. I've made a lot. More than I would*
ever have made in the dompes or cleaning windows.

Rodrigo had been at Estrellitas for a year when Dwight showed up.
Dwight with hair on his chin the color of yellow cornsilk. Dwight who wore
sunglasses inside the dark club. Dwight who bragged about his muscles. He
showed Rodrigo the bulldog with squatty gray legs tattooed on his left biceps and the anchor across his back. It had an insignia with red letters that
Dwight made Rodrigo memorize: USMC.

Their first night, nothing happened. They just sat on the bed and talked.
Dwight told the boy his life was empty and that no one understood him.

"This macho bullshit, it's all an act. I'm married. But she's not satisfying
me anymore. My true feelings, I'm repressing them," he said.

Repressing. Rodrigo repeated the word, memorized it. *Someday I'll use this*
word. Up there. In California.

The next time they sat on the bed and kissed. Dwight put his head on
Rodrigo's chest and cried.

"You understand me like no one else," Dwight said. "I'm taking you
away. Keeping you for myself. Don't want none of these fuckers having their
way with what's mine."

Rodrigo didn't understand. *Fuckers.* He repeated the word in his head.
You understand. No one else.

A few days later, a man with a belly so big it spilled over his waistband, shading his boots, showed up at the club.

"Go with him," Ignacio said. "He'll take you to Dwight."

Rodrigo was told to pack up all his things and leave with this stranger. Maybe Dwight was at another club across the city or the state. Ignacio owned a circuit of places like this, scattered throughout the pueblos of the north, all along the frontera. Chino told him they all work together. The police. The Migra. Even some priests lure homeless boys in off the street and pass them off to Ignacio or some other jefe who trades pollos. That's how it happened for Rodrigo, how he crossed the border into California. A circuit of men—Border Patrol agents, cops, coyotes—slip things by. They work in secret, communicate by hand gestures, wear certain colors, drive certain cars. All of them get paid. Ignacio makes sure of it. Some of them don't want money at all. Instead they ask for a boy for a whole night. Every time he was ordered to be with a man who didn't have to pay or one who wasn't one of his regulars, Rodrigo wondered whose pasaje he was paying for, which boy he had helped sneak across.

Dwight was waiting for him on this side with a blanket and clothes. He took Rodrigo out for cheeseburgers and fries. They drove in the dark over long freeways, their numbers painted on blue and red crests—15, 215, 10. He saw the names of cities—San Diego, Los Angeles, Las Vegas, Riverside, San Bernardino. The car looped over a ramp supported by tall columns, and they pulled off the freeway. They passed a sign that read Buffalo. He thought of Leonardo. *Could he be there?* He wanted to ask Dwight to stop.

They came to the rows of houses, all of them small and pressed close together with flat roofs. They pulled into a driveway and got out. The duplex had a cramped kitchen. Some of the cabinets were missing doors, and the countertop was cracked and broken. In the living room, pushed up against the far wall, was a faded blue couch with lumpy cushions. The bedroom was at the end of the hall and had a high window. Dwight had to stand on a chair to reach the latch in order to open it. In the center on the floor there was a mattress with sheets Dwight had brought from his home. Cockroaches, with translucent wings on their backs like capes, roamed freely around the place.

"Temporary," he said to Rodrigo. "Until the divorce. Then it'll be just you and me. You understand, don't you?"

Understand. Rodrigo repeated the word to himself.

Dwight had stocked the refrigerator and cupboards with food and had bought a can of Raid to kill the roaches. On the floor of the bedroom there were pads of paper and pens. Next to these was a book of games and crossword puzzles and another one, thick, with a black cover. It was titled *1,001 Big Questions.* "If you get bored," Dwight said. He tucked money in between the pages and told him. "For emergencia. Comprende?"

Rodrigo nodded.

They walked down to the end of the block. A phone booth with a rusted door stood under a streetlight that shone hazy yellow. Dwight had written a string of numbers on a sheet of paper.

"In case of something, page me," he said. "Dial this." He took Rodrigo's hand and guided his finger over each of the ten numbers. "After you hear the beep, punch these three more." He guided the boy's hand again, and Rodrigo's finger pushed the silver buttons with blackened numbers, his ear pressed against an oily receiver. "It's a secret code, okay?" Dwight said. "You're my secret."

Secret, the boy repeated. *Code.*

They walked back to the duplex. They sat on the couch and kissed and touched each other. Dwight unzipped his pants and pushed the boy's head down between his legs. When Dwight finished, he cleaned himself up and splashed water on his face.

"I won't be back until next weekend," he said. "Sit tight and lie low till I come. Don't go out. You could get lost. And Migra's been known to do sweeps around here." Then he roared off in his car.

That first night, Rodrigo couldn't sleep. He heard strange noises—the whistle of a distant train, voices shouting down the street, pipes hissing and groaning within the walls. He kept the hall light on to keep the cockroaches away and left the bedroom door open. He tried to fall asleep, breathing in the smell of soap on the pillowcases to soothe him. Rodrigo imagined Dwight's wife washing and hanging them out to dry in the sun.

The rest of the week he cried, thinking about his mother and father. *They don't even know I've left the country. I could be dead, and they wouldn't know.* He thought of his brothers. *Moisés moved around too much, but Leonardo, he stayed still because of his job.*

Maybe Dwight could take me to Buffalo. Rodrigo remembered the green street sign. Buffalo. *If I find him, what will I say, though? About how I got here? What will I say if he asks?*

He didn't understand the book or the crossword puzzles. Instead, to pass the time, he listened to the two girls who sat on the stoop next to his duplex. They had dark skin and beaded braids as violet as bougainvillea petals woven into their scalps. They talked loud, fast English. He tried to memorize the words they said and listened to the way their voices sounded when they laughed.

Dwight came back that Friday night.

"Got the whole weekend to ourselves, Rod. Told my wife I'd be in San Diego till Sunday. Shit, she don't care, man. All she does is sit around the house, playing cards, gambling my savings away at San Jacinto."

He brought a pizza, and they ate. Afterward, they went out for a ride around town. They drove along the río. The moon reflected in the water broken and warped, its light silvery, reminding him of the tinsel cords strung around the zócalo of San Miguel on Noche Santa. He saw the image of La Virgen de Guadalupe painted on the side of a wall, girls and boys standing in line near the entrance of a building with red, white, and green neon bands coiling around a marquee that read *El Yanquee: Donde Se Reunen Las Bandas Sinaloenses.* They drove by a restaurant, and Rodrigo smelled carne asasda, pollo a la parilla, carnitas. Dwight turned the music up and sang out loud, revving the engine at an intersection.

The weekend after, when he showed up again, Rodrigo waited until Dwight was inside before asking him to take him to Buffalo. But something was wrong. When the boy reached out to touch Dwight, he slapped his hand away. He sat on the floor and smoked small white rocks from a glass pipe that lit up blue and mysterious.

"Fucking two years sober out the fucking window," he said, sobbing. Rodrigo tried to understand him. Dwight took his shirt off and cried into the bulldog on his biceps. He stood up and paced, punching the walls and kicking the sofa.

His face and hands turned red. He yelled, waving his arms around and cursing. He pulled Rodrigo by the hair down the hall into the bedroom. He ripped the boy's pants off and pushed him down onto the mattress. He bent him over, the boy's face pressed into the pillows. Rodrigo reached out, swatting the air with his left hand as Dwight raped him. When he finished, Dwight put his pants back on and collapsed on top of Rodrigo. Then he got up, ran out to his car, and took off. He didn't come back for two weeks.

·   ·   ·

The boy stopped talking after that.

Two hours had passed. No customers had come to the door, peering in, looking for Perla. She hadn't flipped the sign over, hadn't set up the register. Instead, she had taken the blanket from the shelf behind the counter and covered Rodrigo up, the faint scent of roses from the "Serenidad" spray still lingering in the threads.

She had found him that morning huddled by the front door. His face was pressed against the iron bars and when Perla bent down to look at him, she saw the greenish bruises below his eye, the purple and red swirls around his neck. *Fingers.* Perla knew. She had seen them before. Consuelo Acosta's husband used to beat her, and she would come in looking for spells to chase his temper away, stretching the collar of her blouse or jacket over her neck to hide the marks, dabbing concealer to cover the black eyes.

Rodrigo's lip was split open. When he tried to smile, it cracked, and he winced. He spit on the ground and cursed in Spanish. Rodrigo trembled so much, Perla was afraid he was in shock. She had to carry him in, tucking her shoulder under his armpit, her arm around his waist, lifting him over the threshold, his feet hovering over the floor. He was so light it made her cry.

What am I supposed to do? He looks like he was trampled by a herd of horses. He was so small; his body swam in the folds of the blanket. He needed help. He needed to see a doctor. She remembered the business card with Teresa's cell phone number tucked away in her wallet. *I could call her.* Or maybe she should take the boy to the police first. They needed to report this man, this Dwight. *He's out there. Probably looking for him. He could be watching us right now. I should call them.* But the boy would say no. To Teresa. To the police. He was an illegal. Nobody but Perla and that man Dwight knew he was here. So she sat with him, cleaning his cuts, dampening a cloth with rubbing alcohol, pressing it against his wounds.

Keep him warm. That's all Perla could think about. *Keep him warm.* She prepared him a té de manzanilla and lit some candles around the botánica to soothe and relax him.

"You don't have to talk anymore," she told Rodrigo, placing the cup in his hand. "I'll sit here with you. You've told me enough."

"No," he said. "I tell you. I trust you."

The boy trembled. *Don't lose him*, she told herself again and again. *Don't lose him*. His face was swollen and blue as an overripe plum. She held his hand and squeezed back her tears.

"Did Dwight give you the burns? On the back of your hand?" She dabbed the bloody scratches on his arms with a cloth, moist and heavy with alcohol. She touched his hands, her fingers running over the scars, trying to erase them.

The boy shook his head. "I do them myself. Because I wanted to die. Catch myself on fire."

Perla's own hands trembled at the thought of the boy lighting up like a match. Of skin melting his ears shut, his eyes. She remembered Agripina. She squeezed the cloth, and alcohol dripped to the floor.

"Dwight. He changed," Rodrigo said, putting his té down. "He scared me. Smoking the drugs. Sleeping for a long time. Almost for days. After the first time, when he raped me, Dwight made me not leave. He came by more. There all the time. I can't go outside."

"Why did you stay? Why didn't you run away?"

"I know nobody here. I don't know where I am. I was afraid of leaving that place. Dwight said if I do people will know I'm a mojado. The cops, they will take me back to Ignacio. The priests, they will take me back to Ignacio. Ignacio will kill me because I'm no good to him. All used up. He's killed other boys. All week long I sit in there alone. Dwight made me close the curtains. The cucaracahas running all around. Making me afraid to sleep. I look out the window when I hear the girls outside talking and playing music. I try to learn English from them. So I can run away."

"How was it that you came here? To see me those times? To leave the note?"

"I snuck out. First time when he was gone. Other times when he was sleeping off his drug. I wanted to pray. I don't want to go to the church because what if the priests find me? So I come here because I remember the

Virgen on the wall. I look through the window, and I see the santos. For a long time I was afraid to come in. I just walk by. The first time when Dwight was crazy, I was scared. I wanted help. I trust you. You're not a priest or a police or a doctor. You look like my Abuelita Josefa."

"You disappeared. Where were you? The last time I saw you was in March. You left me that note in May." Perla got up and walked over to the register. She took the note and showed it to him. "It's now late September. What happened? I wanted to go find you. But I didn't know where you lived."

He said after he came back from leaving the note, one of the neighbors, a woman living in the duplex where the two girls sat, told Dwight she saw him coming back with books and sheets of paper tucked under his arm.

"Dwight got so mad. Hit me. Said he was going to send me back to Estrellitas. I say no. Ignacio will kill me."

So Dwight brought a friend to keep an eye on the boy.

Rodrigo didn't know the man's name. He was much older that Dwight, with thick rimmed glasses, and a bald head that was pale red and spotted with brown freckles. He wore a tank top, and so many gray hairs covered his back that it was hard to see his skin. He smoked cigarettes, one after another. He had yellow teeth and fingernails thick as a rooster's beak. The old man watched the boy during the day. He brought a sleeping bag, some clothes, and a television. There was a stuffed bunny rabbit with floppy ears that the man kept on the floor next to the television. When Rodrigo accidentally kicked it over one day, the man slapped him hard and made him pick it up.

Rodrigo went for days without being able to leave his room. The man sat in front of the television, drinking beers and smoking, watching the place like a guard dog. The only time Rodrigo was allowed to come out was to eat. Only then could he see the sunlight and remember things like day and trees and wind and grass.

"Dwight bought a lock for the door, and the old man only let me come out to use the bathroom. He never did nothing to me. When Dwight came back at night, they smoked their drugs. Dwight had sex with me. Then hit me. Spit on me. Go to the bathroom on me. The old man could hear me crying. But he never did nothing."

Perla wanted him to stop now, to sit quietly and let her clean his scrapes and cuts. She wanted to bandage the scratches and rub rose oil and aloe vera on his chapped lips, but she let him go on.

"One night," he continued, "I hear them talking. I'm lying on the floor after Dwight was finished with me. And I'm hurting so much. I'm so weak. Nothing to eat. I can't get up. I'm wanting to die because why did this happen to me? Fucking dump a body. Dwight was saying that. Fucking dump a body."

The whole botánica was warm now from the candles. *How could you?* she thought, looking at the images of Saint Michael Archangel, San Judas, Juan Soldado. *How could you let this happen here?*

"They kept talking. And I'm lying there like that. Bloody and feeling like I'm dead."

He heard Dwight's car pull away and down the street. He would be gone until the next day, Rodrigo knew. He was alone with the old man again.

"They will kill me when he comes back," he said to Perla.

It was pitch black because Dwight had taken the bulbs from the fixtures. He could taste blood on his tongue. He crawled around, staying close to the ground, close to the band of light from the old man's television coming through the crack at the bottom of the locked door. The light glowed bright green, and Rodrigo remembered the robe of the Virgen on the botánica's wall. The papers with Perla's writings. The book of saints. How much she reminded him of Abuela Josefa and Mexico and his family.

"I crawled around in the room. It's dark. And I was naked and cold. I wanted to die because there's no one for me."

He stumbled while putting his pants on. He was dazed and hit the wall with his head. The old man heard. He unlocked the door and stepped in. Rodrigo could not see his face, only his shadow filling the doorway. A hand reached out to hit him, and he fell to the floor again. The old man threw himself on top of him.

All he could do was reach out, around him, his hand falling into the light of the television, the light tinting his fingers green. The man held Rodrigo's legs down with one hand, choked him with the other.

"My jacket," Rodrigo said, crying. "I feel it in the dark. A big lump. The bag of shells and rocks you put there. I take it. Squeeze like a fist. And swing

and swing. I hear crunching, feel his hands go loose. His glasses fall off and
break. I swing and swing. Over and over until he won't move. I only have
time to get my boots and my clothes. And I run out into the yard. No one
sees me. It's late. I run and run. Past the street into a field. I stay where it's
dark. No cars. I change, and I run. I stay down by the río. Hiding during the
day. All day yesterday. At night I come here. For you. Because I miss my
mamá and papá. You are like my Abuelita Josefa."

Rodrigo pulled the blankets off and rose slowly. His hands shook as he
reached into the jacket's pocket for the pouch. It was stained with blood.
She untied the string and poured out the shells and stones. They had shattered into small pieces, spilling out onto the floor of the botánica, dusting
Perla's shoes.

*   *   *

He could be making all this up. But why? That wouldn't explain the bruises and
scratches. Did he do them himself? Like the burns? Teresa. I should call Teresa. She
knows. Drugs? Was he doing drugs? He could be in shock. Head trauma from too many
beatings. Fluids collecting around his brain. Swelling his head up like a balloon.

It was midnight now. She watched him sleep, his feet hanging over the
edge of the couch, a picture of Guillermo floating above the boy's bruised
body. He wanted to stay at the botánica, to sleep there on the floor. He was
afraid to leave. "Dwight. Out there," he told Perla, pointing to the empty
parking lot. "He'll kill me."

"No," she told him. "Not as long as you're with me. I don't live that far.
Just on the other side of the field. We have to go," she said. "We can't stay
here."

So they waited until dark to leave.

At home, Perla drew all the curtains and locked the doors. She ran a hot
bath for the boy. While he soaked she said, "I'll find something for you to
wear."

Perla had kept all of Guillermo's clothes—his slacks and shirts, the ties
and silk handkerchiefs with his initials embroidered in the corners. She
rummaged through piles of his things in the hall closet to find a pair of
sweatpants. From one of the hangers, she took an old flannel shirt.

He said he wasn't hungry, but she forced him to eat. She made warm tortillas and scrambled eggs, heated more té, valeriana, to calm him. He sat in the kitchen while Perla cleared the dishes and wiped down the counter.

"I don't know what to do, señora," he said just before he fell asleep. "Do I go back there? To my parents? Or do I stay here? Look for my brothers?"

"Don't worry," she told him. "Mañana. Mañana. Right now, try and sleep."

His eyes fluttered before shutting completely. She didn't go to her room. Instead, Perla sat in the easy chair all night. Her eyes drifted from the boy sprawled out on the couch to the front door's bronze knob, the baseball bat resting on her lap.

If you have followed us, I'm not afraid. I'm ready for you. Andale. Here I am.

She woke to sunlight filtering through the cracks in the curtains. Rodrigo was already awake. She walked into the kitchen and saw him outside, leaning against the back porch column, looking out onto the wet blades of grass. He was still in Guillermo's clothes, the sleeves of the shirt covering his hands, the sweats rolled up and kicking around his ankles. The Santa Anas stirred the palm fronds, and they waved back and forth, sweeping the sky clean.

A ghost? But I touched his hand. Saw his blood. What do I do with him? she asked the wind.

It gave no answer. The palm fronds shuddered.

*   *   *

She led the boy down the dirt path through the lot. Dust devils swirled around them, catching scraps of paper and Styrofoam cups, sending them soaring up toward the sky.

Two men sat on the hood of a car near the tattoo shop. One talked on his cell phone. The other had a silver spike poking out from his chin, and black rubber rings stretched out his earlobes. Black thorns twisted around his biceps. Wolves breathing fire, crosses, and Chinese writing covered his forearms and legs. He watched as Perla unlocked the iron gate.

"Hold up, bro," the one talking on the phone said, and he covered its mouthpiece with a finger. "Excuse me," he said to Perla. "What time do they open?"

"Around noon," she said. Perla unlocked and opened the door. When she turned back, she saw Rodrigo standing there, motionless, staring at the two men.

He shuddered when Perla reached out to lead him in. He said, "They're here for me. They're taking me back to Dwight."

"What do you mean?"

"He has tattoos like his." He pointed.

Perla looked at them.

"They're going to kill me," he shouted.

"Wait, Shawn," the man said into his phone again and cradled it between his shoulder and chin. "What'd you say, bro?" He walked up to Rodrigo, who backed away.

"He's sick," Perla said to the man. When she pressed her hand against his chest to keep him from coming closer to the boy, the cell phone fell and hit the concrete. "He doesn't know what he's saying."

"Let it go, Beady," his friend with the tattoos said. "He's fucking high."

But Rodrigo had moved too fast. When she turned around to lead him in, she saw him running away, back across the field. Past the house. Down the street. Perla watched the red and black checks of Guillermo's shirt fading into the hazy air, the dark patch of Rodrigo's hair growing smaller and smaller.

"Do you know what you did?" she shouted to the two men. "He's sick. He needs help. You chased him away."

They ignored her and sat there until the tattoo shop opened.

She stood in front of the botánica the whole morning and only went in when customers pulled up. She stayed open late, waiting until the tattoo shop was closed before going home. That night she slept out in the living room and left the porch light on, watching the shadows of moths dance across the stucco ceiling, wishing she could will them to fly off and find him.

Saturday morning, Perla left a box of cereal, a can of juice, two slices of bread, and a banana wrapped in a plastic bag next to the mailbox. On a piece of paper she left a note telling him to come to the shop. She looked for signs near the front door of the botánica that would tell her whether he'd come back and waited there for her like he'd done before. But there was nothing.

In the afternoon she walked over to the donut shop and asked Vithu and Alice if they'd seen anyone matching Rodrigo's description.

"I come at four in the morning to make the donuts," Vithu said, stepping outside to smoke. He swept his hand across the parking lot. "No cars. Nothing. I'm sorry."

"I've only seen some homeless guys," Alice said. "Sitting out on the tables. But they were older."

On Sunday, Perla woke early. She walked down the street to San Salvador's. She looked behind trash cans and under cars. She stood at the bus stop, lingering until the number 17 pulled up. When no one got off, she peered through the tinted windows and tried to recognize his face among the shadows of the passengers.

She made it to the church ten minutes early and took a seat in one of the pews at the back. By the time the bells chimed for the eighth time, San Salvador's was full. The congregation stood as the procession of altar boys carrying crucifixes and candles made their way to the front with Father Madrid following behind them, smiling and bowing his head. Reaching the altar, Father Madrid blessed himself and proceeded with the Mass. Perla's mind drifted.

Maybe I should have brought him here. Had him talk with Father Madrid. But he's afraid of churches, of priests.

A woman in a purple jacket and thick glasses rose and walked up to the lectern. She adjusted the microphone. Her voice was shaky when she spoke. "A reading from the Book of Habakkuk," she said. Everyone sat down.

She cleared her throat and began.

> *"How long, O LORD? I cry for help*
> *but you do not listen!*
> *I cry out to you, 'Violence!'*
> *but you do not intervene."*

She looked up and scanned the crowd. A baby cried. Someone behind Perla blew his nose.

> *"Why do you let me see ruin;*
> *why must I look at misery?*

Destruction and violence are before me;
there is strife, and clamorous discord.
This is why the law is benumbed,
and judgment is never rendered:
Because the wicked circumvent the just;
this is why judgment comes forth perverted."

The woman stepped away from the lectern and returned to her seat. The choir rose and sang from the balcony above.

Though she tried to concentrate on the Mass, she thought only of the boy. Everything he'd been through. How he'd trembled and bled. The things that had been done to him. All for what? He hadn't hurt anyone. *Why did you leave? I could have taken care of you.*

"Justice comes from within us. Look around." Father Madrid's voice rang loud, booming throughout the church. The embroidered sleeves of his surplice billowed out as he stretched his arms. "Do you see ruin? Do you see misery? Do you see something that needs to be changed? Then ask yourself: Am I doing enough? We must pray, yes. But we must also act. Take responsibility. For your community. For one another. For yourself. Let us go forth and do what is within our power to make things better. Instead of asking God simply to remove our obstacles, let us ask Him to give us the strength to remove them ourselves. Instead of throwing our hands up and saying 'It's too late, I can't do a thing,' let us implore Him to give us the ability to fix it, to change it. Instead of asking Him to solve our problems, let us ask Him to give us the wisdom and clarity to arrive at our own solutions."

Perla cupped her hands and rested them on her lap, the elastic cuffs of her sweater biting into her wrists. She bowed her head and closed her eyes.

When it came time for the Communion, Perla remained seated and watched the congregation rise row by row. People squeezed past her to reach the aisle, joining the single line inching toward the altar. The heads of many of the older women were covered in black and white lace mantillas. The men wore dark blue slacks and clean pressed shirts.

There were so few left Perla recognized. She remembered how there had been a time when she'd counseled parishioners outside near the drinking fountains before Mass, or had sat with them in the pews afterward, giving them recetas and novenas she carried in her purse.

Where did you go?

There had been the Lunas. Sofía and Julio and their six children had packed up and left for Arizona because there Julio could find more work and the family could buy a new house. There was Luz Peña and her blind mother, Carmen, who fell too many times, so that Luz finally had to put her in a home. There was Mr. Slusser, the war veteran who carried his medals around in his pocket, who retired to Washington to live with his son. There were the Pérezes, who moved to Las Vegas, and the Bustamantes, who flew back to the Philippines.

Perla placed her hands on the edge of the pew in front of her. She lowered her head again and listened to the slow shuffling of feet across the thick red carpet.

Why did you leave? she repeated, over and over, to herself. *Why? Why? I could have helped. I could have helped.*

When Mass ended, Perla got up and anointed her forehead with Holy Water. She felt it drying into her skin and imagined it mixing with her blood, giving her wisdom and strength and courage. One by one the congregants filed out. Father Madrid stood out on the front steps shaking hands as they exited.

"It's good to see you, señora," he said to Perla.

"You, too, Father."

"Tell me how things are with your business."

"Good. Same, you know?" She wanted to say something. About the boy. About what she knew. What he'd told her. Instead she said, "I'm still there."

"I'm glad." He took her hand and pressed it in between his own. They were warm, his fingers smooth. She thought of Darío. When he'd first touched her years ago, his palm pressed firmly on her forehead, puffing on a cigar to summon a spirit. "Your store, it's important," Father Madrid said. "It's good for the community. Like I said during my homily." He smiled.

"Thank you."

He raised his hand and blessed her. Perla walked down the steps into the street.

She wasn't going to wait anymore. *I'm going out and finding you myself. Buffalo Street. I'll start there. Stay put. I'm coming to you.*

She pressed the crosswalk button and waited for the light to turn green.

*   *   *

He has to be here. Somewhere.

The blocks of houses and apartment buildings slowly gave way to tire re-pair shops, a taquería, the Panadería Flor de Jalisco, the Excelsior Liquor Store as she walked up Buffalo. She zipped up her jacket and secured her wallet in the front pocket of her slacks.

When she reached the freeway overpass, Perla looked up and saw pi-geons nesting on the support beams, picking at their feathers. Someone coughed behind her, and she turned toward a cluster of eucalyptus trees growing in the narrow ditch running parallel to the sidewalk. The ground sloped down at an angle, and Perla braced herself to keep from falling as she made her way down there. She stepped into a clearing of dirt pounded flat, and the tree branches formed a green canopy above. A doll's head was nailed to one of the tree trunks. Its eyes had been poked out and its mouth scored. There was a cart stuffed with rags and crushed aluminum cans, a sleeping bag, and an overturned bucket with an unlit candle on top of it. Across from her stood a man in a jacket and red pin-striped pants. He was barefoot, his feet black as boot soles.

"Fuck," he shouted at Perla. "Come for your legs?" He raised his hand. "Fuck that. Fuck your legs. Spread your legs."

The rock he held had sharp edges flecked with bronze. She crouched down, shielding her head with both arms when she saw it fly out of his hand. It hit the ground behind her, shattering a baby food jar.

"Bitch," the man yelled. "Bitch. Bitch."

She turned and ran, the branches, heavy with the scent of eucalyptus, scratching her face and hands. *Balms. I could make an ointment with these branches. Doesn't matter if they're coated with train and car exhaust. It would work. I could still smooth out his scars with my hands.*

She made her way up the incline, only turning when she'd reached the sidewalk above to see if the man had followed her. But there were only the swaying branches, a cough, more cursing, and the rush of traffic as she hur-ried back home.

At dusk, Perla walked up and down her street calling Rodrigo's name. She stood out on the curb, holding a blanket, waiting for him. A few minutes later, Rosa passed by. She wore a sweatshirt and shorts with running shoes.

"Is everything okay?"

"Fine," Perla said, still shaken from her encounter with the homeless man beneath the trees.

"Are you sure, señora?" Rosa took a sip from the water bottle she held.

Perla gripped the blanket. "I was helping a customer. A boy. He ran away from me."

"Why?"

"I don't know. I was trying to help him," she said. Perla spread the blanket out on the lawn and sat down.

"I'll sit with you," Rosa said. "Keep you company."

An hour passed before Perla said to Rosa, "You should go. It's getting late. Danielle. Miguel. They probably need you."

"They're at his mom's," Rosa said. "I can get the keys to the van. We could drive around and look for him if you want." She got up.

Perla said, "No, it's too dark now. Maybe tomorrow." She placed her face in her hands and sighed. "I was trying to help him. Just help him. That's all."

"Well, if you need me, I'll be home, okay?" Rosa rose and walked down the sidewalk, the sound of her footsteps mixing with the shrill drone of the crickets in the ivy across the street.

•   •   •

On Monday, she closed up the botánica at five-thirty. She took Rancho Avenue, heading south toward Agua Mansa Road. On the way, she passed a car raised on cinder blocks, passed houses with yards cluttered with toys and empty laundry detergent drums.

It was before six when she got to Galena Court. Perla followed the road, curving around like a horseshoe. She stopped in front of a house where a statue of Saint Francis stood in the center of the yard. There was an altar near the front door, and flowers were arranged in empty veladoras drained of their wax. At the foot of the altar, metal coffee cans with holes punched into their sides held stems of aloe vera plants. She stood on the sidewalk and prayed:

Lord, make me an instrument of your peace.
Where there is hatred, let me sow love;
where there is injury, pardon;
where there is doubt, faith;
where there is despair, hope;
where there is darkness, light;
and where there is sadness, joy.

O Divine Master, grant that I may not so much seek
to be consoled as to console;
to be understood as to understand;
to be loved as to love.
For it is in giving that we receive;
it is in pardoning that we are pardoned;
and it is in dying that we are born to eternal life. Amen.

From the house, a girl walked across the yard and placed an envelope into a mailbox numbered 144. She wore house slippers with cracked soles. She reached the door again and was about to turn the knob when Perla shouted, "Excuse me?"

The girl turned around. Her eyebrows were as thin as dental floss, and blue eyeshadow dusted her lids. She looked at Perla, the edge of her hip bone, sharp as a chisel, poking through the thin fabric of her jeans.

She said nothing.

"I'm looking for someone. A boy. His name's Rodrigo," Perla told her.

"You a cop or Social Services?" She sighed, rolled her eyes. "I ain't saying nothing. Not ratting no one out. Don't want no trouble. I don't know nothing." The girl placed her hand on the door's knob and began turning it. From inside came the sound of a radio playing music.

"A boy. Named Rodrigo," Perla insisted.

The girl walked down the stone steps, past Saint Francis, and toward Perla. "Why you looking for him? He your shorty?"

"Shorty?" Perla asked, confused.

"Kid. He your kid?"

"No. He's someone I care about."

"What's he look like?"

Perla tried to remember Rodrigo's features. "Thin. Very thin. Very gentle boy."

"That don't help." The girl laughed. "Now I know for sure you're not the jura. When the jura rolls up in their shiny black-and-whites they know quick who they're scoping out. Got stacks of flyers and everything sometimes even. The jura lives here, man. Since before my husband and me moved in we heard about Galena and the crazy shit that goes down here. But what are you gonna do? Gotta live, right? Even if it's in this place. With stabbings and break-ins and shit." The girl folded her arms. Bracelets dangled from her wrists.

Then Perla remembered. *The police. The old man. The pouch.* "Break-ins," she repeated. "Like what happened to that old man? Maybe a week ago? Did you know about that?"

"Yup." The girl shook her head. "Whole block did. Cops. Ambulance. Fire trucks even though nothing was burning. They wheeled him out on a stretcher."

"Where did it happen?"

The girl led Perla back behind her house. They walked between rows and rows of damp work shirts and skirts, baby socks and jeans hanging on clotheslines, to a clearing in the middle of the yard the duplexes shared. In the center stood a birch tree, its trunk carved with initials and crooked hearts. They walked on a concrete footpath between two of the units. Screen doors banged open and shut. Silhouettes floated by behind lace curtains or in between the slits of miniblinds. She heard water running and dishes clanking. The air was thick with the smell of chorizo and chiles.

"There," the girl said, pointing to the unit across the street. She turned around and walked back toward the birch tree, disappearing behind the damp laundry.

The screen door hung off its hinges. She could see the gurney's tracks in the grass. Perla jiggled the handle and tried to push the front door open, but it didn't give. She followed the path around the house. There was a trash can full of garbage—empty soda bottles, the cardboard flap of a box of Rice Krispies, bags of potato chips, cans of soup. Footprints were pressed into the muddy ground near a purple sage bush. Steps led up to the back door. It was ajar.

Someone's here.

Perla backed away slowly. She felt the wallet inside her pocket, heavy like a stone. She remembered the crazy man the day before, the rock flying past, barely missing her face. She followed the path back around and crossed the street again.

Just before Galena Court spilled back out onto Agua Mansa Road there was a phone booth. A directory hung from a gun metal gray chain and words were scratched into the strips of paint and on the windows: "SUK," "MANSA FLATS, Y QUE?," "AQUA IZ A FINE RUCA." She reached for her wallet, opened it, and found the business card where Teresa had written her cell phone number. Perla dropped coins in the slot and dialed the number. The buttons stuck when she pressed them. There were clicks, then static, before she heard short rings. Teresa's voice said, "Hello?"

"Teresa, it's me, Perla."

"Hey. What a coincidence. I was just thinking of you today. I need to come by and get more tea." A car drove past the phone booth, loud music thumping from its speakers. Teresa asked, "What is that? Where are you?"

She hesitated. "In a phone booth. Galena Court."

"Galena Court? What are you doing around there? At this time?"

"A customer," Perla told her. "A patient. I was trying to help. But I couldn't."

"What? Who?" Teresa asked.

"Rodrigo," she said. "I couldn't." Her voice trembled, and she began to cry.

Perla recounted everything—the club, the boy being smuggled across, Dwight, the bruises, the burn marks, the duplex where he was held. "I think someone's in there. I saw a garbage can. Footprints. That man Dwight could be in there. Or Rodrigo. He could be sick. In shock or traumatized. When he saw those men by the botánica, he got so scared. He ran. I tried to get him to stay." Her hands shook. "But he left. If he's around here, I can still help."

"Okay," Teresa said. "Okay. Okay. Calm down. Let's think. Juntas. You and me. On the phone. Are you sure this boy was being honest with you? That he wasn't trying to trick you or anything? You believe him? Everything he told you?"

"Yes, I do. That's why I'm here. I'm trying to help him. I just don't know how, what to do."

"Don't move. Stay there," Teresa insisted. "Give me fifteen minutes, okay? Fifteen." There was shuffling in the background, then something slamming shut. "Stay put. Don't try and go back there. Stay there, señora. In that phone booth. I'm coming to you. I'm on my way."

Perla hung up and stood there, gripping the receiver's handle, wishing there was a way she could call the boy and tell him she was there. That she wanted to help him. That he wasn't alone. That he shouldn't be afraid.

The streetlights flickered on, one by one, as Teresa pulled up and parked near the phone booth. "You did the right thing," she said, hugging Perla. "Calling me like that."

Perla said, "I need to know what to do. In case he's in there. But you didn't have to come down here. It's dark. Dangerous."

"You were upset. I could hear it in your voice. I don't want anything happening to you." Her cell phone rang, and she reached into her pocket. "I'm sorry," she said, looking at the light-up screen. "It's Craig." She pushed a button and said, "Hey, honey." She opened her jeep's hatch and pulled out a first-aid kit. "No," she said into the phone. "Helping a friend . . . I don't know . . . I might be a while . . . I'll call you when I'm on my way . . . I love you, too." She hung up and placed the phone back in her pocket.

Teresa walked around the passenger's side of the car and reached into the glove compartment. "Pepper spray," she said, holding a small black cylinder with a bright red nozzle. "Just in case." She felt around the floor beneath the seat and gave Perla a flashlight. "Vamos."

They left the car and walked back across the street.

Perla showed her the duplex, the darkened windows, the gurney's tracks in the grass. "Here," she said, pointing to the trash can behind the house and the footprints in the mud near the sage bush. "See? Someone might be in there."

Teresa walked up the steps first and nudged the door with her right shoulder. It creaked open and, as she stepped into the kitchen, she aimed the can of pepper spray at the dark air inside. "Come on," Teresa whispered, holding out her hand to Perla. She took it, switched on the flashlight, and followed.

Perla felt as if she had inhaled a handful of thorns; the air smelled of disinfectant, bug spray, and stale tobacco. There was a stove with chrome burners and an empty space where a refrigerator must once have been. Perla focused the flashlight on the windowsill dotted with flies, their legs curled into tiny question marks. A round table was pushed up against the far wall, and scraps of cardboard padded its four feet. The sink dripped, a halo of rust encircling the drain.

"I don't think anyone's here," Teresa said. "Watch out. Don't bump into anything."

"Okay," Perla said. She pointed with the flashlight to the pepper spray. "Have you ever used it?"

"Once. I practiced on a face Craig drew on a box."

They walked through a graveyard of dead cockroaches in the living room doorway. Thin beams from the streetlights filtered through the gaps in the blinds covering the front windows, filling the room with a sad blue haze.

"Jesus," Teresa said, letting go of Perla's hand. "This is a pit." She took a few steps forward, touching the walls. "He said they had him locked in a room?"

Perla pointed the flashlight down the hallway. "There."

"Let's have a look."

It was much darker inside the room. The mattress was pushed up against the wall, the sheets unfolded, the pillows flattened.

Teresa squeezed Perla's hand. "Don't let go," she said. "I've got you, señora. I'm right here."

Perla aimed the flashlight at the floor. Her eyes traced a pattern of red dots small as rosary beads fanning out, stretching toward the closet with its missing doors.

"Look," Teresa said. "You see that? It's blood."

Perla imagined the struggle. The old man on top of the boy. Rodrigo's feet kicking. His hand reaching out to grab the pouch.

"He said he hit the man with the shells and stones I gave him," Perla said. "That was probably where they fought." She let go of Teresa's hand.

"What's that?" Teresa asked, pointing the flashlight at something poking out from beneath the mattress. "Look. It's a journal or something."

Perla recognized the cover immediately. It was the book of saints she had lent Rodrigo. She bent down and reached for it. Teresa stood behind her, holding the flashlight steady above her head.

Pressed between images of Saint Margaret of Antioch and Saint Martha were crumpled sheets of loose paper. She saw the curves and slants of her own handwriting, the dried golden rivers of her words. *Perla Maria Portillo. Seventy-two years of age. Born here in Agua Mansa, California. I run the botánica.* When Perla reached out to touch them, to feel the hardened gel, the raised tail of an *n* in the word *Botánica* or the loop of the *o* in Guillermo's name, those letters, those words, liquefied, pulsed, and came to life again.

"Let's go," Teresa said. She placed her hand gently on Perla's shoulder and led her out. "There's nothing here."

Perla gathered the frayed and tattered papers and closed the book. She watched her shadow, long and thin like a ghost, stretch over the wall, then fade into the darkness the room caught and held.

Charity

The summer before sixth grade Travis and his mother, Ruby Dean, moved into the house at the end of my block. The people who had rented it before never bothered to plant any grass out front because they always parked their cars on what should have been the lawn. It was just a small patch of mud and weeds surrounded by a chain link fence.

On the curb, they'd left a mattress that lay there until the day the moving van pulled up and Travis and his mother got out. Our place was three houses down on the opposite side of the street. I sat on the porch, sucking on ice cubes and watching them unload boxes.

That night I rode my bike to the end of the block. On the curb, cardboard boxes were piled on top of one another where the mattress had been. There were no lights on, and it looked as if no one was home. I parked my bike next to the boxes and sat on the curb. I pulled out a candy bar that was in my pocket and ate it. After I'd finished, I tossed the wrapper on the ground.

"You just gonna leave that wrapper there, love?" I heard a voice say. I turned to see a woman standing in the middle of the dirt yard in a purple silk kimono. She crossed her arms and walked over to me. I kept my head down, staring at her terry cloth house slippers, her toes peeking out from the front.

"Lose your tongue?" she asked.

"No," I said.

"You shy?"

I shrugged my shoulders. "Sometimes."

"Sometimes?" She laughed. "What's your name, honeybun?"

"Roberto."

"I knew a Roberto once. Italian guy. You Italian?"

"No," I said. "I'm American."

"There's nobody left that's *American*."

"My parents are Mexican," I said.

"You know Spanish?"

"Sometimes."

"You're a riot, kid. I'm Ruby. Ruby Dean."

She stuck her hand out, and I reached over the top of the fence to shake it. I heard my mother's voice down the street, calling my name.

"I have to go," I said to Ruby. "It was nice meeting you." I bent down to pick up the candy wrapper, and I shoved it in my pocket.

"Pick up after yourself," she shouted as I pedaled away. "I'm not always gonna be quick to catch you."

I said, "Okay."

When I got to our driveway my mother was shaking her head.

"What?" I asked. "I wasn't even doing anything."

"I saw you. We don't know those people," she said. "So don't bother them, entiendes?"

"Yeah, I get it." I parked my bike in the garage, between the wall and our van, and I went inside.

*   *   *

There wasn't much to do that summer. My best friend, Nick, was in Mexico visiting his grandmother, so I found myself watching television for hours. The more I watched, though, the more restless I became. There was an empty field that wasn't too far from my house. I would go there almost every afternoon to ride my bike, smashing beetles with my tires, pretending I was racing in a tournament.

The day I met Travis, I was coming back from the field. He was standing in the middle of his yard on top of an overturned milk crate. He held a green hose with a bright copper nozzle and was watering the mud. When I rode by, he nodded at me.

I stopped my bike. "It's just mud," I said, pointing. "Why are you water-ing mud?"

"What's it to you what I water? See that?" He pointed to a tuft of grass a few feet away from where I stood. "That's grass, in case you don't know what it looks like. If I water this mud the grass'll get bigger and keep grow-ing."

"You need fertilizer." I pointed toward my house. My father and I had spent that Saturday cutting the grass. The tracks from the mower's wheels were still visible on the lawn. "It won't grow without it."

"I bet it will, and it'll make yours look like shit," he said, trying to spray me with the hose. "Get out of here, or I'll kick your ass."

That night after dinner, I sat with my father on the porch. He was con-centrating hard on a crossword puzzle. My eyes traced the evenly spaced vertical rows our mower's wheels had left in the grass. The sprinkler heads popped out from the ground and began watering the yard and my mother's plants. I looked at the hedges lining our driveway, their neat boxy shapes, the roses, and the bougainvillea vines clinging to the columns of our porch. After my father finished his crossword puzzle, he went into the kitchen and sat with my mother, who was listening to the radio.

In the garage, I took the bag of fertilizer we had opened that weekend and secured the top flap with masking tape. Draping the bag over my bike's handlebars, I pedaled toward Travis's house. An El Camino with a bumper sticker that read "My Other Car's a UFO" was parked in their driveway. I knocked on the door long enough for my knuckles to feel raw before Ruby answered. She stood in the doorway, in the same kimono and house slip-pers. She wasn't wearing a bra, and her left breast was showing, the nipple big and pink as a tongue. She covered herself and smoothed back her hair.

"Darling. What can I do you for?"

"I'm looking for the boy that was watering the grass, I mean, the yard here today." I pointed behind me, still looking at her breast.

"Yard?" She laughed. "Are you high, kid? It's mud. You're looking for Travis, my son. What's he done to you?"

I put the bag of fertilizer on the ground. "I wanted to give this fertilizer to him. To help him grow the lawn. I mean the mud." I pointed to the clump of grass. "That."

"You're joking, right?"

"No," I said. "I'm not."

"Well that has got to be the sweetest thing I've ever heard. Let me see if he's here." She stepped away from the door. I tried to get a better look inside, but it was too dark to see anything. Ruby called out for Travis a few more times before finally giving up.

"Guess he's taken off," she said. "Could you come back tomorrow? I got a friend here right now." I heard someone sneeze.

"Can you give him this?" I touched the bag of fertilizer.

"Sure, love. I sure will." She winked at me before closing the door.

I rode down the street just in time to see my mother coming out of our house wheeling the garbage can out to the curb.

ø   ø   ø

My father was at work, and my mother had gone grocery shopping. The smog was so bad that my eyes were stinging. I was standing over the kitchen sink dousing them with cold water when the doorbell rang.

Travis stood on my porch in a pair of cutoff jeans, a stained tank top, and a baseball cap with the brim pulled down low. He was bony and taller than me and wore plastic sunglasses. The first thing he said when he saw me behind the screen door was, "My mom made me come over to thank you for the bag of fertilizer."

"It works good," I said.

"It's used. Don't you have a new one?"

"My dad keeps them in the toolshed, and the toolshed's locked." I opened the screen door. "Sorry," I said. I pointed to our lawn. "He says it's the best."

"What's he, some kind of gardener or what?"

"No," I said. "He sells insurance."

"I'm thirsty," Travis said. "You got anything to drink in there?"

I went to the kitchen and filled two glasses with cherry punch from the pitcher in our refrigerator. Into each glass, I dropped ice cubes, and they popped and hissed as I walked back out to the porch. We sat on the steps, our legs stretched out under the sun.

"Aren't you gonna invite me in? My mom says it's rude when people don't even ask you in."

"I'm not allowed to have people over when I'm alone."

"Why not?"

"I'm just not."

He had a scab on his elbow that he picked at. When it bled, he asked if I had a bandage.

"No," I said. "I don't." I lied.

"Shit." He got up and walked over to the hose and turned it on. He let the water run over the cut, and pale red swirls trickled down his arm. "There," he said. "That works."

*   *   *

That summer, my mother was volunteering down at the library. They held a reading series for kids each Monday, Wednesday, and Friday from ten to two. I'd go with her, roaming the tall stacks and reading all my favorite books, sitting in the overstuffed chairs, enjoying the air-conditioning while she turned the pages of a book and made funny voices to groups of kids sitting around her in a semicircle. The librarians who worked there liked to tease me a lot, asking if I had a girlfriend yet.

"I don't want to go with you next time," I told my mother one day as we drove home.

"Why?"

"Those women bug me."

"Fine," she said as we pulled up to the driveway. "But we'll ask your father, too."

My father wrote down all the emergency numbers I'd need on an index card and showed me how to turn off the main gas line in case of an earthquake. My first day alone, I sat out back, swinging on our hammock, chewing on a plastic straw. It got boring, so at about twelve-thirty I walked over to Travis's house to see how the lawn was coming along.

The same El Camino was in the driveway, and I parked my bike next to it. This time I didn't knock on the front door. I was afraid of seeing Ruby's nipple again. Instead, I walked around back, past metal trash cans filled to the top with garbage. Travis was sitting under a tree, his back to me. He held twigs in both hands and was beating them violently against the trunk of the tree, his head jerking back like he was having a convulsion.

"Hey," I said, touching his shoulder. His hand swung around, and the twig he was holding whipped me on the arm.

I pulled it back quickly and winced from the pain.

"Shit," he said. "Why the fuck are you sneaking up on me like that?" He got up and looked at my arm. "You'll be all right," he said, punching me on the shoulder.

"What were you doing?" I asked.

"What'd it look like?"

I stayed quiet.

"I was playing the drums." He tossed the twigs on the ground and threw his hands up. "The drums! My mom's friend Roy plays in a band, and he says that if I get good he'll take me on tour with him." He pointed to the El Camino. "Says he's gotten laid more times in that car than in any place in the world. He calls it the 'Pussy Prowler,' and he's gonna teach me to drive it someday."

The house had a sunporch with an aluminum door that didn't shut all the way, and we walked through it into the kitchen. There were still boxes everywhere, and it was difficult to see anything because the curtains were drawn. I made out shapes here and there—a cactus in one corner of the dining room, a sewing machine on the kitchen counter. I walked with my hands reached out, trying not to bump into anything.

There was no furniture in the living room except for two lawn chairs near the front window and a wooden console table pushed up against the opposite wall. On the console, next to a lamp with a torn shade, there was a pair of bronze baby shoes.

"Those are mine," Travis said. He walked over to a pile of pictures in between the two chairs. "This is my dad." He held a picture of a man in a crew cut and uniform. "He's in the Army."

"Where is he?" I asked.

He looked like Travis. They both had hair the color of dry weeds.

"He's in Japan," Travis said. "He's been there for two years and doesn't call because it's expensive, and he says the international operators are all assholes. He wrote us a letter four weeks ago saying he's gonna be sending for us soon."

I handed the picture back to him.

A door opened down the hall, and Ruby and a man came out of the bedroom. He was holding a guitar and led her by the hand.

"Didn't I say you should play outside when Roy's here?" she said to Travis. She winked at me. "Roberto, love. How are you, sweetpea?"

"Good," I said, looking down at my shoes.

She introduced me to Roy, who said, "Roy Campos. Howdy, kid."

Travis and I walked back to the kitchen, and he asked if I was hungry.

"Sort of," I said.

He opened the refrigerator and pulled out two packets of string cheese from a bin. Using his teeth, he opened both of them and handed one to me.

He said, "I'll show you my room."

There were no curtains, and strips of aluminum foil covered the windows. In the center of the room was the mattress the previous owners had left by the curb, a thin sheet draped over it.

He said, "This is my favorite part." He ran across the room and tumbled down onto the mattress. "I'm gonna use some sticks I found out back and tie some rope around the mattress. When I'm done we can pretend like we're wrestlers."

"Okay," I said, looking at the sagging mattress, the coils sticking out of the side.

"Are you thirsty?" he asked.

"Yeah," I said. "A little."

We walked back out to the kitchen.

Roy sat at the dining table drinking a can of beer, and Ruby was by the sink smearing butter on flour tortillas.

"¿Qué pasa?" Roy said to Travis. "Have a seat."

Travis opened a cabinet door and brought out a small plastic cup. He gave it to Roy. From a paper bag next to him, Roy pulled out another can of beer. He opened it up, filled the cup, and slid it across the table to Travis.

After he finished the cup, Travis wiped his mouth and said, "It's too warm."

"I forgot I had it in the car," Roy said. He watched Ruby, who was biting into her tortilla. Roy turned to me and said, "You look like a sharp pistol, Roberto."

"Thank you," I said, though I didn't know what he meant. The guitar was against the wall, and he picked it up and started strumming. He wore dark brown construction boots with faded red laces and a flannel shirt with the sleeves torn off.

"Do you know how to play?" Roy asked when he saw me looking at him.

"No," I said. "But my dad likes music."

Ruby took bites of her tortilla and stood over the kitchen sink, staring out the window at the tree Travis had been practicing the drums on. "Don't teach the poor kid," she said. "You don't got the know-how."

Roy just ignored her. "You must got music flowing through your blood, kid." He took the plastic cup and poured some more beer into it. "Travis, get another one."

Ruby said, "Stop ordering him around, Roy."

He waved a hand up at her and said, "Relax, will you? We're just having some fun here."

Travis returned with another cup that Roy also filled with beer.

"A toast," he said. "To Roberto."

Roy and Travis raised their cups. I slowly lifted mine and took a deep breath before swallowing it as quickly as I could.

"That's it," Roy said, slapping me on the back a few times and clapping his hands. "You like it?"

"I guess."

Travis held out his cup and said, "Gimme more."

"Sorry. Bar's closed," Roy said. "Only one drink per customer."

Ruby put the tortillas back in the refrigerator. She turned to Roy and said, "Didn't you say you were gonna help me chop down that mangy tree out back? It's crawling with bugs."

He continued strumming his guitar, ignoring her altogether.

After a while, Ruby walked over to the table and pulled out the last two cans of beer from the paper bag next to Roy.

"I'll be in my room," she said.

"Be right there," Roy said.

"Don't feel much like sharing." She walked down the hall and slammed her bedroom door shut.

*   *   *

I felt the thud of Roy's big hand slapping my back the whole way home. The taste of beer still coated the inside of my mouth. I even felt a little giddy and had trouble steering my bike down the street. All of this gave me a thrill. I was eleven, and I suddenly felt rebellious and dangerous, capable of trouble.

My first impulse when I got back home was to brush my teeth and gargle with mouthwash until my gums hurt. Instead, I sat on the porch and waited for my mom.

She kissed me on the forehead. I tried to breathe heavily and sighed a few times, hoping she'd catch a whiff of the beer. Instead she asked what I'd done that afternoon.

"I saw that new kid that lives on the corner," I said, sighing again.

"From that ugly house?"

I nodded.

She was more concerned about the lawn. "They need to do something with that yard. Plant flowers. It's an eyesore."

When my father came home that evening he asked if I had seen the opened bag of fertilizer.

"I gave it to the new kid," I said.

"What for?"

"Because." I felt cocky, crossed my arms. "They're going to plant grass. Everyone's always saying that yard looks crappy."

"You should have asked first, okay?"

"Yeah," I told him. "Sorry."

After a while, he said, "Is there a father?"

"He's in the Army," I said. "He's in Japan."

"What's she like?" my mother asked. "I saw her the other morning as I drove by. I waved, but she didn't see me."

I thought about Ruby's flashy smile, her winks, her smooth, pink nipple. "She's nice," I said.

"Does she work?" my mother said.

"I don't know."

"Try to find out."

My father shook his head and rolled his eyes.

*   *   *

That Friday morning Travis came over and said I needed to take him to Best Donuts in the Prospect Shopping Center.

"It's too far to walk," he said. "I don't have a bike."

"What do you need to go for?" I asked.

"Breakfast. I can sit on the handlebars. Come on. I'll buy you a donut. My mom gave me a shitload of money." From his pocket, he pulled out a folded ten-dollar bill.

"That's not a lot," I said.

"More than what you got."

"I got more."

"Bullshit," Travis said. "Come on. Let's go."

My parents had made me promise that I would stay close to home when they were gone. Something bad could happen, my mother said. I could get kidnapped or hurt somehow. I looked around my house. Upstairs in my room, I'd picked up my clothes and made my bed. In the living room, the TV was off because there was nothing worth seeing.

Everything around me was quiet and clean. I could feel the heat coming from outside as I stood there watching Travis from behind the screen door. He was sweating, his cheeks as red as my bike's reflectors.

"I'm not supposed to ride past the end of the block," I said.

"Are your parents here?"

"No."

"Then who's gonna tell?"

I said nothing.

"Stop being a pussy."

"Shut up."

"It's ain't that far," he said. "If you don't wanna go, at least let me borrow your bike."

"Fine, I'll take you," I said, reluctantly.

It was slow going when we started out. Travis sat on the handlebars and was heavier than I expected. It was hard to steer, and we fell off a few times and wobbled down Rancho until we eventually made it.

There were only two stores left in the Prospect Shopping Center: Best Donuts, which was owned and run by a Cambodian family whose son was in my grade; and the Botánica Oshún. There were boards up in the windows of the ninety-nine-cent store, and a sign that read:

Moved to a New Location.
Come Visit Us at 4140 Barton Rd #3F, Grand Terrace.

Except for the telephone poles along the sidewalk, there was nowhere to lock up my bike. On a table in the botánica's window stood a statue about the size of a fire hydrant of a saint I didn't recognize. Dimes were taped across his mouth and over both his eyes, and he wore a faded velvet robe with dollar bills pinned along its front, secured by small safety pins. I leaned my bike there, under the glass window.

I told Travis, "I'll wait out here." I held on to my bike.

"Quit being a pussy. Nothing'll happen to it. We won't be long."

I stood there without moving.

"Fine," he said. "Wait then."

He came out with a bag and we sat on the curb near my bike and hardly spoke as we passed a glazed bar between us like a peace pipe until it was gone. The curb began to bother us, and we got up. Travis looked at the saint in the botánica's window.

"Why's it got dimes stuck to his mouth?"

I shrugged. "To keep it quiet?"

"Jesus Christ." He slapped his forehead with the palm of his hand. "It's a statue. What do they sell in there?"

"My mother brought me here once to buy a rosary and some white candles when I made my first Holy Communion."

"Come on." Travis tugged my shirt's sleeve. "Let's go in."

There were no other customers. After we closed the front door, Travis turned to me and said, "Are you scared?"   .

"Why should I be?" I punched him on the arm. "I've been in scarier places than this."

"Prove it," he said.

"Shut up," I said. I shook my head just as a woman walked out from behind a curtain.

She didn't say anything, just watched us as we strolled through the store and peered into the cases. When Travis picked up a small key chain with a picture of Jesus on it from a bin sitting on a bookcase, she said, "Those are a dollar."

He put it down and walked over to me standing in front of a postcard display.

"Ask her about the dimes on the statue," he whispered.

"You," I said.

"Chickenshit."

"What's with that statue in the window?" he asked the woman.

"What do you mean what's with it?" she responded, putting her glasses on.

"Why's it got dimes taped to its mouth?"

"It's Saint Anthony of Padua. He helps when you need to find something or when you need money. Those are ofrendas."

"What?" he asked.

"Offerings," she responded. "Money."

Travis looked over at me. "He thought the dimes were to keep him quiet."

"No," she said, watching us. "He helps."

"How?" I asked her.

"You have to pray. Light a candle. Concentrate." She pointed to her temple.

Then Travis tapped me on the shoulder. "My mom needs her breakfast," he said. "We better go."

When we got back to Travis's, we found Ruby sitting at the dining table in nothing but a bra and panties. I noticed a tattoo on her left shoulder that spelled out *Rebel*. She had pulled the curtains back and the whole kitchen was bright and warm.

Travis tossed the bag of donuts on the table near Ruby. "Are you okay?" he said in a low and serious voice that I hadn't ever heard him use before.

She laughed. "No. Fuck no. I've let myself get old. Ugly," she shouted, slapping the table's top.

I backed into the corner near the cactus and tried not to look at her.

"When I was younger, I was a different girl." She reached into her purse and pulled out a pack of cigarettes. She lit one and blew the smoke up toward the ceiling. "I had charisma. That's what your daddy said. That's why he fell for me. He said I had charisma, and that I could have had any man I wanted. Look at me." She swept her arm across the room, fanning smoke. "I got so much charisma, don't I? So much I got no man. I still ain't heard from your daddy. Part of me don't even care if I do anymore. Roy's gone."

She got up and walked to the counter and tossed the cigarette in the sink.

Ruby gripped the edge of the counter, and I could see her white knuckles, the purple netting of veins under her skin. "When I told him he should stick around more, maybe bring some clothes over and spend the night once or twice, he got pissed. Said I was trying to claw my way into his life. Said I was too old for him anyways and that he had this chick on the side named Maribel, so I told him to fuckin' die. I felt so good saying that. Fuckin' die, I said. And your dick's small, anyways."

She walked past us through the sunporch and out to the back. Travis and I followed her. In the middle of the yard, the tree towered in front of the three of us. Ruby pulled out a machete from a toolbox. She took three swings before she finally hit the tree.

Travis reached into the toolbox and pulled out a pair of hedge clippers that looked just like my father's and he joined her, both of them taking swings.

Ruby turned to me. Her eyes were swollen from crying. I thought about Roy, imagined him getting drunk and making out with some other woman in the back of his El Camino, then taking off to serenade someone else. Travis looked at me, his cheeks red. He gripped the hedge clippers tightly, and his other hand was balled up in a fist.

Ruby blew a few strands of hair away from her face, then licked her lips. "You just gonna stand there like that? Or are you gonna help?"

I found a pair of scissors and started swinging with them.

            •   •   •

He didn't have to ask me twice. That night he tapped on my bedroom window and said he needed a ride. It was past midnight, and my parents were asleep in their room. Travis loosened the fasteners that secured the window's screen by bending them with the tips of his fingers, and I jumped out.

We took my bike from the garage and rode in silence the whole way, past dark streets and darker houses, hiding behind trash cans and in the shadows of trees when a car passed by or a dog barked. The empty fertilizer bag was slung over his shoulder.

By the time we reached the Prospect Center, I was drenched in sweat from all the pedaling. From the bag, Travis pulled out a heavy rock. He stood in front of the window with the statue and all I remember seeing is the rock flying out of his hand, flying through the near black sky, the glass shattering and the pieces falling to the ground.

He cradled the statue in his arms and climbed up on the handlebars. I held the back of his shirt to keep him from falling forward and tried to steer with one hand.

"Pedal faster," he said.

I dropped him off in front of his house, and he walked away without saying anything to me. The statue's money flapped in the breeze, and when a bill fell to the ground, Travis bent down to pick it up. Even from my bike, I could see that the dollar bills pinned to the statue were fake.

I didn't see much of Travis the rest of the summer. Every time I'd go over to ask if he could come out, Ruby would answer and say that he was resting or that she had him doing chores out back and couldn't be disturbed.

Then that fall they moved away. The only thing they left behind was the statue. They'd placed it out on the curb, leaning it against the mailbox. The fake dollar bills were gone but the safety pins remained. I decided I was going to return it to the botánica. From my driveway, I watched as a man in a truck pulled up to their house. He took the statue and placed it upright on the truck's bed, using pieces of twine to keep it from falling out. When he pulled away, I got on my bike and followed him, pedaling as fast as I could. Waving my hand in the air, I tried to get the driver's attention. I whistled a few times but gave up when I heard loud music coming from the cab. I rounded the corner just in time to see the statue toppling over and banging against the side of the bed before tumbling out onto the street and breaking apart. The driver didn't notice. He just kept going. I stopped and got off my bike. One by one, I picked up the pieces, forming a neat pile of white stones on a patch of green grass.

Feast of
Saint Gregory the Wonder Worker

Bishop and Confessor

Patron of desperate situations and forgotten

and impossible causes.

Invoked against earthquakes and floods.

It was early morning. Perla dressed and combed her hair in front of the bathroom sink. On the third shelf of the medicine cabinet were her pills, Teresa's name on each bottle in small black letters along the bottom half of the labels. She hadn't talked with her since last month, after they'd come back from Galena Court.

"It's not your fault," Teresa had told her. "You reached out, tried to help." They had stood in the kitchen drinking lemon tea sweetened with piloncillo. She had tried to calm Perla down, to keep her from blaming herself for what happened to Rodrigo.

Teresa's lucky, Perla thought as she took her pills. *She has X-rays and blood tests. All that expensive equipment. Nurses who keep files and call patients. I have none of that.* She had things of earth and sky. Things born of root and bone and flesh. She had sprays and amulets, saints and gods with tempers and needs. She had teas and colored veladoras and remedios scrawled on tattered index cards. *He needed something else. And I didn't have a candle for it.*

          ⁕   ⁕   ⁕

Her first customer was a thin girl wearing a tight turtleneck sweater. Her pants hugged her hips, inching down low enough for her thong panties to show. In the strip of skin just above her waist was the tattooed image of a winged unicorn. The girl's hair was dyed bright red with stripes of purple and green, and she smelled of cloves. A pink bear squeezing a heart covered one side of her purse.

"Do you sell anything with fairies?" the girl asked.

"Glass figurines." Perla led her to a shelf near the window.

The girl pointed to a pixie with flowers in her hair sitting on a rock. "Could I see that one?"

Perla took it from the shelf and set it on the counter for the girl to examine.

"I love fairies," she said, looking at it. "How much is it?"

"This one is ten dollars."

"Tight," she said. "I'm gonna be next door for a while. After I'll come by to get it."

She left just as Alfonso's truck pulled up outside. Perla watched as he climbed out and crossed the parking lot. He looked taller than she remembered, and he had grown a mustache and lost some weight.

"¿Qué tal?" he said, stepping behind the counter to hug her. "It's so good to see you."

"You, too." Perla smiled at him and patted his hand. "I've missed having you around. It's lonely here without you." She led him to the chairs near the door.

"I can't stay long," he said. "I wanted to stop in and see how things were in the old place. It looks different to me in here. Smaller."

"It's still the same. But next door's changed."

"Tatuajes, eh? They do tatuajes?" He took his baseball cap off. "Are they nice?"

"They're okay. The owner, he says hi sometimes. They can be loud, though." She pointed to the television. "The needles they use. I hear them buzzing all day. Make these wavy white lines on the TV when it's on." Perla pointed to a statue resting on top of the set. "But I have Santa Clara there for help."

He rose and walked over to the window where the San Antonio statue used to be. Perla had left the space empty since the break-in, afraid the same thing would happen if she put something there.

"And San Antonio?" he asked

"I was robbed," she said. "They busted the window. Took him."

He shook his head, whistling through half-closed lips.

She watched his eyes sweep over the whole of the botánica, passing over the cracked and chipped paint on the ceiling, bubbling in some spots from too much moisture, the mismatched glass cases, the outdated cash register, the overstocked shelves.

He whistled again, then sat back down next to her.

"How are things over in your new place? What's it like?" Perla leaned in, took his hand, and held it.

"It's good," he said. "Really good. Business is better. The owners of the plaza are nice. They have security guards who sit up in a little tower in the middle of the parking lot. At night, they patrol. It's real safe. Real clean. We're happy there."

"I'm glad," she said. "I miss you, but I'm glad the business is better."

"If I would have stayed here, we would have gone under. It was a hard decision, but we had to go." Alfonso got up and said, "Speaking of which, I have to run."

"Stay a little longer," Perla pleaded.

"I can't. I'm on my way to Riverside." He looked at his watch. "I have an appointment." He put his baseball cap on. "I'll stop in again soon, okay? When I'm not in a hurry. In the meantime, if you need something, call us. You have our house number. Here, let me give you the store number." He reached for a scrap of paper and wrote it down. Perla tucked it in her pocket.

She put her arms around him and kissed his forehead. "Andale," she said. "Go. I'll see you soon then."

"Yes," he said. "I'll be back. When I have more time."

Alfonso walked out the door to his truck.

She needed some fresh air. The botánica was empty. Perla locked up and walked toward Best Donuts. She passed by the tattoo shop. Beaded curtains covered the windows. Magazines were stacked on top of a coffee table across from a leopard-print couch with red pillows. The girl who had been in earlier in the morning sat on a chair. Her pant leg was rolled up, and a man with fuzzy sideburns sat beside her on a stool with wheels. He wore latex gloves and was passing an electric needle over a patch of skin on her calf. When the man looked up from the girl's leg and saw Perla standing there, she quickly stepped away and continued walking toward the donut shop.

She wasn't hungry and didn't want to go inside. Instead she stood in the doorway and watched Alice take the empty pastry racks and stack them on top of one another. Perla went over to the newspaper vending machines a few feet away. Her eyes fell on an article printed on the front page of the *Agua Mansa Courier*:

Two San Bernardino County police officers discovered a badly burned body along the banks of the Santa Ana River near the Pepper

Avenue Bridge yesterday morning. The unidentified body was that of a young male, slightly built, and approximately 5'4" in height. Anyone with information as to the victim's identity is asked to call the San Bernardino County Sheriff's Department.

·   ·   ·

The last time she'd opened the closet was when Rodrigo had spent the night. His clothes—stained jeans, a blue sweater, and his jacket—were in a plastic bag next to Guillermo's boots, tan and stained with oil and paint. She took the boots, went out into the living room, and sat on the couch.

Despite wearing two pairs of socks, they still fit too loose. She pulled the laces tight, feeling them squeeze the circulation around her ankles, and knotted them. The boots were heavy with steel-toed tips, and when she stood and tried to lift a foot up, her muscles strained. She went out to the garage and found the backpack stuffed into a storage bin. Perla grabbed a pair of sneakers and socks and went into the kitchen for a white candle and a white cloth.

Along the streetlights lining Rancho Boulevard, the city had strung red-, white-, and blue-striped banners tied to the posts with gold cords. On each was written: AGUA MANSA SUPPORTS ITS BRAVE TROOPS. GOD BLESS AMERICA. The banners flapped violently in the chilled morning wind, and their shadows bent and whipped across the concrete like long black lassos as Perla made her way toward the río.

The sun peeked just above the hills near the arroyo. The sky was purple, and the clouds shone bright yellow. Utility trucks and buses rumbled across the bridge, doing sixty down La Cadena toward Highgrove. She looked at the tall columns. Thick concrete blocks anchored them to the sandy river bottom. Paper bags and old tires were caught in the weeds along the banks.

Like where they found you.

She secured the backpack to her shoulder and followed a trail down the embankment. In the distance, other trails disappeared between weeds and bushes. Some led to the concrete blocks underneath the bridge. Others melted into the water. Still others looped back around into themselves. Reeds bent over the widest section of the river, sprouting up like small is-lands. She set the bag on the ground, then reached inside for an empty mayonnaise jar. The color of Guillermo's boots changed from tan to dark brown when she stepped into the water. It rose just above her ankles, soaking the insides of the boots, her socks, her toes, as she went farther out, past the long green shoots hugging the shore. Where the water was the deepest, the clearest, Perla crouched down and jabbed at the sediment with her finger, and plumes of brown soil rose up. She scooped up some water in the jar and screwed the lid back on.

She turned back now, and walked up the embankment, water sloshing in the boots. She leaned against the rocks at the edge of the rise and, from the backpack, took out the dry sneakers and socks she had brought and changed into them. She wrapped the wet boots and socks in a plastic bag and placed them in the backpack, then zipped it up.

She heard the slow groan of tractors and looked across the river, saw them churning land and felt the ground quiver as the cranes scooped out mounds of dirt to level out the soil. The roofs of the two-story houses pointed up at the sky like arrows. They rose past the brick wall that separated the perimeter of the new development from the path of the arroyo. Perla imagined what it must have looked like hundreds of years ago: the river wide and deep, dark blue and teeming with fish, tribes of hunters living in round huts woven from straw and grass, animals grazing in the fields where houses would soon be.

The sun's white light bounced off the water. Beneath the bridge, the river was little more than a few scattered puddles. It didn't move. It settled around the tall grasses and old crates tossed from the side of the road, and she pictured it continuing to the ocean, gathering force as other tributaries merged with it, widening it, the water swift and strong, carving and smoothing out the sides of hills and mountains.

*   *   *

A school bus stopped near the Galena Court street sign. Children climbed up the steps, one by one, when the double doors swung opened. The driver wore a sweater draped over her shoulders, and music played from a radio near the steering wheel. The bus pulled away, the heads of the children bouncing up and down in their seats.

Sale circulars and flyers were taped to the screen door's handle. She made her way around the back. Laundry hung on the clotheslines—sheets with faded images of bears and butterflies, a waitress uniform, towels, and bibs.

From the backpack, she took the white cloth and draped it on the steps leading to the back door. In the center, she placed the jar of river water next to the white candle that she lit. She followed the concrete walkway around the house, sprinkling Holy Water from the vials she'd filled after Mass and reciting the Twenty-third Psalm. Next to the purple sage bush by the back steps, she cleared a spot by brushing away some dried leaves and pulling up a bundle of weeds. She flattened the soil with her knuckles. With her finger she drew a small circle. In the center she placed the stone head of Elegguá.

The knob was missing from the door, and splinters poked her wrist when she reached out to touch the hole in the wood. She could see into the kitchen. Perla looked down at her altar. The río water had settled now. She stared at the top of Elegguá's head, took a deep breath, then pushed the door open and went in.

The kitchen table was gone; only the scraps of cardboard remained, kicked into a corner behind the back door. The dead cockroaches had been swept away. The floor in the living room was stained, and broken shards of glass crunched under her feet. In the center of the room was a bike with a missing wheel. There were plastic soda bottles, sleeping bags, and a green kerosene lantern on top of a plywood stand. By the door was a trash bag stuffed with garbage, brown liquid seeping out of one side onto the floor. Graffiti covered the walls. Someone had written: TURK, WHERE ARE YOU GOING? THIS IS HOME.

The air smelled of garbage and cigarettes. She continued down the hall and stepped into the bathroom. The tiles by the toilet were cracked and broken. There were yellow spots of urine in the bathtub, soiled baby diapers, and syringes in a trash can.

The mattress was still in the bedroom, but it was stripped of the sheets and pillowcases. She avoided stepping on the spot stained with blood, walking around it to the door. In a corner of the closet beside a paper bag stuffed with fast food wrappers she saw a pile of clothes: underwear; a shirt with a grinning orange cat; a pair of jeans with daisies sewn into the knees. The sleeves were buried beneath a black trench coat with metal clasp buttons. The flannel material was still soft, the colors still bright and deep. She recognized the pattern—black and red checks. They were the sleeves of Guillermo's shirt, the one she had given Rodrigo to wear the day he vanished.

Perla's hands shook as she took the sleeves and placed them inside the backpack.

Outside, the concrete path was dry, the drops of Holy Water long since evaporated. The water inside the jar had settled, and the white candle burned low and warm in the glass votive. Elegguá watched everything from the bushes with his cowrie shell eyes. She didn't know what to think any-more—whether to stay or go, whether to call the police office in San Bernardino or not. She knelt beside the altar and cried.

*   *   *

Before opening on Saturday, Perla walked to Wyatt Elementary. She sat down on the bleachers in the park next to the school. The playground was empty. In the distance, the wind pushed the swings, and she imagined phan-tom children sitting on the seats, kicking their legs, pumping themselves higher and higher.

When you were alive, viejo, I came here every afternoon and watched the kids run-ning around on the asphalt, chasing big red balls and crows that flew down from the sky. Sometimes I brought my lunch and sat from morning until their last recess. From these benches, I could never see their faces, so I would pick one out from the crowd and say to myself, "That one there. That's ours." I'd imagine myself standing over by the gate with all the other parents. Waiting there. For our baby.

Perla got up and walked over, pressing her hands against the fence sepa-rating the park from the school. She knew he was gone now. She could feel it. She ached, remembering his bruises, the way his face looked, swollen and blue from the beatings. She saw the teeth marks on his back and the ciga-rette burns on his hands.

That wasn't him. He's fine. He's still alive. He found his brother. She squeezed her eyes shut tight and gripped the metal fence and concentrated. *His brother will take care of him now. He'll be fine. He'll go to school. Learn things. Grow up and be successful. His parents will be proud.*

Perla breathed in deep and exhaled. She wished that life for him. She wished it again and again.

She moved away from the fence and sat back down. She looked out across the asphalt playground stretching before her, flat and smooth, like a wide road without lanes.

There were no customers waiting when she got back to the botánica. She looked at the chipped corners of the display case, the nicks and scratches on the wooden bookcases, the silver strips of duct tape patching up a hole in the wall, and the clunky rotary phone sitting on a stack of phone books, some dating back to when the area code was still 714.

She reached for the book of saints she had taken that night at the duplex with Teresa. Rubber bands were stretched over the cover to keep the sheets of paper from falling out. She touched it and began removing the rubber bands but stopped herself.

A snow globe sat at the very edge of the main glass counter across from her. Perla had bought it from a deaf girl who handed her a card asking for a donation. Inside, there was a small blue lake shaped like a kidney bean with miniature ducks swimming on its surface. White and blue swirls of powder swished about—covering the tops of the fake plastic trees and people by the lake, the cars, the mountain peaks in the background—when she turned it upside down. They were lucky to be in there, she told herself. In that perfect world, where people breathed water instead of air, where nothing ever changed and you could only go so far, where the only interruption was the occasional shake right before a downpour of glitter.

Braceras

Our house is crowded with naked bodies. Some lean against the walls. The ones that don't have legs, the ones that are just torsos with heads, lie on top of the dining table near my mom's sewing machine. Bare arms are scattered around my dad's favorite recliner; I imagine women trapped beneath the floor trying to claw their way out.

My mom started sewing about a year ago to earn some extra cash and to busy herself. She said she was at that age when women need things to do, things to keep their hands and minds busy and going once their children are grown. She sews up tears in nurse's uniforms and cheerleading outfits, alters skirts, and lets out waistbands. Her clientele consists mainly of the neighbors on our block and, every now and again, the stray person off the street who happens to come across the flyers taped around town.

This morning, I find her working on Norma Sánchez's quinceañera dress. She takes a spool of thread, unwinds a piece, and breaks it off with her teeth. She's beautiful even in the dull morning light. Her hair's pinned up, and curls fall down and cradle the backs of her ears. She wears her nice charcoal pants and a lavender blouse with a pattern of orchids along the collar. She's all done up, waiting. My dad's blowing into town.

He's gone all the time. We go months without seeing or hearing from him. When he comes home, he sticks around for a few days, sits in his recliner, and watches soccer on TV. He takes my mom out to a restaurant, then they come home, play their oldies, and dance around the house in their slippers, sipping vodka tonics and smoking cigarettes, the air in the kitchen looking like El Yanquee nightclub, heavy with love.

He takes off in the middle of the night without saying goodbye. He calls us from the road the next day. "I'm delivering to Sacramento. Then it's on to Seattle. I'll send some cash in the mail," he says. We'll get a money order from him, more than enough to last until he blows back in again.

He's always moving. That's the way it's been with that man, my mom says. Pata de perro, she calls him. Vago. Ever since we started going out, he's been like this, she says. I knew it when I married him.

I know some things about him, too, I want to say.

It gets me mad, him not being around like he should. There are times I want to tell my mom to just kick him to the curb. To move on and stop depending on him. He's never around. When he is, he acts real big and bad, trying to lay down the law. Calling shots. Lecturing me about the way I dress or about doing something with my life like my kid brother who's in the Marines.

"What are you gonna do? Paint for the rest of your life? Be some hippie starving artist?" he tells me when I'm out in the garage assembling my supplies.

"So now you're my guidance counselor? Why don't you try being around first instead of away doing who knows what?"

He shoots me a look and gets real close to me, his face flushed. "Watch that mouth, desgraciada. Don't forget who pays for all this. That makes me the man of the house."

"I know what you are," I say, putting my paintbrushes down. "I got your number," I say. "I don't go for your good guy act. They all do. But I don't. No, sir."

*   *   *

Everyone in Agua Mansa knows my dad, Enrique Medina. Enrique the big-rig driver. Enrique who parks the rig in the empty lot at the end of our block when he's home. He's the nicest man. A real sweet guy you want on your side. You need something, Enrique can get it for you. He's solid. A good citizen. Honest. He'll never shade you. Last Friday of every month is when Enrique rolls back into town, people say. Go to the Lickety Split. The booth in the back by the jukebox. You'll find him there. Playing cards and knocking back some cold pistos. Telling stories about his life on the road. Go up to him, tell him you need something—a good mechanic, a coyote to smuggle a cousin or paisano over, a few bills until the check comes. He's hooked up. A straight-up Santa Claus. Enrique Medina's everywhere. He's real connected, they say. He should run for mayor. Real suave with his fancy watches and rings, his silk shirts and bolo ties, and those cowboy boots with shiny silver tips.

He's a real together guy, they say. Takes great care of that family of his. His wife only works because she wants to. She doesn't need to. His son's a Marine. But the daughter. She's a problem. Was in a few fights when she was in high school and got suspended. Just paints murals around town. Riding around on that chopper of hers. A studded leather jacket and combat boots like some thug. She's been a handful for Don Enrique. Poor man. He works so hard to give the family everything and she goes and acts up like that. How could she? He's such a sweet papá. It must break his heart sometimes.

Growing up, I used to believe all the talk about my dad. My brother and I always had everything we needed. Not like our friends whose parents struggled to pay their bills. We never had to worry. It was a fun childhood. Stacks of Christmas presents wrapped up all sweet and nice. Birthday parties with cakes and piñatas spinning from the patio beams. Whenever he came home from one of his long hauls, there was always a present for me beside him in the rig's cab. Me climbing those chrome steps. Hot engine air blasting up my legs. My dad smiling, behind the wheel. Blowing the horn and my brother and I would cheer and clap our hands. It was all real perfect.

This one time my mom got sick. She had to be in the hospital for a week. Some stomach infection. I was four, and Raúl had just turned two. We were still too young to be in school, and there was no one around to take care of us. One morning, he woke us up early. He changed Raúl's Pampers and left him in his pajamas. He made me get dressed and then stood behind me near the kitchen sink. He sprayed my hair with water the way my mom would and combed it, brushing so hard he tugged back the corners of my eyes. But by the time we were walking out the door, the ponytail had started to unravel, and my hair poofed out on one side.

We took a drive in his Nova and ended up in Rialto, in front of this faded ocher house. The backyard was a dirt lot, and there was an old trailer parked under a lemon tree.

My dad had a key. He opened the door, and we walked in.

Stuffed animals and dolls were arranged on the love seat against the far wall. On the TV was a picture of a boy a year or two older than me. He was dressed in a white shirt and a navy tie. Stuck to one side of the frame was a red ribbon. Second Prize, it read, Jefferson Elementary, First Grade Spelling Bee.

My dad pushed some of the stuffed animals aside and told me to sit down. "Watch tu brother," he said as Raúl tried to crawl under the coffee table. "I'll be back."

He walked down the hall. A few minutes later, my dad came out with this woman who was dressed in a pair of tight jeans with a label that read *Kit Kats* sewn onto the back pocket. Her auburn hair was swept up in a bun, all neat with bobby pins and clips. She was younger than my mom. She bent down and took my hand.

"¿Eres Lluvia?" she said.

I nodded.

"¿Y qué pasó aquí?" She touched my ponytail and the side of my head.

My father laughed. "I tried it."

"Hmm. We'll fix it." She winked at me and smiled.

After my father left, she picked Raúl up, and we walked down the hall. We passed the room that must have belonged to the boy. There was a blanket with a race car on it draped over the bed and a radio and a stack of books on the floor. The woman led us to a room at the end of the hallway. She sat my brother on her bed. Near the door was a small vanity. There were tubes of lipstick in gold and silver cases. Bottles of perfume and jars of powders and creams sat on top of a glass tray. I saw tweezers and nail files and a bag of cotton balls.

When my brother fell asleep, she took some pillows and arranged them around his body. "So he won't roll over and fall off," she whispered.

She led me to the bathroom and undid my ponytail. She took a wooden stool and placed it in front of her.

"Anda," she said, gently nudging me.

I stepped on it, the edge of the sink coming just below my chin. She combed my hair back, and I watched her face and mine framed by the mirror's thin silver border. The shower curtain behind her had a pattern of flamingos frozen in flight. She gathered and swept up loose strands of my hair the way my mother did every morning.

On the day my mom was to be released, my father brought along Raúl's stroller. He gave the woman some money and kissed my brother and me goodbye before leaving. After he woke from his nap, the woman placed Raúl in the stroller, and we walked to a McDonald's a few blocks away. She bought us Happy Meals and sat at a booth inside the restaurant while we jumped around the Playland with our shoes off. She watched us through the window the whole time—her elbow resting on the table, her chin in the palm of her hand. She smiled and blew kisses at us. Raúl was wearing shorts. When he fell on the ground and hurt his knee and cried, she ran out to him. She poured her cup of soda out on the ground. She took some of the ice cubes and wrapped them in a napkin. She placed them over his scrape and tried to calm him down.

She picked Raúl up, showing him a picture of Ronald McDonald and Grimace painted on one side of the slide. "Mira. Mira a los payasos," she said in a silly voice. She took Raúl's hand and made him wave at them. He laughed.

On our way home, we stopped off at the grocery store. My brother was out of apple juice, so we got him a carton and a box of animal crackers. When she asked what I wanted, I pointed to a display of construction paper, colored pencils, and rulers near the registers.

Back at her house, I sat on the floor and spread my papers out. I drew a picture for her of the Playland—the jungle gym, the ball pit, and a slide spiraling up to the sky where I'd sketched billowy clouds and a sun with a smiling face. I showed the three of us next to the slide holding hands.

I was sleeping when my father came back. I got up from the couch and walked into the kitchen. She was leaning up against the stove. My father had one arm around her waist. His other hand was shoved inside her blouse, moving around under the tight black fabric. He was kissing her neck. Her eyes were open, and she was looking at the refrigerator door. She'd taped the drawing I'd given her there, right next to a school lunch menu printed on fluorescent fuchsia paper.

Before we left, she hugged us tight and kissed our cheeks. She made sure to wipe away her lipstick marks and smoothed back my hair, then buttoned my brother's jacket.

"Be good to your mamá," she said. "She'll still be weak."

On the car ride from the hospital, my mom whispered, her voice small and scratchy, that she was glad to be going home. She coughed and spit into a paper cup the nurse had given her. I reached over the seat and put my hand on her shoulder. She took it and with her other hand flipped the sun visor down and adjusted the mirror so that she could see me. She tilted her head to one side.

"I missed you," she said.

She spent the next few days in her robe and walked around the house in those booties they give you at the hospital, the ones with the rubber padding on the soles.

When she was feeling better, she combed my hair in the bathroom. I couldn't bring myself to look at her reflection. At least not right away.

·   ·   ·

A natural, my art teacher Miss López had called me when she saw the pencil sketch of a poodle I drew when I was a freshman. A natural artist.

"You gotta nurture this power," Miss López told me.

That's what she called it: power.

"You know the Clínica Mujer?" she asked me a few weeks before graduation. We were behind the art building soaking paintbrushes in laundry detergent buckets full of cold water.

"On Alta Vista?"

"Yeah."

"What of it?"

"Well, they asked me to paint this mural on the side of their building. Why don't you help me? I'll pay you."

"I've never painted a mural before."

"Relax. It's easy," she said. "You ever painted a room in your house before?"

"Once," I said.

"It's the same thing. Except you're doing it outdoors and doing it on a scaffold using more than one color of paint."

"Fine," I said. "I could use some extra cash."

The mural was of a group of women holding a banner reading "Al Futuro." To the Future. We used vibrant colors, greens and yellows and reds. We put a rainbow in the sky and hot air balloons and doves perched on the branches of citrus trees. We included all different types of women—Latina, black, white, Asian. We showed their faces strong, their eyes looking straight ahead. They're holding hands, all of them united.

Miss López was the one who suggested I start up the mural thing around here. After we finished up at the Clínica Mujer, she turned to me and said, "You're good at this. Why don't you keep at it? You could paint murals for restaurants and shops. It's great advertising for them."

"Alone?"

"Yeah. Alone. You can use my supplies to get started."

I inherited drums of exterior acrylic paints, tackle boxes full of paintbrushes with wide fat angles and thin tips, drop cloths, and industrial-sized cans of turpentine. Her scaffold was made out of two A-frame ladders and two thick sheets of plywood.

"It's kind of a pain in the ass," she said, showing me how to set it up, how to adjust the ends of the pieces of plywood on each rung of the ladders. "It's not very wide. But it's easy to transport because it's collapsible."

I got my neighbor Frankie D to help me move everything from Miss López's garage to mine.

"What you setting out to do, girl?" Frankie said, laughing. "Opening a paint supply shop?"

"I'm gonna dress this town up," I said.

"With used cans of paint?"

"No, stupid. With murals."

I start first by looking at the space. I try to get a feel of the rhythm around it, try to sense the flow of energy to figure out what colors I should use, what shades of green or red or brown. I touch the walls with my palms, become familiar with the bumps and grooves, with the cracks and chips.

None of that seems to matter, though. Because the trend around Agua Mansa, especially with the veterano cholo types, is low-riders and eagles and Aztec princes and princesses decked out in feathered headdresses and skimpy loincloths. Like right now, the piece I'm doing for Lucky's Quick

Mart is an eagle in flight with American and Mexican flags in the background, the word UNITY written across the bottom. I've done so many like this that it's automatic for me. But Miss López told me to try not to resist. Muralists, she says, are artists of the people. Their work is public art, art that needs to reflect the people, their hopes and desires.

I stop and look at my watch. It's later than I thought. I'm glad because I can't wait to get home today. My dad left early this morning, and I don't have to worry about dealing with his attitude.

When he drove off, my mom cried again, of course.

"He forget that?" I asked, pointing at a shirt of his she held.

She nodded. "And you know me. I always get like this when he leaves."

"Let it go. He'll be fine."

"I know. It's just, you hear these stories. About accidents on the road. I always think, 'What if next time he doesn't come back?' Sometimes at night I lie in bed thinking of him. Out there. All alone."

He's not alone, I wanted to tell her. He's probably got a lady in every city from here to Seattle. I probably got a grip of half brothers and sisters. I thought about the woman in Rialto years ago. The picture of that boy resting on top of the TV.

Instead I stayed quiet. I let her keep seeing what she wants to. Just like Raúl. Every time I try and get him to talk to me about Dad, he changes the subject or makes up an excuse about having to go.

Let them, I think to myself. Let them see what they want.

The eagle's giant wings are spread out across the side of the store, and they look so real, like they could carry me away across that painted sky, far bluer than the hazy one above me now. Drums of paint crowd the top of the scaffold, and I move them to one side and step back to survey my work. Gathered in the parking lot is a flock of seagulls. They look different from the ones I remember seeing at the beach the last time I was there. These are dingy, their feathers messy and ruffled. They're awkward and clumsy, picking over piles of trash, out of place in the middle of the asphalt.

From below the scaffold, a voice says, "Hey." An old woman stands there, holding two plastic shopping bags filled with groceries. Thick-rimmed sunglasses cover her eyes, and I can see my face in their lenses. "How much do you charge?"

"Depends," I say.

"I want a mural on my building. He says your prices are good. How much?"

"Depends on what you want. On the detail. On any of the supplies I may need."

"Okay," she says.

"What are you looking for?"

"A Virgen. The Virgen of Guadalupe."

"Where?"

"Botánica Oshún in the Prospect Center." She pauses. "Do you know how there's that one side that faces the empty field?" She points across the parking lot in the direction of the gulls.

"What of it?"

"People are dumping sofas and broken chairs, leaning them on the wall and taking off. It's getting full of graffiti and cuss words."

"I've got about two more days here. I can come by later this week to check it out."

"Good," she says. "I'll be expecting you."

.   o   o

I stand in the bathroom washing smeared paint from my arms. In the medicine cabinet, there's a shelf with his shaving creams and gels, his razor blade with stubble still caught in the blade. I want to take all that and chuck it out the window.

After I'm done eating, the phone rings, and my mom grabs it. She says something before hanging up. She stands there with her head cocked at an angle, and it makes me remember the car ride from the hospital.

"Who was it? Telemarketer?" I ask, washing my plate in the sink.

"No," she says. "It's just this voice. A woman."

"Wrong number." I put my plate on the rack to dry. "Why are you spacing?"

"She was asking for your father."

I stay quiet.

"It's nothing," she says. "Just nobody."

She walks over to the sewing machine and goes at it. She doesn't let up all night. I hear the whirring from my room. Stopping. Starting. Stopping. Starting. And it sounds painful and angry. I turn my stereo on and flip

through some CDs stacked on the floor—Rammstein, Wumpscut, Skinny
Puppy. I put one in and blast it, taking in the fast industrial beats. Like buzz-
saws and jackhammers battling it out with drums and heavy guitar riffs. I
stomp around my room until I'm sweating and out of breath, singing along
to KMFDM's "Juke-Joint Jezebel."

·   ·   ·

Mom's still asleep when I hop on my Yamaha and head off to the botánica.
When I get there, the old woman's standing behind the counter opening up
a white jar.

The first thing she says to me is, "Keep it simple."

"Duh," I whisper.

"I want a sweet Virgen." She fills small plastic Ziploc bags full of green
powder. "Something special," she tells me.

None of the pictures I had of the Virgin were very detailed, and it was
hard getting a clear shot of her face. I was going through a shoe box of old
photos and came across this one of my mom sitting on a chair in a house I
didn't recognize. It must have been at a cousin's party, I guessed. I could see
balloons in the background and a boy wearing a party hat. In the picture,
my mom looks to one side, her mouth open. She's laughing. Her hands are
clasped over her knee. She's real young. I can tell this was way before my father.

That's the face I use for the Virgin. The image itself is the standard one,
like any you'll find on a thousand other walls. La Virgen's in the center of a
circle of gold and yellow rays. She wears a deep crimson dress and, over
that, an emerald cape with gold trim and a pattern of gold stars that covers
her head and body. Her hands are cupped under her chin in prayer. Her face
looks away to the side, her eyes downcast. An angel holds the crescent
moon on which she stands.

"This is what I got," I say.

I unfold the sketch and hand it over. She walks over to the window
where the light is better. I stroll around the store, looking into the glass
cases where red and aqua stones are displayed next to necklaces of feather
and yarn. I see jade pendants and ankhs and crucifixes. I flip through the
novenas and prayer cards of Saint Christopher, Saint Martín de Porres, and

Saint Ignatius, arranged in a clear tray with individual slots. A small figurine of an angel wielding a sword stands guard on the other side of the register. Cut pieces of glass encircle the statue's base, and the sunlight bouncing off them casts rainbows across the ceiling.

"It's nice," the old woman says, handing it back over to me. "Very nice."

"When should I start?"

"You always dress like that when you work?" She reaches over the counter, tugs at the straps of my overalls, and glances at my boots.

"Yeah. Do you always dress *like that?*" I point.

"Yes. I'm comfortable. Are you comfortable?"

"I'm fine," I say. "I'm always fine."

"Then you should start now before all the good light is gone." She points at the door. "I'll pay you up front tomorrow. Cash." She turns away from me and continues filling her plastic bags. "Anything else you need, just let me know."

        ·   ·   ·

For a small fee, Frankie D helps me haul all my supplies to the sites where I do my murals.

"Why'd ya get that thing?" he says, pointing to my Yamaha. "If you knew you were gonna be dragging all this shit, you shoulda just bought a pickup. Hell, a rig like your old man's."

"I like to feel free," I say. "I like the wind in my face."

He helps me set up the ladders. When I tell him it's fine, that I can handle it, he says, "I don't mind. Got nowhere to go. Precious took the baby to the park."

When we're done, Frankie picks up his tools and pulls out of the parking lot toward home.

I don't see much of the old lady the first few days on the job. She seems to spend a good part of the day in the store while I'm working. She leaves the back door open for me in case I need to go to the bathroom. I cut through there, past the shelves stocked with rolls of paper towels and jugs of glass cleaner. A small Shiva statue sits on the second shelf. It's in between bottles of hand soap and a box of trash bags, and every time I walk by, I touch its forehead with my thumb.

Today she comes out of the store and hands me a glass of lemonade and watches as I work on the rays around the Virgin's shoulders. It's morning and already I can tell that the day's going to be a warm one.

"You've got a pretty name," she says. "Who chose it?"

"My dad," I say, turning to look at her. "What's it to you?"

"I'm just wondering. Does he like your murals?"

"What's with the twenty questions?"

"Nothing. I'm just curious."

"Haven't seen you since I started. Where've you been hiding yourself?"

"Doing work," she says.

"It's just you that runs the place?"

"Just me."

The Yamaha's parked a few feet away. I take a sip of the lemonade and watch her go over to it. She touches the gas tank, runs her hands across the seat, stoops over and examines the chrome tailpipe and the back tire.

She asks, "You like motorbikes?"

"That's why I got one," I say, finishing up the lemonade and crunching a piece of ice.

"Why?" She doesn't look up at me when she asks this.

"Why what?"

"Why do you like them? Don't you get scared zooming around so fast? I've seen how these things fly. Why didn't you get a car instead?"

"Because I don't like getting stuck in traffic, okay? I like my bike. I like to be able to get on it and take off."

"Where to?"

I hand her the glass of lemonade. "Here. Thanks."

I turn around and continue painting.

A few days later, the old woman brings out a lawn chair. She sets it up directly behind me and pops open an umbrella. Last night she watched a segment on the news about sunburns and skin cancer.

"I have to be careful," she says, adjusting herself in her chair, draping a towel over her shoulders. From her pocket, she takes out the same pair of sunglasses she was wearing the day she commissioned me and puts them on. "Don't you get scared? Working out in the sun?"

"No."

She calls me hija and says she has an oil inside the shop. "It doesn't have sunscreen, hija. But it can give you some protection."

"I'm cool," I say. "Look." I hold both arms out. "See? No cancer here."

"Huh. Not yet. Then ten years from now you get this spot and next thing you know it's all over."

She keeps the towel wrapped around her shoulders and walks back into the shop. A few minutes later she comes out holding a small vial and a glass of lemonade.

"Come down." She goes over and sits back in her chair.

"I'm working here."

"Yes," she says. "You're working for me. I'm the boss. And if I say you come down here, you come down here." She unscrews the cap and pours some into her hand and rubs with both palms.

"What is it?" I ask

"It's an oil for strength. To attract good vibes. Give me your arms."

"How am I supposed to drink the lemonade?"

"After," she says.

I stand before her and hold out both arms. She begins by kneading the oil into my skin. I smell mint and cucumber, and it makes my skin feel cool. My muscles expand and relax. She pinches my knuckles, unravels the knots I feel there.

"Thanks," I say when she finishes.

"Es nada."

I turn around and face the mural. The Virgin's body's already sketched in, the traces of black lines forming the hands and the head. She looks out across the junk field.

From behind the old woman says, "You're Enrique Medina's little girl, aren't you?"

"Yeah."

"He's real popular around here."

"So I hear."

"He gets around, your father. All over the place."

I say, "It's what he does. What he's good at."

"Yeah," she says. "I know."

For a long time we're silent. Then I ask, "What do you think? You like how it's coming along?"

"It's nice," she says.

"Good," I say. "Because I'm not changing a thing."

She laughs at me. "I like you," she says. "You've got a strong spirit."

                            *   *   *

The house is empty when I get home. Everything's eerie with just me and the mannequins standing around, greeting me when I shut the door. I decide to take a shower and clean up before dinner. When I walk into my mom's room to grab a clean towel from the stack on her bed, I notice a bottle of pills on the dresser.

"What's going on?" I ask, holding the pills when she gets home.

She shakes her head and sits on the couch. "That," she says, tiredly. "That's nothing."

"Looks like a lot more than nothing." I stand in front of her when she doesn't answer. "Mamá?" I say softly when I see she's crying.

At first, she says, it felt like nothing. Abdominal pains. Like when you've eaten something that didn't agree with you.

"I took Tylenol," she says. "And it went away." She looks at me and hesitates before going on.

"But?"

"I thought it was a yeast infection. So I bought something at the farmacia. But nada. The doctor ran a test a week ago. She says it's an infection. She gave me antibiotics."

"That's it?" I look at the pills.

She stays quiet, kneading her purse's straps.

I sit next to her. "Tell me, Mom."

"She says it's gonorrhea."

"Jesus," I say. "Jesus Christ."

"She said I better call all the people I've slept with. I'm not some puta coming off the street, I told her. Maybe I got it from using a public toilet, I said. Or touching a doorknob."

"That fucker," I say.

"Who?"

"Him. Dad. That pig. That whore."

She shakes her head. "It wasn't him."

"What do you mean? Yeah it was. You don't get this by sitting on a toilet. It was Dad."

"Leave him out of this. I'll take care of it. He's a good man. Worked hard. You and your brother had everything. It's not his fault."

"It's not his fault? So whose is it? Yours? Are you running around screwing other men?"

"No," she shouts. "No." Her purse falls on the floor.

"Then?"

"Don't disrespect your father."

"He's disrespected you. This family. Open your eyes. He's fucking other women. Has been for years. Stop defending him. Stop painting this picture of him all sweet and perfect."

She gets up from the couch and walks over to the mannequins. "Why do you say all these things? Where are you getting this from?"

"Everyone around here knows, Mom," I say. "Everyone except you."

She takes the bottle and hurls it against the wall. It shatters, and the pills fall to the ground, rolling under the dining table and the couches, his recliner, and the TV. She throws herself on the floor, pounding on it with her hands, scratching it until some of her nails break. I crouch beside her, and I hold her in my arms. I hold and hold her.

*   *   *

The mural's done. The old woman comes out with a camera. She adjusts her glasses and takes some snapshots.

"Stand there," she orders me. "To the side."

I lean up against the wall, my thumbs hooked to the belt loops of my carpenter pants. She snaps a few like that before having me push the bike in front of the mural. I sit on it, and she snaps more, the camera clicking fast.

She gives me an extra hundred bucks and tells me, "Stop looking like a biker. Go to a school. Study art."

"I can't," I say. "I don't wanna leave my mom."

"You don't want to leave your mom. Your mom doesn't want to leave your father."

I look up at her, surprised. I flip my baseball cap backward and say, "What do you know?"

"I know your father's a cabrón."

"Everybody around here's a cabrón."

"It's more complicated, isn't it? There are feelings involved. History. There's too much history."

Before I leave, the old woman writes my address down and says she's going to mail me some copies of the pictures. She says she recited a prayer for me and my mom last night. To help us in our situation. She lit a candle to Saint Rita of Cascia, she says. The patrona of difficult marriages, of sickness and desperate causes.

"Tell your mamá," she says as I start my motorcycle up and rev the engine. "Tell her La Santa Rita will help her."

○   ○   ○

"I'm cutting off his balls," I say to my brother when he calls. I'm in the house alone. My mom's at the market. "I swear I'm cutting off his balls the next time he walks through the door."

"That's real mature, Lluvia," he says.

"There you go taking his side again."

"I'm not," he says. "See, this is why I hate talking with you about this. Because you always accuse me of defending him."

"You do. You should be pissed. Pissed he did this to her. That he's been lying all these years."

"I am pissed. I'm just saying to put yourself in her shoes. Imagine how frustrated and confused she's feeling right now. What would she do if she kicked him out?"

"She'd *do* just fine," I say. I look out and see my mom putting her purse and some grocery bags on the dining table.

"Who is it?" she asks.

"Raúl," I say.

"Here," she says, reaching out to take the receiver from my hand. "Hi," she says. "I know," she tells him. "I do. I will, I will. I love you."

She hangs up the phone and is quiet for a long time. She goes over to the dining table and starts putting the groceries away.

"Your father's coming in tonight. He called when you were out this morning," she tells me. "I don't know what to do."

I look at the naked mannequins, posed like beauty pageant contestants, their smiles painfully awkward, their eyes blank and empty. "I wanna take you somewhere," I say.

"Now?"

"Now," I say, leading her by the hand out to my motorcycle.

"Let's take the car," she says when I start it up. "You know that thing scares me."

"No," I tell her. "Get on." I give her my helmet.

"I have to put the groceries away. I have things to do before your father gets here."

"Just get on, Mom." I rev the engine, and she steps back. "Come on."

She looks back at the house, then at me. She puts the helmet on, climbs on the bike, and we take off down our street.

The botánica's closed when we pull up to the shopping center. I park my bike in front of the mural and shine the headlight on the wall, illuminating the image.

"Look, Mom," I say. "Look what I made."

She walks up to the wall slowly and touches the fresh paint—the harsh grays and blacks of metal and stone, the muted greens and browns of earth and soil, the gentle blues and purples of water and sky, and the gleaming golds and silvers of light and Heaven.

In the far background are the sharp and jagged peaks of the San Bernardino Mountains, with white veins trickling down their sides for snow. Stretching from the mountains are fields of citrus trees. The groves fade into new housing tracts, the trees themselves transforming into the skeletons of houses. The dirt rows where migrant farmworkers pick lemons and oranges melt into the concrete streets of Agua Mansa. The city spreads out before you, a grid of gray avenues and boulevards lined with shops and buildings—Tina's Taco Haven, the Agua Mansa Palms, San Salvador's church, our house. The streets are shaded with eucalyptus trees and pines and oaks, electrical wires tangled among their branches. There are cell phone towers disguised as palm trees, their steel trunks tagged with graffiti. A paletero pushes his ice cream cart down Redondo. Ranflas cruise up Descanso. On Meridian, a school bus releases a group of kids carrying Dora the Explorer and Spider-Man back-packs. The 10 runs from left to right with cars and motorcycles and trucks. The north–south streets run down, flowing like tributaries into the Santa Ana in the foreground, widening and expanding it. The río skirts the border of the city, passing through channels and the tall green stalks of wild horsetail and arundo canes. In the bottom right corner, just as the wall is about to end, the water changes. It becomes a strip of turquoise fabric tumbling from the lap of Santa Ana herself, who sits on a bench stitching gold stars onto it by hand.

High above, past the branches and power lines, La Virgen floats on a bed of clouds sprinkled with roses in the center of the sky. The angel still holds her up, his fingers still curled around the crescent moon on which she stands. I kept the dark crimson robe and the emerald cloak dotted with stars. But now, instead of cupped, her hands are open, her arms stretched out. She looks straight ahead and over us all.

"It's you," I say. "Do you see?"

My mother is silent, then she says, "It's me." She says it defiantly. "It's me. Me."

"There was this picture I found of you," I say. "You're so happy in it. You're not wearing a wedding ring. It was before you got married, before Dad."

"I knew what he was when I married him," she tells me. "And that makes me mad the most. I knew and ignored it. I told myself I could change him."

"None of it's your fault," I say.

She turns around and looks out across the junk field. She says, "I keep thinking about those other women. Just like me. Out there somewhere. Waiting for him to get back to them."

"What do you wanna do?"

She puts the helmet on and buttons up her denim jacket. "I don't want us to be there when he comes home tonight. Let's go."

"Where to?" I ask, starting the bike up.

"Let's go," she repeats, getting on. "Let's take off."

My hands squeeze the grips. I rev the engine and we drive away.

I take the freeway on-ramp, and we head west on the 10 toward the ocean. I'm doing ninety, one hundred, then one hundred and fifteen, weaving in and out of traffic so fast that everything's just flashes of color. There's only us and the roar of the engine and the wind. My mother shouts and squeezes my waist tight, and she doesn't let go until we're far enough away.

Feast of
Nuestra Señora de Guadalupe

Holy Mother and Queen of the Americas

Patroness of Mexico, the Americas,

and the New World.

The sirens woke her at one in the morning. Perla got up and stood in the hallway, the water heater gurgling in the closet by the bathroom. In the backyard, lights throbbed, turning the leaves of the avocado tree pink then green then pink again. She tried to look over the fence but could see nothing. After a few minutes she gave up and went back to bed.

The morning was cold and clear and the sky bright blue. Dewdrops covering the tips of the creosote bushes sprinkled her legs as Perla walked through the lot toward the shopping center. On the street corner stood a middle-aged woman and a young girl. The girl held her arm around the woman's waist, and now and again she would stroke the woman's shoulder. Both of their heads were bent, staring at something on the concrete.

On her way to the donut shop to get her morning coffee, Perla passed the tattoo parlor. A fiberglass Santa Claus with a tan button nose and bright red cheeks stood guard near the entrance. Alfonso had never been in the habit of decorating the ninety-nine-cent store for Christmas, but he had moved, and these loud men were now next door. So much around her had changed this year. The botánica had been vandalized and robbed. Rodrigo was gone. *Only me. I'm still the same. Still around.*

Inside Best Donuts, Alice was placing maple bars in a pink box lined with waxed paper. "Did you hear what happened?" she asked, pointing toward the corner with a pair of metal tongs. "Some kid. Coming home last night. He was hit by a car and died on the spot. My grandpa was here baking. Said he heard tires screeching. Didn't think much about it. When he was outside smoking a while later, there were all these cops everywhere."

Perla looked through the lace patterns of snowflakes airbrushed on the windows at the women on the corner. An old man was with them now, arranging a bouquet of flowers around a wooden cross staked into the ground.

"Awful, isn't it?" Alice said. She handed Perla her coffee and left to help someone standing at the edge of the counter.

Perla opened at nine-fifteen. Her first customer was Nancy Pérez.

"How's everything with your father?" Perla asked.

"Worse." Nancy paused, then said, "He's in a coma. Darrell and I are driving to Vegas tonight. You know? I've been a real jerk all these years. I feel so bad. For everything."

Nancy's eyes filled with tears. She put a pair of sunglasses on and crossed her arms. "Anyway, I thought I'd stop by. Maybe buy something. A candle or whatever."

Perla sold her a scapular of Saint Jude for her father to wear, a prayer card of Santa Bárbara, and a white candle to light. She placed these in a paper bag and set it before Nancy.

Nancy opened the bag and peered inside. "My mom will appreciate this. I'll tell her you say hello."

"Please do," Perla said. "And tell her I'm sorry. I'm sorry what I told you to do last time you were in here didn't work."

Nancy looked down at the ground and shook her head. "It was too late by then. But you did all you could. Thank you."

She walked out the front door and drove away.

Later on, Perla helped a woman whose daughter was in the service. From her purse, the woman pulled out a wallet and pointed to a picture of a girl in a military uniform with medals pinned to her lapels. Behind her was a furled American flag, the folds thick.

"She's going away," the woman said. "Her name's Catalina Gómez. She's being sent to the war. I want to give her something. Protection."

Perla reached for the tackle box on the shelf behind the register. She sifted through the compartments filled with silver medallas until she found the one she was looking for.

"Here," she told the woman. "San Cristóbal." Perla threaded a leather shoestring through the eyelet of the medal. "Tell her to wear it all the time. It's the only way it can keep her safe."

When the woman handed Perla a five-dollar bill to pay, Perla took it and gave it back to her. "No," she said. "No."

The woman bowed her head and clasped the medal in both hands. "Once she's home safe," she said, smiling, sweeping her arm across the store, "we'll have a party. And you, everyone, everyone will be invited."

A couple who were leaving the state came in next. They needed help selling their house, they told Perla.

"Where are you going?" she asked them.

"Para Washington," the man said. "Mucho trabajo." When he smiled, Perla saw a thin ribbon of gold outlining a front tooth.

"We have to sell the house fast," his wife said. "My mom, she told me we should buy a statue of San José and bury it in the front yard. Will that work?"

"Bury him upside down," Perla explained, taking the saint from the shelf. "Then the property will sell right away."

It was late afternoon and she was shelving some candles when Rosa arrived.

"I think I'm almost ready for another cut," Perla said to her, tucking loose strands of hair behind her ears.

"Okay. Sure," Rosa said. "You know, I have enough. To rent out a station."

"That's good. Will you be working in a salon now?"

"Eventually. But I'm gonna have to wait awhile." Rosa paused, then touched her stomach. "See, I'm pregnant again, and it looks like I'm gonna have twins. Twins!" she shouted and laughed out loud.

Perla took her hand. "Rosita, that's great."

Rosa said, "I was gonna wait to tell her, but I called my mom right after I found out. We talked for a long time, and she apologized, you know? For the way she acted. She said she was proud of me. Of my life. She said I'd sacrificed a lot, and I'd made good choices."

Perla said, "I'm glad you two are talking again. You'll need her help when they come." She pointed to Rosa's stomach.

"Not just hers. You told me way back then. You said to come back here when I needed this." She pointed to the shelves. "Well, I'm gonna need it. And I'll need your help, too. So get ready, okay?"

After she left, Perla took the book of saints from the shelf below the register. She pressed it against her chest and tried to remember what she had written on all those scraps of paper. Perla pictured him, forming her words over and over, chanting her life like a prayer.

She went over to the front window to watch the crowd on the corner. A man in a baseball cap sat on a lawn chair, sipping out of a sports bottle, talking on a cell phone. Girls in sweatshirts and boys in football jackets held each other or buried their hands in their faces and cried. There was a teddy bear squeezing a heart next to the cross on the ground, and balloons and poems and prayers written on pieces of paper were taped to the street sign.

She opened the door and walked across the parking lot.

Near the corner the woman and the girl stood beside the old man who held a handkerchief up to his nose. The girl looked up at her. She pointed to the book of saints Perla held and asked, "Are you from the church?"

"No," Perla said. "I just wanted to find out. What happened?" She looked over at the old man and the woman. "Qué pasó?"

"Lo mataron," the old man said. "Lo mataron anoche." He pointed to the cross where the name *Joey Ramírez* was written in thick black letters.

The woman was heavy with curly brown hair and chapped lips. She wore a sweater with the word *Forgiven* knitted across the chest. Dark purple spots covered the bottom part of the sweater. "My son," she responded. "Joey. My son. He was coming home from his girlfriend's house last night. Crossing." She pointed to the street. "A car ran him over and took off."

"Venía llegando," the old man said. He tried to adjust and straighten the cross when a gust of wind blew it over. He took his shoe off and used it to drive the cross further into the ground.

"They need stoplights here. Not stop signs. They just drive through those," the girl said, twisting her hair into a bun and tying it with an elastic band wrapped around her wrist. "But nobody's gonna do nothing. If there'd been a stoplight here my brother wouldn't have been killed. Nobody'll do nothing, though. Just watch."

Three boys standing by her whispered to one another and shook their heads. They looked away when the dead boy's mother began to cry and wring her hands.

"He was walking across the street when the car hit him," she shouted. "And it threw him off the road. He crawled. He crawled here. And he died right here. His blood," she said. She pointed to the stains on her sweater, then to a spot on the concrete where no one stood.

Seven-day veladoras surrounded it, one lined up next to the other, forming the outline of a body. Nuestra Señora de la Caridad del Cobre, La Mano Poderosa, San Martín de Porres, and Santa Marta outlined part of his left arm. There was San Judas Tadeo on the heel of his left foot, La Anima Sola near his inner thigh, and El Santo Niño de Atocha by one knee. El Sagrado Corazón, El Cristo Rey, and San Martín Caballero crowned his head and shaped part of a shoulder.

Someone had leaned a picture of Joey against the stop sign. In it, he knelt, wearing gold football pants and a purple jersey. A helmet sat on the grass in front of him. In the background were empty bleachers.

"So much of his blood on the sidewalk. And they washed it away and it went down into the gutter. His blood is in the gutter." The woman pointed to her sweater again.

"I'm sorry," Perla said, gripping the book. "Did they catch who did it?"

The old man said, "No."

"Why would they do that? Hit someone and leave?" the girl said, untying her hair again, and it fell around her shoulders. "Pieces of shit. I hope someone they know gets run over."

"Lena," the old man said. "Cálmate."

"I'm pissed, Grandpa." Lena kicked the metal street sign over and over with the tip of her sandal. "I'm fucking pissed."

"My Joey," the woman cried out. "He never hurt nobody. He was coming home. Just coming home." She turned away from the crowd and took a few steps toward the shopping center's driveway.

Perla walked up behind her. She touched the woman's hand and said, "Why don't you come inside." She pointed to the store. "Let me make you some tea."

Perla led her into the botánica and seated her in the fold-up chair near Santa Bárbara. "There," she said. "Rest now."

"Yes. Okay."

"I'm Perla."

"I'm Angela," she responded. Her hands trembled.

Perla set the book on the counter and went to the kitchenette. From the cupboard beside the sink, she took a mug, filled it with water, and heated it in the microwave. She made Angela manzanilla tea and poured in a few drops of whiskey from the bottle tucked under the sink.

"Here," she said, handing her the mug. "This will relax you."

Angela took sips, looking around the botánica, at the shelves, the statues, the packets of incense and herbs hanging on the pegboard. "It's nice in here. It's peaceful," she said, her voice fast, her words catching in her throat.

She got up, paced around the store, and stood in front of the Santa Bárbara statue. She leaned over the arrangement of candles and the bouquet of flowers gathered at the base and touched the figure's face. "The last thing I said to my Joey. What was it? The last thing. I can't remember. I was in the kitchen sewing a hole in Lena's cheerleading outfit. He left. Out the door. He walked past me. He was wearing a lot of cologne. I remember the smell. Why can't I remember? We didn't fight. We got alone fine. I love Rocío. I liked her for my son. I wasn't mad that he was going to see her. I think I said something," she said. "But I can't remember. If only I hadn't been concentrating so much on that tear in Lena's outfit. I could remember what I said. What did I say?" She looked at Perla, then at Santa Bárbara.

"My husband died many years ago," Perla told her, in the words she had once written for Rodrigo. "At home. He died in our bed. The night before, he'd been up watching a movie on TV. He was always watching TV late into the night. I rolled over and told him to turn down the volume. I was so mad and sleepy that I yelled. It was the last thing I said to him. He turned it off, then rolled over and kissed me. It was dark, and he couldn't see me lying next to him so his kiss landed on my ear. All I remember is the feeling of his breath blowing into my ear."

Angela sat back down. The mug wobbled in her hand when she drew it to her mouth to drink. She said softly, "We've only been here a little over a year. My husband. The father of my babies. We're separated. He wants me back. I only wanted to get away from him. That's why we came here. My Joey, he was so happy about the move because he'd gotten into trouble at his old school. He was excited. New friends. A new start, he'd say. For all of us. He was turning seventeen this year." She touched her blood-caked sweater.

Everywhere inside the botánica things were piled on top of one another, stacked high, thrown together. There were the cases and shelves and all the merchandise in the stockroom. There were boxes lining the floor behind the register, spilling over with bags of incense sticks, bottles of bath salts, and the candles from the day's delivery. Rows of statues stood in frozen meditation, a long and ancient line of martyrs and prophets, healers and teachers. *So much*, Perla thought. *There's still so much left.*

Perla leaned in close and asked her, "Do you know who I am?"

Angela's hands still touched her son's dried blood. She shook her head slowly.

"I can walk on water. The dead," Perla told her. "Spirits and saints. They talk to me. I just have to listen."

Angela lowered her head and began to weep.

"Look at me," Perla said, placing the rosary around Angela's neck. "I'm here to tell you something. I'm here to tell you your baby, he's fine. Where he is."

On the counter were rosaries in small white boxes lined with padding. She had sold or given away so many over the years and wondered where they were—if they were hanging from the rearview mirrors of cars like Teresa's or stuffed in drawers or just maybe someone was holding one now, pressing the beads and concentrating on the Mysteries.

"Don't worry," Perla said. Taking a pad and pencil, she wrote something down from memory—a receta, a saint's name, a prayer for the dead. "Listen to me," Perla told her. "Listen now. I'll help. I'll tell you what to do."

Angela stopped crying and wiped her tears away as she held the rosary.

Outside, night was falling, and the faces of the people gathered on the corner were gray as stone and indistinguishable in the approaching darkness. Some paced restlessly, and others huddled together for warmth. Perla watched the silhouettes of the candles on the sidewalk, the specks of light in the glass cylinders burning distant and lonely.

Perla felt them there, all those who had come and gone, who had sought her help and guidance. She felt them standing with her, their fingers wrapping around her own, their hands working with hers. From the shelves she took two veladoras—one plain white, the other green with a picture of the Virgen de Guadalupe. She struck a match and the flame extended out like a torch, lighting both candles at the same time. She handed the white veladora to Angela, then took the other.

"Follow me," Perla told her.

They walked out of the shop and across the parking lot. There were a few people scattered about, wandering between the empty field and the cluster of candles on the corner. The front door of the tattoo shop opened and two men wearing latex gloves, their fingertips stained with green and black ink, approached and hovered near the group. They wore dark blue work shirts, their pants creased and stiff, and they smiled and hugged Angela and said something to her. Alice and her grandfather joined them. Her apron was dusted white with flour, and she wiped her hands before taking

Angela's. The jade pendant around her neck caught the light from the vela-doras when she reached out to hug Lena. Alice's grandfather stood near An-gela, smoking, his face wrinkled and small, as he watched the traffic on Rancho slow down. One by one, the cars turned off their engines and head-lights. People got out and made their way to the corner. Some cut through the empty lot, stepping through the scrub, carrying flowers and lit candles.

Little by little the crowd grew until it filled the empty field, spilling into the parking lot and onto the street. There were members of San Salvador's church there, co-workers and friends of Angela, Joey's high school princi-pal and some of his teachers. A reporter from the *Agua Mansa Courier* went around interviewing everyone, writing things down in a small notebook.

Perla thought about the scraps of paper she had given Rodrigo. What would she say about him if anyone ever asked? What would she come to re-member about all that had happened here?

She watched Rosa walking through the crowd with Miguel Angel and Danielle, stopping now and again to let others pass in front of them, as they made their way to the altar. They placed some flowers there and the card that Danielle herself had made. Perla imagined the babies growing inside Rosa. She saw their lungs taking shape, tissues forming their brains, and a web of thin blue and red veins netting around a pair of small new hearts.

So many. So many of them.

Perla began moving through the crowd, reciting a prayer, touching their hands and faces when the people gathered around her. They had felt ache and disappointment and had borne witness to passing and loss. This was just a moment, Perla told them. Death was always stirring. It hid in the wind, in those palm trees, on the banks of the Santa Ana río. But if you stood there long enough, if you stood there and watched and listened, you could see what that river had once been, and you could see so much life in the still wa-ters that remained.

Perla and Angela added their candles to the rest, and the light from the veladoras grew. A yellow glow rose up from the ground where they were clustered. It burst out in thick beams, shooting up to the sky, curving around the edges of buildings and houses and bending between tree branches and power lines, before it found its way back down. It descended upon them, and Perla watched as, one by one, they each shone brighter, wiser and forever changed, stronger now.

Acknowledgments

So many people helped me to get here. So many were with me from the very first word. So many joined in the middle or at the very end. I thank you all.

To my agent, Elyse Cheney, for her faith and brave support of this project and of me from the moment we met and for patiently listening to what I had to say. To my editor, Kate Medina, for guiding and pushing, for taking a chance on a kid from Tijuana, for seeing what I couldn't, and for never settling. To Stephanie Hanson for never failing to give the kinds of comments and input every writer dreams of. To everyone at Random House who got behind and pushed, who wrapped their many arms around this book and me. To Robin Rolewicz for the warm wishes and for doing so much behind the scene. Thank you, Abby Plesser, for your wisdom and grace and presence throughout, for keeping things moving swift and steady, and for the phone and e-mail pats on the back that kept me smiling.

I couldn't have asked for a better team.

To Geoffrey Wolff for never failing to tell me that I had the chops to pull this off, for the long talks in his office, and for reminding me what true commitment and artistry are. To Michelle Latiolais for being a brilliant master of language and mood and for showing me again and again until I got it right. To Arielle Read for so, so much. Your advice and encouragement always got me through. Mil gracias, "mi corazón." To the International Center for Writing and Translation and the Humanities Center for their generous financial support, which allowed me to do research for this book. To Judith Ashton, Laura Gómez, and Julie Tilton at San Bernardino Valley College for getting things going way back then and for showing me how to persevere and how to matter in this world.

I'm better because of you.

To Amanda Rea for never letting me believe otherwise and for the keen eye and witty retorts. To Ariana Simard for being interested from the very beginning. To Kristen Williams for the Dump Cakes and Hello Dollies, for the fried shrimp and lasagna and the down-home East Texas love that kept me happy and full. To Michael Jaime-Becerra for being first, for opening the door and letting me follow, for his graciousness and his big heart, and for the uncanny coincidences that bind us. Only you and I get it, compa. To everyone in the MFA Program at UCI for the critiques and camaraderie. To Sandra Cisneros and my fellow Macondistas, the wild bunch straight out of San Antonio, Texas. To Leslie Larson and Carla Trujillo for their advice and for the long conversations that made me feel better. To Liliana Valenzuela for her brilliant job of translating this novel.

You've filled me up big-time.

To the Shallers of Glendora, Dusty and my best friend Mike, for all the fun we had getting here, and for the more we'll have getting there. To Jason Spivak for his guidance and friendship, for carefully keeping tabs on me from so far away, and for taking me along on those gigs during the Hollywood years. Jefe, un abrazo fuerte. To Elle Thornberry for the rowdy life that kept me insane and uncontrolled, tattooed and angry, for the bar fights and loud music, and for the wild times that made those nights gleam.

You've stayed with me and always will.

To Susan Straight for the books and stories, for the food of the soul that is inspiration and sweet hope, for the beats and rhythms to dance to words, for teaching me to look where no one else could, for teaching me to listen when no one else would, and for making me write it all down. To Kyle for making me reach, for seeing the potential when I was too exhausted, and for carrying so much of this with me as I fought to give a voice to these ghosts. I couldn't have done this without you. To my mother, Maria Luz, for giving so much and asking so little, and for always believing when everyone else had given up. To the memory of my father and my grandparents for crossing when it was rough, for working with their hands and dreaming with their souls so that I could do this, and for shining a light.

This I give to you. With everything. Everything.

picador.com

blog
videos
interviews
extracts